# THE RAGUSA THEME

## Ann Quinton

PIATKUS

*Also by Ann Quinton in Piatkus Books*
Storm Islands

Copyright © 1986 by Ann Quinton

First published in Great Britain in 1986 by
Judy Piatkus (Publishers) Limited of
5 Windmill Street, London, W1

British Library Cataloguing in Publication Data

Quinton, Ann
  The Ragusa theme.
  I. Title
  823'.914[F]      PR6067.U5/

ISBN 0 86188 534 1

Typeset by Phoenix Photosetting, Chatham
Printed and bound by Mackays of Chatham Ltd.

To Stuart, Neill and Kathryn

I should like to thank the following friends for all the help and information they have given me:

Vedija Ibrahimovic-Parker, without whose help pertaining to all things Serbian this book could not have been written.

Anthony Parsons, Principal Trombone, BBC Symphony Orchestra.

D.S., who, because he is a Customs Official and has signed the Official Secrets Act must be nameless!

# Chapter 1

'*Crescendo et rallentando!* Ladies *und* Gentlemen, *por favor* – ve 'ave *komen* to the climax!' Willie Bode, or to give him his full title Herr Doktor Wilhelm Bode, Principal Conductor of the Europa Symphony Orchestra, rapped smartly on the music stand with one hand and mopped his brow violently with the other. The heat was getting to Willie and he was losing his cool in more ways than one. And, as usually happened when he became excited, his grasp of the English language, tenuous at the best of times, deteriorated severely. It was one of the favourite pastimes of the younger members of the orchestra to count how many different languages he managed to get into one sentence. The record so far is six, not including 'American-ese'.

I was convinced that he was never sure himself in what tongue he was conversing, that he actually thought in an amalgam of languages, but there were those amongst my colleagues who thought it was all a pose; that Willie Bode was capable of speaking fluently in at least half-a-dozen languages if he so desired. This point seemed to be borne out by what followed. Willie flourished his baton.

'Back to Bar 127 *und maintenant* ve shall be 'aving *der*

build-up *à la* finale, *fortissimo und molto ritenuto!*' Then, in the impeccable English that occasionally issued from his lips and completely threw us, he continued: 'The co-operation of the second violins would be much appreciated'.

I declare he was looking directly at me as he spoke and I blinked and shifted my fiddle against my damp jaw. Beside me Ivo sighed exaggeratedly and flicked back the pages of our score.

'Don't tell me you're feeling the heat too,' I hissed out of the corner of my mouth as we positioned our bows at Willie's command. 'I thought as a native you'd revel in it.' Ivo Tomasic, Yugoslavian born and bred and now returned to his native land for a series of triumphant concerts, grinned and flashed his beautiful brown eyes at me.

'Kate, *moja draga*, I am just thinking of what is out there.' I knew what he meant. Being a member of a prestigious orchestra can sometimes pall and today was one of those times. Inside the thick, white-washed walls of the Revelin Fort we sweated away in the fusty, dust-ridden atmosphere rehearsing for what was to be one of the highlights of our tour: a concert to be given in the opening week of the Dubrovnik Festival.

Outside, the whole of the Old City lay encircled within her magic ring of walls, shimmering in the July heat haze and lapped by a turquoise sea. In a string of terracotta and white towns and villages tumbling down the Dalmatian coastline, she is the gem at the centre and well named the Pearl of the Adriatic. Beyond, a short distance across the lucid water, the tree-girt island of Lokrum dreamed in the sunshine; a bathers' and sun-worshippers' paradise.

But that was another world away. My world this morning had shrunk to the stifling, claustrophobic concert hall that had been gouged out of the interior of the Revelin Tower; the tower that guarded the north-east aspect of the city walls and had witnessed many strange comings and goings in its eight-hundred-year history. I tried to concentrate on the music but even Beethoven failed me today. The triumphant, pulsating fourth movement of the 7th Symphony which usually carried me along on a high that left me shaken and exhilarated failed to move me. Our music-making was stale, like the air inside the tower and the strings were definitely sharp, all of them. The heat was playing havoc with pitch and even constant re-tuning did little to alleviate the problem.

Eventually Willie gave up the struggle and called it a day. Musically we didn't really need the rehearsal. Our programme consisted of a well-known, well-loved repertoire. The rehearsal had been called primarily to sort out the seating arrangements on stage, always a problem on tour when faced with strange concert halls with inadequate orchestral space. Willie and Sammy Cohen, our leader, had spent the earlier part of the morning fussing around like a couple of deprived mother hens, but they had finally arranged things to their satis-faction. It was a crush though, and Sammy was worried about the acoustics. The stage was apron-shaped and the audience on either side of the apron would get little or no view of the conductor or the soloist, because of the gigantic pillars situated at each corner, but would be in close proximity to the side ranks and the percussion and might see more than it was meant to. There would be an additional strain on those members of the orchestra who were used to being tucked out of sight and now suddenly found themselves the focus of attention by a certain section of the audience.

With the prospect of the rest of the day free to spend

3

as they wished, the jaded musicians miraculously and suddenly revived. With enthusiasm, instruments was cased and there was a general exodus down the broad, stone staircase. If we had thought it hot inside the tower, the searing heat that greeted us as we moved from interior dimness to the midday sun was stupefying. I wandered with a group of my colleagues onto the terrace that overlooked the Old Harbour; we were all good friends and all of us string players. It was strange how we invariably socialised strictly within our orchestral groupings. The strings stuck together, the woodwind formed another clique and so on. It wasn't that we didn't get on together. The orchestra was one big, happy family with all the companionship, bickerings and ramifications attendant on such a structure; but although we did mix to a certain extent, we seemed to gravitate naturally to our fellow instrumentalists, divided not by sex or age but by whether we blew, bowed or banged. I believe this is true in general of all orchestras, and this hypothesis would make an interesting study for any budding sociologist.

I drifted over to the balustrade and gazed down at the panoramic view of water and boats spread beneath me. Distant figures crowded on the quayside waiting to board the ferry to Lokrum and a broad-beamed fishing smack shuffled through the harbour arms. Lokrum beckoned. It hung suspended on the near horizon, a smoky green hump rising out of the clear water, and I almost imagined I could smell the aromatic scent of pine and juniper from here. I remembered my father telling me that this was the island on which Richard the Lionheart was supposedly shipwrecked on his way back from the Crusades; though how anyone could manage to run aground in these calm seas was beyond the imagination.

'Kate, are you coming?' I dragged myself back to the twentieth century. 'You were miles away. We're going

4

back to the hotel for lunch and then collapsing on the beach afterwards. Come on.'

'It's far too hot to eat and such a drag back to the hotel,' I said. 'I think I'm going to wander round the Old City and then go across to Lokrum. How about joining me when you've finished stuffing?'

'That's Lokrum over there, isn't it?' Cor Vinke, our Dutch cellist, squinted into the sun. 'The fairy-tale island you've been on about, where shapely sirens sit on the rocks combing their locks and luring poor men to their fate?'

'Cor dear, you're in the wrong country. But I should imagine toplessness has reached these august shores by now.'

Then what are we waiting for? We'll meet you down there', he gestured to the quayside, 'this afternoon and you can take us on a conducted tour.'

'Are you really not coming back to the hotel first?' asked Sarah, who is my closest friend in the orchestra.

'No, I really can't be bothered. I'll just loiter in the shade and grab me a limunadu somewhere.'

'Your fiddle is here and your swimming gear at the Splendid,' she pointed out, tossing back her tangle of black hair.

'How true. You wouldn't be a dear . . .?'

'You're not seriously suggesting I lug your violin as well as mine on that bus?'

She was quite indignant and I knew what she meant. The Splendid Hotel was situated on the Lapad Peninsular not far from the Sumatrim Beach in the new part of the city. It was a twenty-minute journey from here on a hot, crowded Libertas bus humming with packed bodies and exhaust fumes.

'I'll take it.' Ivo plucked the offending instrument from my hands and tucked it under his arm. 'But you should eat, you know Kate. You'll fade away.'

5

As I am nothing if not robust and not your anorexia candidate at all, I chose to ignore this remark.

'Sarah, could you possibly manage to bring back my swimsuit and towel?'

'Of course,' she gave me a quick grin. 'If they become too heavy I'll hang them round Ivo's neck and he can wear them next to his heart.' I ignored that remark too.

'Shall I stay with you?' asked Ivo. 'We can explore the Old City together.' I shook my head. I wanted to be alone and Sarah sensed my mood.

'Don't be obtuse, Ivo. Can't you see that Kate wants to wander down memory lane. You may be Yugoslavian but I declare Kate cares more for these old sticks and stones than you do.'

They departed in a gust of good-natured bantering and I sat down on a bench under the shade of a palm tree. It was quite true what Sarah had just said. I, Kate Bracegirdle, Scottish born and bred, was far more familiar with Dubrovnik than Ivo. It, and indeed, the whole of Yugoslavia held me in thrall. It was a thraldom that went back three generations. My grandfather had been one of the few British agents dropped into the country during World War II to make contact with Tito and the partisans. Practically every male Yugoslavian over the age of fifty will confide, if given half a chance, that he fought by the side of that great hero, Josip Broz, and took part in the guerrilla warfare that raged in the interior, but my grandfather actually did just that. He met the great man himself, liaised between him and the Allies and spent a gruelling eighteen months living as a fugitive, treking through those cruel, bleak mountains. The great hardships and privation he endured did not stop him from falling under the spell of this beautiful land and her divided countrymen, and this attachment was compounded in my father.

My father is a research chemist, an expert on phosphoric acid and he often travels abroad commissioning chemical plants. He has worked on just such a project in Yugoslavia. This was at Mitrovica on the Kosova Plain, an underdeveloped area in the centre of the country. Despite poor working conditions, he grew to respect and like the Serbians there, many of them of Albanian origin and Muslim roots, and he contrived to visit places his father had known in the war and make himself familiar with what had been, up to then, only hearsay. My mother, brothers and myself had flown out to join him for a short holiday and he had brought us from Belgrade to Dubrovnik. I had been in my early teens then and the romance and beauty of the place had grabbed me; I also fell under the spell. I had been back once on holiday and now was here again on a working visit; playing with the second violins in the Europa Symphony Orchestra.

I still couldn't quite believe it; that I was a professional musician earning my living doing the thing I loved best of all – making music – although I had been with the orchestra nearly two years.

The Europa Symphony Orchestra was founded in 1947 and had originally been a youth orchestra. It had been conceived and endowed by one Cornelius D. Hoffmeyer, an American industrialist of vast wealth who had been with the American Forces in Europe in the aftermath of World War II and had been shocked by what he had witnessed. He had decided then and there to channel some of the family wealth into a project for uniting the nations, and he chose music as the great intermediary. Music transcends all barriers; a trite cliché but true, and Hoffmeyer's idea was to gather together promising young musicians from as many countries as possible and weld them together to make a formidable musical entity. Some said it was conscience money; that

7

much of the Hoffmeyer fortune was based on armaments, and not just dealings with the Allies either. Be that as it may, Cornelius became known as a some-what rough-necked philanthropist; one who jumped in with both feet and bludgeoned people into doing his will, but who abhorred political trafficking. He was quoted as having said he 'didn't want no politics in his orchestra and anyone who was into politics was out'. This was probably hearsay but he certainly achieved what he had set out to do in his lifetime.

Cornelius was an ardent Anglophile so the orchestra is based in England, and a series of trust funds and annui-ties ensures that even in today's economic climate, it has a sound financial backing. We are actually paid a salary, small it is true – a mere retainer say some – but at least this is more than most members of other orchestras receive, the normal policy being that one is paid only for rehearsals and actual performances. We get paid for those too, on top of our nominal salaries which means that we have a modicum of financial security and do not have to free-lance so much. Of course, that goes on too; we hire ourselves out to other orchestras and chamber groups when asked, take regular teaching sessions and those more distinguished amongst the older fraternity take master classes and give solo recitals.

The Europa ceased to be a youth orchestra many years ago. The policy is still to recruit amongst the young musicians newly qualified from musical colleges, but nobody is turned out or made to feel they should be looking for pastures new when they reach a more mature age. Sammy Cohen, our leader, and Harris Fordham, our principal percussion, are both founder-members, and our ages range from the early twenties to near retirement. There are more British and American members now and not so many Europeans, particularly

Eastern Europeans, but we still form a cosmopolitan little empire.

Ivo Tomasic joined the orchestra nine months ago. He was born in the little town of Pristina, situated, strangely enough, in the area in which my father had worked; but he had departed from his Serbian hearth at an early age, apparently under some sort of a cloud, and had studied in Zagreb and Belgrade before graduating to the States and thence to London and the Europa. His command of the English language is well-nigh perfect and he has lived away from his roots long enough for him to have severed most emotional ties. He is brilliant, moody, erratic and handsome in a swarthy, gypsyish way and I think I am in love with him. Can one be half in love with someone? I am certainly very attracted to him and he to me, but something, perhaps his volatile, slightly unstable temperament, has held me back from a full committment. That, and the fear that a closer relationship might damage our professional association. We are partnered amongst the second violins; we share a music stand and work in close proximity. We get on well together – we have to, working in such intimacy – but at the back of my mind is the fear that if we become intimate in private life and it didn't work out our musical partnership would also be finished, and I am still new enough in the profession not to want to jeopardise my career in any way.

When I first joined the orchestra, wet behind the ears but eager to experience anything and everything, Jenny Seaman, the tall, languid cellist with a Home Counties accent, had taken me on one side and given me some advice.

'Do you or don't you?' she had enquired, and when I had looked mystified, had elucidated with a gleam of amusement in her protuberant blue eyes, 'sleep around?'

9

'I don't see what business it is of yours,' I had gasped, trying to cover up how she had startled me.

'I'm only trying to give you some advice. In a set-up like this you are either everybody's or nobody's.'

I knew she had been deliberately trying to shock me and I had retaliated by trying to turn the tables on her. 'Which are you?'

'I am the exception to the rule,' she had drawled, examining her short, capable nails. 'I have a beautiful, on-going relationship with Tom Meyer, the principal clarinet.'

I had winced at the expression but had soon found out what she meant. She and Tom were as one, married in all but name. I learned later that she came from the stockbroker belt and, rebelling against her upper-middle class background, had chosen to become an itinerant musician rather than a Sloane Ranger, much to her family's dismay. It had regarded life in a respected orchestra as just a step above living in a hippie commune, and Jenny had succeeded in thoroughly shocking it. But she was a gifted string player and had soon made her mark in her chosen world and, to her chagrin, she became an object of prestige to her relatives. She countered this by openly flaunting her sexual liaison with Tom and this was, I think, the sole reason why she would not marry him. To live in sin was one thing; to be licensed to wash and darn his socks was not the image she wished to project at all. I wondered whether she would ever want to have children and if this would make her change her mind. There are several married couples on the orchestral circuit and they seem to manage their private and professional lives very successfully.

I had soon realised the truth of what she had warned; there was a lot of sleeping around amongst the members of the orchestra. I suppose it was inevitable, given the percentage of young members and the intimate conditions under which we lived and worked, particularly whilst on tour. Carley Norton from Boston was the most notorious in this respect. Blonde and delicate with an ethereal, touch-me-not look about her, she was certainly anybody's, sleeping around with all and sundry. I remained unconvinced but very much in awe of her promiscuous life-style.

I, Kate Bracegirdle, from a respectable Dundee background, product of a happy, stable family, did not wish to emulate her behaviour but I did often wish that I looked more the part; more artistic – more exciting. I am sturdily built, with a mass of dark, springy curls that just miss having auburn highlights. As a great-aunt of mine once said: 'Kate is noo a red-head but she'll have ginger bairns'. With my locks I have the inevitable complexion; ruddy, prone to freckles and a lost cause as far as acquiring a suntan is concerned. Already, after only a few days in this country, I was an unbecoming shade of pink and quite sick with envy of the varying degrees of brown displayed by my friends and colleagues.

The sun was beating against my eyelids now, having moved round beyond my tree cover. I opened my eyes and shifted along the seat. A flurry of pigeons strutted the ground and perched confidently on the stone balustrade, cooing and murmuring amongst themselves. They were plump and sleek. The feline population of Dubrovnik might be scrawny and half-starved; the pigeons obviously did better for themselves.

I felt tired and yet strangely restless. I was back in my beloved Dubrovnik but somehow the tour was not turning out quite as I had anticipated. There was nothing I could put my finger on, nothing that had actually gone wrong so far; just a feeling of unease, a slight disappointment; I suppose you could call it a pricking of my thumbs. I had been so thrilled when I had heard we were to go on tour in Yugoslavia, and a leisurely tour at that. Often we go on a series of one-night stands and one gets to the point where one doesn't know where one is – just continuous coach journeys, anonymous hotels and concerts followed by repetitive receptions.

This tour had actually started in Trieste, then we had gone on to Ljubljana, Zagreb and Sarajevo before coming to Dubrovnik. After the concert here in two days time, we have a free fortnight which we can either use to holiday locally or go off and do our own thing. We should have played a concert at Titograd but this had been cancelled at the last moment. After this break we have another concert here as part of the Dubrovnik Festival and a final concert in Belgrade to round off the tour.

There had not been quite the usual happy atmosphere. We pride ourselves on being a united group but there had been some strained periods this time; frayed tempers, displays of temperament – the worst coming most shockingly from Sammy Cohen, our leader, who, though he feigned to be rather precious, normally held the whole show together. I suppose it was because of Richard Godbold. He is, or rather was, our business manager. This was the first time we had been on tour without him and his absence was felt. I had better explain.

Richard is in his late fifties and was originally a clarinet player before tragedy struck in the form of arthritis which attacked the joints in his hands. He isn't too badly crippled, not yet, but any defect in that line spells curtains for a musician. He had always shown a flair for managing people and he turned his talents to the business side, at first combining the two, but as his disease progressed he gradually ceased playing and became our full-time manager. The orchestra was his life, full stop; and because he was so well liked he had the complete support of all its members, who were delighted that he had found a new outlet for his musical talents. Over the last nine months the debility had spread to his hip-joints and his mobility is threatened.

We went on tour last winter, a short tour in the Benelux countries, and for the first time Richard Godbold had an assistant; a whizz-kid by the name of Miles Bretherton. I say whizz-kid but he must be in his early thirties and his rather consequential manner, after the placid handling of Richard, put many people's backs up, mine included. Instead of asking, suggesting or discussing as Richard did, he just gave orders and it didn't go down at all well. He was supposed to have come from a similar job in Australia and had a musical background but he was not Australian though apparently his family had been settled there for some time.

There is something just a little bit phoney about him. Perhaps it is in his appearance. He is tall and fair with blue-grey eyes and looks a typical English Public School product; he has absolutely no trace of any accent whatever, be it Australian or Winchester, and he is always impeccably dressed. One wished that he would sometimes look just a little mussed, would drop the mask occasionally so that one could see the real man underneath, for to me he gave the impression of someone living behind a carefully constructed façade. I must admit, right now, that I am almost entirely on my own in this interpretation of him. Most of the female members of the orchestra display weak-knee symptoms if he so much as glances in their direction. He holds himself aloof and yet at the same time he tries to ingratiate himself with certain factions.

Anyway, to most people's consternation, certainly mine, Richard had taken a turn for the worst and we found ourselves at the start of this tour with a new business manager: Miles Bretherton. It was supposed to be only a temporary arrangement. Richard was having a well-earned rest and would return at a later date, but I had my doubts. One couldn't fault Miles Bretherton's carrying out of the job; everything had functioned smoothly so far and he had flown out beforehand to work out arrangements with the various local musical entrepreneurs in whose cities we were due to perform.

There was the clatter of footsteps down the stairway leading from the Revelin Tower and a shadow moved across my line of vision. Talk of the devil – it was Miles Bretherton. Had my musings managed to conjure him up in reality? He was wearing, would you believe, a collar *and tie*, an *actual tie*; in this heat, at this time of day! He saw me and swung in my direction.

'Hello Kate; have they all run off and left you?'

'I wanted to be alone,' I said rather pointedly but he didn't take the hint. He dropped down beside me upsetting a pair of pigeons who had been carrying on a quite shocking courtship at my feet, and they shied off a few yards and regarded him with beady eyes and pulsating chests.

'They are very tame, aren't they?'

'*Golub*,' I said dreamily.

'I beg your pardon?' He looked startled.

'It's Serbo-Croatian for pigeon. Don't you think it describes the sound they make splendidly?'

'The perfect onomatopoeia.' Trust him to have the correct word at his fingertips.

'Are you still working? Squeezing the last few shekels out of our obliging hosts?'

'I shall ignore the latter question but ponder on the

supposition behind the first. I am not working and am yours to command.'

'What would a nice girl like me want with the likes of you?' I said in a broad Scots accent and the best leer I could muster. He narrowed his eyes and changed the subject abruptly.

'You've been here before, haven't you? You know the country well?'

'A little bird has been busy. But yes, I have been before and there are family connections. Why?'

'Then I presume you will be off on your travels after this first concert, visiting friends and places you know?'

'Actually I was planning to stay right here in Dubrovnik. It is a good centre for touring, if I'm so minded, but I probably shan't go far. I need to recuperate after this last week.'

'This tour is a doddle and you know it. How about dragging yourself together and joining me for a drink?'

I was very tempted. Then I saw the look on his face; complacent would be putting it mildly. He was expecting me to fall over myself in my eagerness to accept his invitation.

'No thanks. Another time perhaps, but I have things to do.'

I sauntered across the terrace and through the archway, aware of his gaze boring into my back. I was annoyed and flustered and I wished now that I had gone with the others.

The steep path leading down to the Placa was chequered with shadows, grey and purple smudges overlaid the bleached stones and I kept close to the buildings that overhung the street. I stopped to buy peaches as large as grapefruits and washed them under one of the spouts jetting out from Onofrio's little fountain; then I sat down to eat them in the shade of the colonnade

15

outside the Sponza Palace and watched the world go by.

In the middle of the square a group of tourists was braving the midday sun to have their photos taken in front of Orlando's statue. This is a slender column sporting a very ancient-looking knight in armour. At his feet swarmed the ubiquitous pigeons, keeping their balance with difficulty on the stone flags that paved the area. These are burnished to a pearly patina by generations of feet and are as slippery as blocks of ice. Holidaymakers of many nationalities strolled back and forth across the square and in and out of the shops lining the Placa, which is the main street. No motorised traffic is allowed into the Old City and everyone goes walkabout along the Placa. There was a continuous kaleidoscope of colour and above the people's heads hung the banners announcing the summer festival, flaunting scarlet against the white stone and cerulean sky.

This is the heart of Dubrovnik, the old city of Ragusa from which the Argonauts are reputed to have set sail. It has never been destroyed or damaged due to the simple expedient of always opening to whatever enemy was knocking at its gates. This policy has certainly paid off in the form of a perfect medieval city surviving untouched to the present day, and accounts, in part, for the heterogenous collection of people that form the Yugoslavian nation.

After a while I roused myself and strolled into one of the little kafanas where I passed more time sipping sweetened lemon juice. So much for my plans for sightseeing.

The ferry to Lokrum was crowded and it was with difficulty that we all managed to pile onto the same boat, especially as our party was swollen by friends from brass and woodwind.

'Whew, that's better!' exclaimed Sarah, collapsing under the awning. 'I declare you could fry an egg on that quayside. You had the right idea. Another few moments on that bus and I would have passed out. No matter what time of the day or evening, those buses are crowded and they don't seem to impose any limit on the number of passengers they carry. I'm sure half the Serbian youth just spend their day travelling backwards and forwards for the sheer hell of it.'

I looked into the plastic carrier she was carrying. 'Oh good, you've brought my green one.'

'Who are you trying to turn on?'

'I only wish it did. I haven't really the figure for swimming gear.'

'Nonsense, you're nicely rounded, not scrawny like me.' She was thin, it was true, all angles and corners, even her face with its jutting cheekbones and patrician nose, but it all added up to a vibrant personality.

The ferry chugged out of the harbour entrance, past the tall, oblong Fort of St John which now houses the Maritime Museum, picked up speed and spun across the crystalline water. The white, embattled walls receded in a froth of wake and we swept along the north shore of Lokrum past the pines and crowded greenery that pressed almost to the water's edge, fighting for a toe-hold on the low rock fringe lapped by a viridian and ultramarine sea. The jetty on Lokrum is built in a little indentation on the coastline towards the far end of the island, and there were several private yachts and launches moored in this natural harbour.

It was just as I had remembered it: the broad stone path leading up from the jetty in a series of slopes and steps that diversified into a maze of tracks that threaded through the trees and intersected the island. And the smell; the warm, spicy scent of pine, juniper and scrub was a tangible aroma that enveloped you as soon as you stepped ashore, attacking your senses with a heady, haunting perfume. We walked beneath the trees a short distance and scrambled down onto the rocks which at this time of the day were in welcome shade.

The water was deliciously cool and so clear it was unbelievable. Shoals of tiny fish swam in and out of our plunging bodies and darted into purple caverns under the rocks. I climbed out, towelled myself and lay half propped up against a shelf of rock. After a short while Ivo joined me. He shook his mop of hair like a dog and when I protested he laughed and dropped down beside me.

'You're looking very delectable, Kate. That green complements your colour.'

'Is that a nice way of drawing attention to the fact that I'm rapidly becoming shocking pink?'

'You look very nice. Very English and distinguished amongst all these Mediterranean types. But watch you don't get burnt.'

'You certainly look the part.' I eyed his smooth, bronzed skin. 'Nobody could mistake you for anything but a native.'

'Is that so?' He didn't seem particularly pleased at my comment and stared unseeingly across the water towards the bare, rocky mainland.

'What are you doing after the first concert?' he asked sometime later. It was the second time today I had been asked the same question, but this was no idle enquiry. He was going to press me into making a significant decision about our relationship, and although one part of me was eager to comply with what I sensed he was going to suggest, yet I hung back and parried the question.

'I suppose you'll be going to see your family?'

'Now, what makes you suppose that? My family and I are alienated. I haven't seen them for years.'

'But surely . . . I mean, now you're back in Yugoslavia you'll want to visit them, they'll be eager to see you. . . . They *do* know you're here?' I added as he kept grim silence.

'Listen, Kate, I told you. I left home a long while ago. I have no wish to return to my home town and I can assure you I would not be very welcome. There was some trouble . . .' Now it was his turn to flounder.

'What sort of trouble? Do you mean you got on the wrong side of the law?' I was never one to let sleeping dogs lie.

'Nothing serious,' he said hurriedly. 'Just a few of us local youths got involved in a little pot-smoking and high living and there was a bit of a scandal.'

'Drugs? You mean you were involved with drugs?'

'Don't look at me as if I'd suddenly sprouted horns. I tell you, it was nothing serious, just youthful high spirits mostly. But I got the chance of this place to study at Zagreb Academy, and to cut a long story short, I was as glad to shake the dust of Pristina off my feet as they were to see me go. The fact is that I am *persona non grata* as far as my family is concerned.'

'How sad,' I said, thinking of my own happy family life. 'But you're not wanted by the police or anything are you?'

'What makes you think that?' He was eyeing me intently and I felt uncomfortable.

'Well, you do seem to be keeping a low profile. I mean, this is your native country . . .'

He had stayed carefully in the background since we crossed the border, even to the extent of standing aside and watching us struggle with Serbo-Croatian when he could have acted as interpreter.

'You are making the same mistake as all foreigners, outsiders. Just because this country has one name now and is ruled by a central government, you think we are one nation. We are not. We are a collection of vastly different races and cultures, somehow welded together under one baton. As a Serbian I am as alien to these Croatians . . .', he gestured widely with his arm '. . . as you are.'

'Well, thanks for the lesson,' I said tartly.

'Children, children! Anyone who didn't know you better would think you were quarrelling!' Sarah's head popped over the rocks and she shook her damp, tousled curls.

'Nonsense, we were having a deeply intellectual discussion.' Ivo bounced to his feet. 'But now I propose we sample the local pivo. Who's coming?'

We wound our way back through the trees to a little kafana where we comandeered most of the tables and chairs set out in the dappled sunshine. Sylvester, our coloured trumpet player, had joined our party this afternoon with Adrian Palmer and Marianne Ducros, our principal and sub-principal oboes. Adrian Palmer was a particular friend of Ivo's and about the same age. He was intense and moody but capable of bursts of levity when he would indulge in buffoonery of a high order. Ivo made a business of sitting with him and ignoring me and they cracked jokes and made disparaging remarks about the beer in mock German accents. I didn't care. I sat back and let the buzz of conversation drift over my head. I listened instead to the cones cracking overhead and the chirruping crickets.

I had shot my mouth off about the beauty and splendours of Lokrum so that when there was a concerted move for another swim before returning to Dubrovnik I led them to, what is for me, the *pièce de résistance* of the island, the little landlocked lagoon on the south side of the island. We walked along paths that tunnelled through green foliage, skirted the building of the old Benedictine monastery that became a summer residence of the Archduke Maximilian of Hapsburg and now houses a natural history museum and a restaurant, and strolled across sunbaked open spaces dotted with oak and sycamore, past hedges of oleander in full bloom. I saw butterflies that I could not identify; a black one with white markings and red tips to the underside of its wings, and a pretty little mauve one that cavorted amongst the giant cacti.

The approach to Mrtvo More, or Dead Sea, as the lagoon is officially called, is deceptive. The path winds down between gnarled olives and pines in a series of uneven rock steps and one is not prepared for the sight at the bottom. The little lake is almost perfectly round in shape, a lapis-lazuli bead set deep in a circle of rock that on three sides rears up to a height of sixty to seventy feet; rugged cliffs sporting sizeable pines that lean out of cracks and fissures in a blaze of greenery and a top-knot of dense scrub. Where we stood was a shallow beach of rock and shale that formed the remaining curve of the circle.

'My, this is something!' breathed Sarah. 'It is quite beautiful and so unexpected.'

'Is there an outlet to the sea?' asked Sylvester, dumping his gear onto one of the rock slabs and already halfway into the water as he posed his question. 'It looks as if there could be an under-water channel over there near those caves.'

'I don't think so,' I said, 'but there must be some sort of osmosis. The sea is only over there.' I gestured to the wall of sheer rock that faced us, backed by the burning blue sky.

'What are we waiting for? Come on.' Ivo dropped a kiss on my ear and a thrill went through me. 'What a clever girl, Kate; a perfect spot. What a pity it is not ours exclusively.'

There were plenty of people about; in the water and on the narrow strip of beach, and children paddled in the shallows. Then I saw what he meant. Draped across a rock was Sammy Cohen holding forth to Harris Fordham and Willie Bode, and at his feet, looking incredibly elegant in a pair of scarlet shorts, was Miles Bretherton. I felt an irrational surge of disappointment, as if my own private Shangri-La had been desecrated. Sammy saw us and beckoned us over.

'Is it all right if the rank and file join you?' I asked rather rudely. Sammy waved us to the rocks surrounding him rather in the style of a potentate bestowing favours and Willie Bode enthused about the scenery.

'Eet ees *wunderbar, n'est ce pas? Der wasser*, der *sonnenschein* and de beautiful peoples.'

'I hope you're referring to us, Herr Bode.'

Willie looks rather like an emaciated, demented version of Geraint Evans. He has masses of dramatic black hair heavily stippled with white and his face is festooned with eyebrows. Perched upright on a rock he bore an absurd resemblance to a manic heron. Beside him Sammy, with his droopy, pouched eyes and barrel chest covered with a fuzz of grey hair, looked like a businessman recovering from an over-indulgent lunch break. Apart from a languid wave and raised eyebrows Miles had not spoken but he watched me closely as I sidled over to Sammy intent on provocation.

'Sammy, you look devastating. If I was into older men you wouldn't stand a chance.'

'*Were* dear. It should be *were*, not *was*,' said Sammy pettishly. He likes to encourage the impression that he is

22

dipping his toes into the gay scene but this is not borne out by facts. We once had a galloping homo in the second violins but when he misread the signals and made advances to Sammy, you couldn't see him, Sammy, for dust. He was horrified and scared stiff at the same time. As Sarah has said, he is an old woman, not an old queen. For all that, he is held in esteem by almost everyone, although Peter Brownstone, our principal horn, resents his manner. He too has been with the orchestra many years and I think he fancied his chances at following on in Richard Godbold's steps as a player/manager. He is always querying Sammy's decisions and throwing his weight around, especially when tour preparations are in progress; but he probably thinks that his position as a member of the Orchestral Management Committee entitles him to this. Surprisingly enough, he has knuckled down under Miles Bretherton's direction and has not been too awkward during this tour.

'Look at that!' We followed Adrian Palmer's pointed finger. High up on a ledge of rock near the top of the cliff facing us across the lagoon was the figure of a youth. 'He's surely not going to dive from there!'

Even as we watched, in degrees of fascination and horror, the figure sprang forward and arched into a perfect swallow dive. He was joined by two companions who appeared over the summit of the cliff and hurtled themselves down after him. I held my breath until all three surfaced.

'It must be very deep over there.'

'Let's go and see.' Ivo led the way into the water. It was warm and salty and blackly mysterious over the far side under the lee of the rockface.

Later, when we had all swum to exhaustion point and were sunning ourselves on the rocks, Miles produced an enormous watermelon, hacked it to pieces with the aid

23

of a penknife, and handed it round.

'No thanks,' said Ivo with an exasperated shudder as the dripping pink flesh reached him. 'I could do with a fag.' He fumbled in the pockets of his jeans.

'Don't be a fool, Tomasic; you know smoking's not allowed,' snapped Miles. 'There are notices all over the place in English *and* Serbian telling you so.'

Lokrum is a nature reserve and the lighting of fires or the use of matches in any way is strictly forbidden. It was quite understandable. The place was like a tinder-box. One spark and the whole island would erupt.

'Keep your cool. I haven't got my cigarettes with me.' Ivo smiled at Miles who responded with hostility.

'It means no smoking of any sort.'

'Well, he's hardly likely to produce a Meerchum out of thin air, is he?' I said brightly but both men ignored me. They were staring at each other and I had the feeling I was on a different wavelength. Then Ivo laughed and turned his back on Miles and I wondered just who was getting at whom.

Miles yawned and turned his attention to his brief-case. Yes, he actually had a briefcase with him on the beach!

'I've got a copy of the programme for the concert if anyone is interested.' We crowded round. The Europa Orchestra got quite a good plug, translated into several languages, the English version being a quaint paean of praise, and the musicians were listed by name at the back.

'Kate Bracegirdle,' read out Cor Vinke. 'Are you sure you're Scottish? Shouldn't there be a "Mac" in it somewhere?'

'Actually my family originated from Lancashire many generations ago but I can assure you I am Scottish born and bred.'

'A name like that really lowers the tone of the entire

24

programme,' said Sylvester with mock disapproval. 'Can't you even make it Katherine?'

'I was christened Kate,' I said haughtily, 'and it's all very well for you to talk. A name like Sylvester de Monterey looks good in print but what does your audience see in real life – a big buck nigger.'

'Kate!' exclaimed Amanda Brown in horror and Sylvester fell about laughing. She is the newest recruit to the orchetra and still very much feeling her way in the matter of the amicable insults and repartee that punctuate our conversations.

'He would be most indignant if you called him anything else,' I said and Sylvester went into his Black Mammy routine, waving his hands and rolling his eyes. He is a brilliant musician and can produce sheer magic out of his trumpet which looks like a toy from a Christmas cracker in his banana hands. Unlike many brass players who come to the classical repertoire via the brass band, Sylvester has a pure jazz background. He still free-lances occasionally in the jazz world and I think it has lost a very gifted performer in him, but he enjoys the cachet and snobbery of being part of a classical orchestra, especially as he is the sole coloured member.

'What are we doing tomorrow?' enquired Sarah idly. 'I declare I could easily turn into a sybarite in these surroundings.'

'You vill practice,' said Willie sternly, '*und* tomorrow evening ve vill rehearse.'

'Oh no.' There was a general groan from most of us present, and Willie continued, 'I am not happy *mit der* Stravinsky.'

We were playing Petrushka as part of our programme and I must admit the acoustics and dry atmosphere of the Revelin Tower had not helped the percussion, who play a vital part in this work.

'This is an official rehearsal call,' said Miles Bretherton standing up and looking very officious. '6.30 pm in the Revelin Concert Hall. And you will get paid for it,' he added seeing the look of mutiny on one or two faces. 'Don't be late.'

Did I feel a pricking of my thumbs again? The rehearsal was to go ahead as scheduled but we were not all to be present.

# Chapter 2

After Willie, Sammy and Harris had left to catch the
ferry back to the mainland the rest of us lazed around a
little longer. Miles Bretherton had elected to stay on
with us, a fact that irritated both me and Ivo. I was
delighted to see that Miles was turning an angry shade of
pink. Would he be sore tomorrow! When we eventually
got back to the Old City, the green men in the clock
tower were striking 6 and we decided to walk the walls.
The city walls are open to the public from 10 am to 7 pm
but it is far too hot even to envisage the trek during the
day. We should just have time to make it round before
they closed, and it should be a little cooler now.

'How many washers is it?' asked Cor. 'I don't think
I've got enough.'

I must explain that washers is the slang term amongst
us for currency. No matter what country we are in the
local currency is known as washers and there are so
many to the pound.

'Fifty dinars. I'll bail you out.'

We bought our tickets, entered by the Ploče Gate and
struggled up several steep flights of internal steps before
coming out on the wall, which is quite narrow with a
frighteningly low parapet in places. We walked round in

a northerly direction marvelling at the views of the Old City spread out like a coral and russet fan at our feet. I could go on and on about the breathtaking panorama; it would be corny but true. The roofs tumbled in profusion below us, higgledy-piggledy, up and down, in and out, with no seeming plan in their layout. Everywhere one looked, the humped terracotta tiles blazed in the evening sunset; gables, ridges, curves nudged each other and fought for the sky, and one caught fascinating glimpses of little balconies crammed with geraniums and vines; and fig trees leaning out from gaps where no trees could surely possibly be grown. In the distance the dome of the cathedral glowed greenly.

The path wound downwards and then we were on a section of the wall that passed above the end of the Placa, and we watched the fore-shortened figures strutting up and down like something out of a Lowry painting. Then we were looking down into a square courtyard that was enclosed by a two-tiered colonnade hung about with swags of bougainvillaea and trailing vines. Tables and chairs were set out in this square and from tubs in the corners orange and lemon trees reached up towards us.

'What a fantastic looking restaurant' I said wistfully. 'I'd love to have a meal there.'

'You're on.' Miles spoke at my shoulder. He had latched on to me when Ivo went on ahead with Adrian and although at first I had been annoyed he had been an easy companion, not talking much, very intent on his photography.

'Then I hope the Europa pays you more than it pays me. It looks very expensive.'

'Nothing seems very expensive in this place. This must be one of the few countries left where the pound is still strong against the local currency. It's hard luck on the

Yugoslavians but good for us. We'll definitely have a meal before we leave.'

The wall climbed upwards again. Ahead, to our right, loomed the massive Fort Lovrijenac, formidable on its rocky plinth rearing above the Pilé suburb; then we were on the seaward side of the Old City. Below us the water, an incredible navy blue, lapped at the walls themselves. On an outcrop of rock a cluster of fishermen huddled over their rods, tiny pin-men from here, and a launch swept past trailing a curl of incandescent feathers in its wake; a child's toy on a pond. Around us the swallows screamed and soared. The Yugoslavian swallows are a larger, more vociferous breed than their English counterparts. Dark brown and cream, they swept above our heads and hurtled low beneath the walls shouting and scolding like a pack of schoolboys. The going got steeper and I paused to get my breath back. Beside me Miles leaned on the parapet and stared across the water towards Lokrum. His hair, darkened with sweat, hung in a wedge over one temple and he seemed preoccupied.

'Which orchestra did you work with in Australia?' I asked.

'Only a small provincial one in the suburbs, you wouldn't know it,' he said hurriedly.

'Not the Sydney Opera House?'

'Good Heavens, no.'

'So this appointment was quite a step up for you?'

'I suppose you could say so.' He refused to be drawn so I tried another tactic.

'How did you get into this line of business?'

'It was just one of those things.' He shrugged. 'I have always been interested in music, in fact, at one time I hoped to be a professional musician myself.'

'And what happened?'

'I wasn't good enough.' He gave me a crooked smile.

29

'Would you believe it, everytime you draw your bow across your violin and make such exquisite sounds, I am green with envy?'

'You were a string player?'

'Clarinet.'

He refused to say any more but I wasn't satisfied. I just could not see him as a musician. He certainly had no rapport with the temperament of us professionals. I was convinced there was something odd about him.

'Perhaps you knew someone of influence in the music world?'

'You mean, did I have a big boot behind me? Perhaps I did. Why?'

'You appear to be very competent but I think you are in an alien environment.'

He looked at me then, very carefully. 'How astute, Miss Bracegirdle.' He brushed the hair off his forehead. 'We appear to have lost the others. Shall we try and catch up?'

At the top of a particularly steep incline was a little stall selling limunadu and there we found the rest of the party. The stallholder had chosen his site well. I should think he made a sale to just about everybody who walked the walls. After a welcome break we pressed on. The path curved round the south side of the harbour. The outlook on the land side was not so salubrious. Houses were in a state of decay, slum tenements, and everywhere were the signs of a poorer section of the community; but even here there were the little patches of garden, scratched out of the stones themselves, with their rows of cabbages, peppers and tomatoes.

The wall came to an abrupt end and we went down a steep flight of steps that brought us down to an almost subterranean tunnel, that ran along at ground level. It was dark and noisome.

'Phew, I think we've got into the sewers by mistake,' said Sarah holding her nose. 'Wherever does this lead to?'

We eventually came out somewhere at the back of the cathedral. This is closed to the public for the time being whilst repairs are carried out to the foundations which were damaged by the bad earthquake of a few years ago. I was feeling quite exhausted by this time and nobody wanted to spend any more time in the Old City so we bused back to our hotel and the pleasing prospect of showers and a decent meal.

I was kept awake that night by the sound of Sammy Cohen playing his violin. He has a Guarnerius. It is loaned to him by an ancient noble Italian family who actually own it, but he treats it as his own personal property. It very rarely leaves his sight. Whilst the instruments of all the other members of the orchestra are transported in a special pantechnicon Sammy carries his himself, humping it on and off planes and coaches and hugging it to himself as if it were a baby, and nobody else dare lay a finger on it. He has a second violin which is transported with the others but I don't think he ever plays it. His Guarnerius has a beautiful tone, quite unique, and when Sammy plays I listen.

Sarah and I shared a twin-bedded room next door to Sammy's single one. On the other side of his was another single room occupied by Miles Bretherton and beyond that a double room in which slept Ivo and Adrian Palmer. On the other side of the corridor were four more twin-bedded rooms shared by members of the Europa. The rest of the orchestra were on a different floor. Sarah had fallen asleep almost as soon as she had got into bed but I lay awake a long time and just as I was drifting off an achingly sweet cadenza from the room next door

31

drew me back. I got out of bed and padded across to the balcony which ran along the entire length of that floor, flimsy partitions separating the individual rooms and suites. Sammy was playing inside his room but the door leading onto his portion of the balcony was open and the music drifted out, shivering into the night air. I sat in the corner and listened. Outside, a palm rustled in the slight breeze that had risen, and below, a few coloured lights picked out the shiny, black water glittering in Sumatrim Bay; but my attention was all for the music.

Nobody knows quite where Sammy came from originally. He claims he was dug out of a ghetto somewhere in Central Europe. He has been rootless all his life but his one ambition is to have a house of his own when he retires. He talks about it as another would expound on his favourite hobby and I think a large part of his earnings goes towards this goal. Where this mythical home is going to be nobody knows either, but it is the pot at the end of Sammy's rainbow. I did not recognise what he was playing. It was sad and haunting and spoke of the sufferings of his tribe. I let the music flow over me and it was so poignant that I could hardly bear it.

Then there was an interruption in the form of some sort of fracas coming from one of the rooms further along this floor. Sammy went on playing but for me the spell was broken. There was a spate of angry voices and a balcony door was pushed open. For a few seconds I thought I could smell smoke, sweet and cloying. I had a feeling the commotion was coming from Ivo's room and I slipped back across my room and went out into the corridor. I was right. The corridor was dark and still and a row of blank doors faced me but behind Ivo's was the sound of raised voices. I tapped, and when no one replied I pushed open the door which was not locked and went in.

Miles Bretherton was standing in the middle of the room, his back to me, almost blocking off my view but I could see Ivo slumped on a bed, shaking his head and laughing. Miles was speaking in a low, angry voice.

'. . . fools! You ought to have more sense! Pull yourself together Adrian.'

Adrian was gabbling excitedly and gesticulating wildly. His speech didn't make much sense but he seemed to be trying to get across some brilliant idea he had had for improving the quality of the woodwind tone. Miles pushed him roughly onto the other bed and then seemed to become aware of my presence for the first time. He spun round and glared at me.

'Kate! You're not in on this too?'

'What?' I was stupefied but beginning to get horrible suspicions.

'Pot. These two beauties are stoned out of their tiny minds.' He picked up the thin, soggy-looking cigarette laying limply in the ashtray and waved it under my nose. At once I smelt again that sweet, elusive smell.

'It's wafting out of the window.'

'Damn. I was trying to get rid of the smell in here.' He strode over to the balcony and wrestled with the door.

'C'mon Kate. Come and join us.' Ivo pulled me down onto the bed. The whites of his eyes were red and he looked flushed and had a dry cough.

'Ivo, I didn't realise you were still involved with drugs. How could you be so stupid – what's the point?'

'Quite.' Miles had managed to shut the door and was back at the bedside. 'Get up Kate.' He yanked me to my feet and snarled at Ivo and Adrian: 'Don't you realise the penalties if you get caught? It can be five years in England and a hefty fine. God knows what it is over here, perhaps *you* know?' He spoke savagely to Ivo who shook his head and giggled.

33

'We weren't doing any harm. It should be lega-legalised.'

'Well it's not, and you should have more sense. I couldn't care less if you want to end up as a junkie but think of the orchestra. What do you think would happen if the authorities found out? Our reputation would be in shreds and we should be banned. Come on Kate.' He gestured to the door.

'But what about them? I mean . . .'

'We won't get any more sense out of them tonight. Let them sleep it off.' He snapped off the light switch and the last thing I saw as he pulled me out of the room was Adrian gently bumping his head against the wall and crooning to himself.

'Miles, you're hurting me!'

'Sorry.' He released my arm. 'What brought you on the scene?'

'I heard a commotion. You were making rather a noise.'

'Thank God no one else heard. You knew about his smoking?'

'He told me that he had been in some trouble years ago, before he left home to study. I didn't know he was still involved,' I said miserably. 'Will they be all right?'

'Yes,' he said tersely. 'I only hope I've found all of it.'

'You mean . . . ?'

He dug in the pocket of his dressing gown and produced the remains of the cigarette he had filched from the ashtray, a packet of cigarette papers and a tiny packet of whitish powder. 'This is what it is all about, Kate. Now you know.'

'What are you going to do with them? If they're found in your possession . . .'

'Don't worry, this little lot is going straight down the loo. Now, back to bed; you're losing your beauty sleep.

And just try to use your influence to keep your boyfriend on the straight and narrow.'

'I'm not his keeper,' I said stiffly. He was watching me carefully and I'm sure I could see amusement lurking in his eyes. His hair was ruffled and he looked altogether more human and approachable. It did not go with the expensive silk dressing gown he was wearing.

It was not until I was back in my room and listening to the ladylike snores of Sarah that I realised that I had forgotten to put on my own dressing gown. I was clad only in a somewhat transparent nightdress.

Ivo and Adrian did not appear at breakfast the next morning but to my amazement Ivo joined me on the beach later on, apparently none the worse for his indulgences of the night before. I had thought about it a lot, worrying it over in my mind and had decided that the best policy was a discreet silence, but Ivo was having none of it. He bounded up and flopped down beside me. The Splendid has a private beach nestling in a curve of the Lapad Bay and I did not intend to venture far that day.

'Kate, I'm sorry about last night. Am I forgiven?'

'You remember what happened then?'

'Kate, I adore you when you get on your high horse. Now stop being so prizzy and give me a kiss.'

'Ivo, stop it, everyone will see . . .'

His answer was to roll me into his arms and kiss me very thoroughly. Pot smoking had not impaired his technique. I felt myself dissolving and weakening and fought to keep up my resolve.

'Why do you do it? For the kicks?'

'There's no harm in it. I tell you Kate, it was a lot of fuss about nothing.'

'But . . . Miles . . .' He closed my mouth with

another kiss, then sat up hugging his knees.

'That snoopy bastard.'

'Ivo!'

'I suppose it hasn't occurred to you to wonder how he got onto us so quick? Mister Miles Bretherton is very *au fait* with the smell of hash; I wonder how?'

He had a point. The answer was obvious; Miles Bretherton must have indulged at some time. So much for his holier than thou attitude.

'Where do you get it from?'

'What?' He was being deliberately obtuse.

'The hash, pot, marijuana or whatever?'

'Now that would be telling. You go on being your innocent little self and don't worry about these things.'

'But I do worry. Suppose you had been caught by the hotel manager?'

'I'm flattered that you care. Now stop worrying Kate. I've fixed up a treat for this evening. I've got two tickets for the Lindo Folk Ensemble Concert. I know one of the performers; she comes from a village near my home town and she managed to get them for me.'

I had seen posters advertising the Lindo Ensemble. They are a group of dancers and musicians recruited from all areas of the country and they perform national dances, songs and music. They are an elite company and I had wanted to see them. Then I remembered.

'What about the rehearsal?'

'That will be over in plenty of time, and we won't have far to go. They perform on top of the Revelin Tower – there's an open-air theatre there.'

I spent the rest of the morning lazing on the beach and at lunchtime I left the hotel grounds and wandered up to the public Sumatrim Beach. This was packed with bodies and positively reeked of the coconut suntan oil with which the locals seem to smother themselves. My objective was a little café along the road leading up from the beach, which sells limunadu, coffee and ices and a marvellous range of mouth-watering cakes. I had almost reached it when I saw a grey Volkswagen car with Milicija on its side parked in the road and two policemen standing nearby talking to a third person who was hidden by the angle of their bodies. Then one of the policemen moved and I saw that their companion was Miles Bretherton.

My first thought was that he had been arrested. They'd found the pot in his possession, he hadn't managed to get rid of it, and he was being carted off to some Yugoslavian prison. Then I saw that the two grey-uniformed policemen were looking quite relaxed and Miles was actually smiling. Even as I watched he clapped one on the shoulders and called out something as they got into the car and drove off. I caught the word '*hvala*' which means 'thank you' and then he saw me.

'What's the matter, Kate? You look as if you've seen a ghost.'

'Those were policemen – they haven't found that stuff?'

He threw back his head and laughed. 'Don't be ridiculous, I was just asking them for directions.'

'They speak English?'

'My Serbo-Croatina is coming on in leaps and bounds. What about you? Are you doing a Garbo again?'

'I'm far too young to know what you are talking about. There seems to have been a mass exodus to the new complex at Babin Kuk and I decided I'd rather stay here. I was just going to sample some of those cakes.' I nodded towards the café.

'I'll join you.' There were tables and chairs set outside, but they were in the full sun and it was cooler inside. I had a limunadu and Miles a beer and I hesitated a long while over the choice of cakes. There were strud-las and Baklavas and swirling pyramids covered with chocolate but I finally settled for a wedge of what looked like marshmallow sandwiched between sponge.

Miles sipped his beer and eyed me fastidiously as I ate.

'Are you not hungry?' I asked.

'I had a snack back at the hotel.'

I was beginning to feel more than a little resentful of the superior Miles Bretherton. I always ended up feeling gauche and immature in his company. Who did he think he was anyway? I was more than half convinced that he had wheedled his way into the orchestra by false pre-tences, and I decided to lay a trap for him. But first I deliberately licked my fingers which were sticky with sugar and was pleased to note the pained expression that flickered across his face.

'Miles,' I said, putting my elbows on the table and resting my chin on my hands, 'I've been wanting to talk to you about our repertoire.' I stared at him fixedly.

'That's the province of the musical director.'

'Yes, but you've got influence. When are we going to do the Battle Symphony?'

I'd got him. For a couple of seconds he looked completely blank, then he was in control of himself again and parrying the question.

'You think we should?'

'I know the experts class it with his earlier works but I think it ranks with the 5th and 7th, don't you?'

'The experts are usually right.'

'But the fourth movement is pure genius; Beethoven at his best; all that virtuoso stuff for the strings. We really should do it.'

'I'll have a word with Willie some time.'

I turned away to hide the triumphant smile that threatened to take over my face. He had given himself away. The so-called Battle Symphony is an obscure piece of programme music by Beethoven; a sort of alternative to the 1812 Overture. It is a composition that few professional musicians have grappled with either in the hearing or the execution, involving a vast orchestra with a lot of timpani representing canons and excerpts from God Save the Queen and God knows what else. It makes Beethoven enthusiasts blush and most professionals regard it as a work best forgotten. It only has two movements.

Blissfully unaware of his gaffe, Miles continued: 'Have you recovered from last night?'

'Yes,' I said shortly. I did not want to discuss it with him.

'I hope you're not getting too involved with Tomasic.'

'It's none of your business! You're here to manage the financial affairs of the orchestra, not meddle with the members' private lives!'

'Calm down. I'm only trying to prevent you from getting hurt. Ivo Tomasic is in a different league from you. He treads dangerous paths.'

'When I want advice I'll ask somebody else.'

'I'm only trying to help, stop him from influencing you – he's not a very stable character.'

'You think he will corrupt me?' I asked icily.

'All right Kate, I'm sorry. I should have kept my big mouth shut. How is he today?'

'Perfectly normal, if that means anything to you. We have decided that it takes one to know one.'

'Now just what do you mean by that?'

'I'm talking about drug experimenters.'

'You mean . . . ?' Instead of being annoyed as I would have expected, he looked amused. I decided that I had had enough of Miles Bretherton's company. I picked up my handbag and stood up.

39

'Well, I mustn't detain you any longer. I expect you want to get going.'

'Do I?' He looked bemused.

'You were going somewhere, remember? You were asking directions.

'Quite, I mustn't waste all that hard-won information.'

The sun was still beating down outside and by the time I got back to the hotel I felt like a grease spot. I showered and lay on the bed and much against my will I drifted off into a deep sleep.

I dressed carefully for the evening bearing in mind that whatever I wore for the rehearsal would have to do duty for the concert later. I chose a full, gathered skirt and a low-backed embroidered blouse and with them I wore high-heeled sandals and filigree chandelier ear-rings that had originally come from here. Sarah teased me unmercifully. She was in a restless, disruptive mood and she got across Sammy before the rehearsal even started by drawing her bow across her violin in piercing cacophony.

'Sarah dear, do stop torturing that poor instrument,' he ordered.

'Poor Sammy. I declare when you get your little grey home in the west even the doorbells will charm in harmony.'

Sammy shuddered but his reply was lost in the crescendo of sound as we all attempted to tune up.

Willie Bode, looking distracted in shirt sleeves, bawled us down. '*C'est terrible*! Quiet please. May we have an A from our oboe.'

There was a dead silence. Then all eyes swivelled to where Adrian Palmer was sitting. Only he wasn't there. His oboe was propped up on his empty seat. A frisson went through the entire orchestra and I felt a prickle at the back of my neck. That Adrian, the principal oboe, was missing was extraordinary enough; the fact that his instrument was there and not him seemed to add a sinister dimension to his absence.

'Well . . .' Willie's eyebrows were nearly lost in his hair. ' . . . since Mr Palmer is not honouring us with his presence tonight perhaps I could have some co-operation from someone else?'

Marianne Ducros hurriedly put her reed to her lips and gave us a note.

'Do you know where he is?' I asked Ivo, who was looking worried.

'I think he was meeting someone; he must have been delayed.'

'I think he's gone back to the City Walls,' volunteered Jenny Seaman. 'He was very peeved yesterday evening that he hadn't got his camera with him and he said he was going back to get some photos some time. He probably forgot the time.'

The rehearsal continued without Adrian. We concentrated on the Stravinsky. Andras Flegman was playing the solo piano part. He is a percussionist but also a competent pianist and he doubles up in compositions requiring a pianist as part of the orchestration. His decisive rendering of his part of the Petrushka score helped to lift it off the ground. The insistent repeated single note high up on the piano keyboard that comes not far into the work beat like a warning tocsin into my brain. The music had never seemed so savage before, and there was no mistaking the tragedy enacted; the unleashing of primative emotions and the pathos of the ending.

Adrian Palmer didn't turn up. I kept looking over to the woodwind deck expecting to see that he had slipped into place but his seat remained empty and he hadn't returned by the time the rehearsal finished.

'Come on. Let's get out of here,' said Ivo, putting his instrument into its case. 'We can leave our violins backstage for now.'

As we hadn't eaten and would miss dinner at the hotel we went to a little restaurant near the Ploče Gate and ate a hurried meal of raznjici, which are pork kebabs, with salad and thick slices of bread and a carafe of local wine.

When we came out it was pitch dark and stars were sparkling overhead. We joined the mass of people converging on the Revelin Fort and made our way up through the hall where we had been rehearsing such a short while ago and out onto the top of the tower. A stage had been built out against one of the walls and the battlements provided an unusual backcloth. Tiers of seating built on a framework of scaffolding swept back to the other crenellated walls and we took our places, not far from the front, on the hard wood and metal seats.

'What a marvellous setting,' I said looking at the spotlighted walls and breathing in the atmosphere of anticipation and excitement that was building up.

'You wait until you see *Hamlet* performed at Fort Lovrijenac. That setting makes Elsinore look like a toy castle.'

'They do it in Serbo-Croatian?'

'They do.'

'That should be most interesting,' I said trying to imagine how the famous soliloquies would sound rendered in a different language. There was a burst of colour and music and suddenly the stage was full of whirling bodies and stamping feet and I gave myself over to the entertainment.

The musicians stood on the left-hand side of the stage. They were all male and included some very young boys, and their accompaniments ranged from a full backing of clarinets, guitars, mandolines, double bass, fiddles and tabor drums to a solo performance on a one-stringed mandolin. I was fascinated by this last. These one-stringed mandolins or fiddles are the national instrument of Yugoslavia. One hears them played whenever there are gatherings of folk groups and replicas of them figure largely on the souvenir stalls. The range of haunting, wailing notes that can be coaxed from the one string by the vibrant sawing of the little bow is quite astounding.

The dancers themselves in their beautiful national costumes were equally enthralling; the men in their boots and fur caps and capes and the women a kaleidoscope of colour. One of the dances had no music at all, just the steps called out to the beat of the feet, and several were augmented by the singing of the female performers, in which the Eastern influence could be easily discerned.

The dances fell into roughly three categories. There were the dances from northern Yugoslavia; Istria and Slovenia, which had a strong Austrian flavour both in the costume and the rather heavy music. There were the eastern European, with Slav-type music and costumes; and the Turkish/Albanian-style dances from Macedonia, Montenegro and Serbia, with their wailing Eastern music and costumes showing a Muslim influence.

'Which is your friend?' I asked, as the first half rose to a spectacular conclusion.

'The second one along in the front row.'

I don't know how he could tell. It was a Serbian dance and the men and women were heavily veiled and swathed from head to toe. It was hot enough in the still night air for the audience to feel uncomfortable. How the dancers managed to bear the weight of their costumes, let alone dance in them, I couldn't imagine, with their thick boots and what looked like fur rugs slung from their waists.

'Come below and meet her,' said Ivo as the interval commenced. 'We'll get a drink and meet some of the company.'

The bar was tucked away in a corner of the concert hall below and the performers were already mingling with the audience when we reached there. Ivo led me over to a small group and tapped one of the women on the shoulder.

'Mija, *kako si*?'

'Ivo! *Dobra sam, a ti*?'

'Kate, this is Mija Novakovic. Mija, *ove je* Kati.'

'Hello, I am pleased to meet you.' She had shed some of her layers of clothing and was bareheaded. Her hair was an improbable shade of dark red and her greenish, hazel eyes were heavily outlined in black, but beneath the make-up she was a very attractive young woman. She smiled at me warmly as we shook hands.

'Your English is very good.'

'It is our second language now and I go on the tour a lot. You are enjoying the concert?'

'Very much. It is quite enthralling and I can't wait to see the second half. You must be exhausted.'

She shrugged. 'It is our way of life.'

'I will go and get us a drink,' said Ivo eyeing the crowd round the bar. 'I think you two can manage to communicate all right.'

We communicated very well. By the time Ivo returned, looking a little battered and clutching three glasses to his chest, we were deep into a conversation on Serbian regional dances and Mija was telling me about a dance that was performed by men only at local weddings which involved handkerchiefs being set alight. We sipped our drinks and made polite conversation for a few more minutes and then Ivo said apologetically to me:

'Do you mind if we talk in Serbian for a bit? There are

44

things I want to discuss with Mija and I don't think her English is quite up to it.'

'Of course not, carry on. I'm quite happy just surveying the scene.'

They chatted away at what seemed a great rate. It is strange how people speaking in another language always seem to talk so fast; perhaps English spoken by us sounds the same. I caught the odd word here and there that I understood, and I think I figured largely in the conversation. I was content to stand aside and let the talk drift round me. I was still punch-drunk from watching the spectacular first half of the show.

I studied Ivo. There was no mistaking his origins now he was among his fellow countrymen; the same olive skin, expressive eyes and intensity. He would look fantastic in the clothes the male dancers were now wearing; embroidered shirts, red breeches, boots and short, swinging cloaks. How different he was this evening from the hyped-up character of last night.

'Kate, Mija has come up with a marvellous offer.' He grabbed my arm as if he would invest me with his enthusiasm. 'Her sister owns a holiday chalet further down the coast. It is not being used at the moment and we can borrow it for the next fortnight!' He saw my hesitation. 'Don't you think it is a terrific idea?'

'I – I don't know. It's so sudden.' Good heavens, I sounded like a Victorian heroine but I felt that I was being pressurised, swept away by a proposition that needed careful thought, not an impulsive decision.

'You hadn't got anything else planned, had you? Just think, Kate, it will be a lovely break. Just you and me – at long last. You can't hold out on me any longer you know.' The look he bent on me made me weak at the knees.

'Where is it?' I asked feebly, playing for time.

'Baošić, on the Boka Kotorska,' said Mija. 'It is very simple, a small village but very pretty.'

'The Boka Kotorska is that series of fiords that cut inland beyond Herceg-Novi,' said Ivo. 'It is one of the great tourist attractions of this area.' I remembered seeing it on the map. 'How about it, Kate? You'll come?'

'I don't know. I must think about it.' Ivo looked mutinous, then turned to Mija and rattled off again in Serbian. The five-minute bell had already gone and Mija had to get backstage.

'It is lovely knowing you,' she said taking my hand. 'You will like Baošić.'

She hurried away from us and Ivo called after her,

'*Videćemo se sutra!*'

'What are you saying?'

'That I'll see her tomorrow. I must make arrangements.'

'I haven't said that I'll go.'

'But you will, won't you Kate?' He looked at me pleadingly.

'Come on, we must get back to our seats.'

I was thankful to immerse myself once more in the performance. Ivo could be very persuasive, and secretly I wanted to be persuaded. Tomorrow I would make a decision, or rather, Ivo would make it for me. Tonight I was still my own woman.

At the end of the concert we picked up our violins and joined the exodus from the Revelin Fort. We left the Old City by the Ploče Gate and plunged down the steep, ravine-like road that led back to Pilé and the bus stop. Steep walls of rock, both natural and man-made sections of the city walls, reared up beside us dwarfing man and vehicle alike, and far above a slit of inky black sky glittered with stars.

The bus was, as usual, crowded and when we alighted at the Sumatrim terminus we were sticky and crumpled. It didn't seem possible it was nearly midnight, it was still so hot and very humid. Any breeze that blew off the sea was stilled at this time of the night. We sauntered down the road to the hotel and after a few stops for amorous dalliance we made it into the foyer.

There were a lot of people still about. I was surprised to see several members of the orchestra waiting around; it was almost as if there was a reception committee waiting for us.

'Where have you been?' asked a worried Harris Fordham.

'They looked as if they've been busking,' drawled a pinched-looking Carley waving a hand at our violins.

'How can you be so flippant at a time like this?'

'Is something wrong?' I was suddenly aware of the strained atmosphere, the look of shock on everyone's faces, and then I saw the policemen, several of them and all toting enormous guns on their hips. 'What has happened?'

'I'll tell you what has happened,' Miles Bretherton came towards us, his face taut and wary. 'Adrian Palmer is dead. His body has been found below the Old City walls.'

# *Chapter 3*

Beside me Ivo made a noise that was half grunt, half groan and I turned on Miles Bretherton.

'It's not true! It can't be true!'

'I'm afraid it is. I've identified the body.'

'Why wasn't I sent for?' snarled Ivo. 'Where is he?'

'You weren't around and I was the obvious person.'

'How did it happen? Where?'

'He fell from a part of the wall on the seaward side of the Old City. His body was found in an alleyway between two empty, derelict buildings. It could have lain there undiscovered for some time but a gang of boys who were trespassing and playing where they had no right to be stumbled on it. Have you any idea what he was doing on the walls when he should have been at rehearsal?'

'He wanted to go back and take some photos,' said Ivo who was looking very pale.

'His camera was found nearby, smashed,' said Miles, and I winced. It was later that I remembered that his photography was not the explanation Ivo had offered earlier for Adrian's absence, but I supposed that it was the more obvious one.

'But how could it have happened?'

'The parapet wall was very low just there and I

suppose he leaned over to take a photo and slipped.' I shuddered and Miles took my arm and led me to a seat. 'Sit down a minute. You've had a terrible shock. I'll get you a brandy, and then the police want to question you. They're interviewing everyone.'

The brandy was slivovic, the local plum brandy, and I put it down untouched. The chief police officer spoke English; stilted, stylised English, but understandable. I wondered how we would be treated by the police force of a Communist state but my worries were unfounded. He was, and indeed all his colleagues were, charming and competent and not half so officious as many of their English counterparts. After a few routine questions I was dismissed but Ivo spent much longer with them. He was taking it very hard, which was understandable, and his face looked very pale beneath the surface tan.

'Go up to your room, Kate,' said Miles; 'there's nothing more you can do. I sent Sarah up a little while ago.'

'Miles . . .' I drew him out of earshot of the police and the other orchestra members still wandering around looking poleaxed. '. . . he hadn't been smoking, had he? I mean, he wasn't high and that caused him to fall?'

'I should hardly think so. Look, the police are quite satisfied that it was an accident; let's not complicate matters.' He sounded weary.

'Of course not. What about his family?'

'He had an elderly mother and father – I've been on the phone to them, they're flying out tomorrow. He had no brothers or sisters or other close relations.'

'Poor Miles, this is rotten for you. What will happen?'

'I suppose there'll be the Yugoslavian equivalent of an inquest but I should imagine it will only be a formality; they'll settle for accidental death. I think his parents want his body flown back to England.'

The police officer called Miles over and I left the reception lounge and walked slowly up the stairs. Sarah was staring tragically at her reflection in the dressing-table mirror when I reached our room. We stayed up, huddled on one bed, talking for ages and when we eventually settled down for the night I was convinced that I wouldn't sleep. But I did, and nightmares stalked my slumber. I was a swallow flying low over the Old City walls and below me I could see bodies; body after body lying tumbled on the ground below. I dived down and inspected each corpse; everyone was a member of the orchestra. They were all there; the principals, sub-principals and rank-and-file of each section; only one was missing – Adrian Palmer.

I awoke some time later and clawed my way back to reality. My heart was pounding and sweat was trickling down my face. I squinted at the luminous dial of my watch. It said 3 o'clock. I swung my legs off the bed intending to get a drink of water when I heard a scrabbling at the door. I froze, half in, half out of bed and listened. Someone was tapping quietly on the door and I heard a disembodied voice whispering my name.

'Who is it?'

'Ivo. Please let me in Kate; it's urgent!'

I hesitated for a few seconds, then unlocked the door and opened it a little way. Ivo insinuated himself into the room.

'What's the matter?'

'Sarah – is she likely to wake up?'

'She's dead to the world once she's asleep.'

'Good, can we go through to your balcony?'

'Ivo, what is it? What's the matter?'

'Ssh!' He led me across the room and through the verandah doors which were standing open.

'I've got to get into my room.'

'You've locked yourself out?'

'No, I've been moved to another room on the floor above this, and the police have locked up our old room, but I've got to get in – there's something I must get hold of.'

'Didn't they give you the chance to move your things out?'

'This is something of Adrian's – the box he kept his reeds in.'

I remembered the box. Adrian, like many oboe players, made his own reeds and he kept them in a black wooden box which went everywhere with him.

'But what do you want that for?'

'Kate, he kept his supplies in there.'

'You mean . . .?'

'Yes. I can't risk the police finding it, or his parents. They'll be taking possession of all his things tomorrow – today.'

'Then what are you going to do?'

'Try and get along the balcony. I should be able to get over the partitions and I just hope they haven't locked the verandah door.'

'Suppose you wake the others up?' I gestured to the adjoining rooms. 'They'll all have their doors open – it's so hot.'

'Then I'll have to be very careful, won't I?' He flashed me a grin and edged his way carefully along the balcony. As he merged into the darkness I listened to his progress. The odd footfall, the rattle as he negotiated a partition and a creak and rustle and then silence.

He seemed to be gone ages and when he suddenly appeared, looming out of the darkness, I was quite startled.

'Did you get it?'

His answer was to hand me the object he was carrying. I was surprised at how heavy it was.

'The louvre doors were fastened but it was easy to force them. I don't think anyone heard me.'

'What are you going to do with it?'

'I want you to keep it for the time being.'

'Me?' My voice squeaked. 'Are you crazy? I'm not having anything to do with it.' I dropped the box onto my bed as if it were red hot. In the other bed Sarah stirred and muttered something.

'Ssh. Kate please! It's only for a little while till I can get rid of it. Nobody's going to search your things, nobody knows it exists. But I wouldn't put it past our dear Mr Bretherton to go through my belongings if he gets half a chance. He's just waiting for an excuse.'

'Where can I put it?' I said unhappily.

'Lock it away in your suitcase and forget about it.'

I didn't think I would be able to do that. It was weighing heavily on my conscience already, but I did as I was bid. He lifted my suitcase down from the wardrobe shelf and I picked up the black box and tried the lid.

'It's locked.'

'Of course it is and there is no need to open it at the moment. Make sure you keep your suitcase locked.'

We stowed it away and I returned the key to my handbag.

'You'd better go.'

'What a pity Sarah's sharing with you. All right, I'm on my way. You will come to Baošić with me, won't you?'

'I don't know. We may all be under arrest by tomorrow. Now, for goodness sake go before you wake up the entire hotel.'

I opened the door and pushed him out. He hadn't awakened the whole hotel, only one of the people who slept on this floor. As he slipped down the corridor, Miles Bretherton stood silhouetted in his doorway, the light behind him making a nimbus of his blond hair. I wondered how long he had been there. Long enough to witness Ivo leaving my bedroom, of that I was sure. I shot back into my room and resisted the temptation to slam the door.

I overslept the next morning, the result of two disturbed nights, and woke feeling strained and languid. Everyone was very subdued and any mention of Adrian Palmer was carefully avoided at first.

The concert was to go ahead as arranged. At first there had been tentative suggestions that the rest of the tour be cancelled but these were overruled. Fortunately we carried an extra oboe player with us on this tour. Mahler's 1st Symphony is part of our repertoire and it calls for four oboes, so Sean O'Toole, a new recruit to the orchestra, joined us and tried out his hand in small parts. For this concert Marianne Ducros would have to play principal oboe and they would all move up one. We were due to play the Mahler again in Belgrade at our last concert and for that another oboe player would have to be recruited. For the time being we could manage, but even the mention of a possible cancellation had provoked a shocking outburst from Peter Brownstone. He glared round the dining room and went on at length about the debt we owed our Yugoslavian hosts, the irresponsibility of even thinking of disappointing our audiences, and he even brought in something about East/West relationships.

'Calm down, Peter,' said Sven Larsen, our deputy leader. 'It has only been suggested that out of respect to Adrian Palmer that concert should be cancelled or postponed.'

'That is nonsense,' snapped Peter, rubbing at his horn-rimmed glasses. 'Just because one young irresponsible member of the orchestra goes and gets himself killed you want to jeopardise the whole tour; and all the goodwill we've built up.'

'Peter, that is quite unforgivable,' said Sven looking very distressed. 'I can only think that shock has clouded your judgement.'

Peter subsided and attacked his food with muttered asides but he had the grace to look slightly ashamed. I thought it was a good thing that Sammy had not put in an appearance at the breakfast table.

'Anyone would think he had his own money tied up in this tour,' hissed Sarah. 'Callous brute.'

We dispersed after the meal but many of us stayed within the hotel environment. Ivo was in a state of shock and very edgy. Even my company seemed unwelcome to him. He said he had things to do and was missing for most of the day. No policemen were in evidence and I didn't see Miles Bretherton. I believed he was going to the airport at Cilipi to meet Adrian Palmer's parents off the plane.

I drew comfort from my music. I practiced rigorously, concentrating on my double stopping and actually managed to forget events for a while though they waited like a black cloud ready to pounce on me when I dropped my guard. I did not see the arrival of Adrian's parents. I did not want to witness their distress. Common decency told me that I should talk and commiserate with them, especially as Ivo, Adrian's particular friend, had opted out of the task, but cowardice kept me penned in my room. I couldn't really believe that Adrian was dead. I kept remembering him as he had been in the last few days; his high spirits on Lokrum, his drugged euphoria of the night before last, his black, surly moods. It seemed impossible that someone who had been so visibly alive could be snuffed out just like that. One false step, a slip – and curtains. I was also horribly aware of the wooden box locked in my suitcase. It was burning a hole in my conscience and I wanted out.

As it was an official engagement the entire orchestra was transported by coach from the hotel to the Ploče Gate for the concert. Everyone was tense and feelings ran high and there was none of the usual camaraderie in the dressing rooms. I struggled into my black dress and looked despairingly in the mirror. I do this at every concert. Black does nothing for me. The colour does not suit me and at best I look like a little girl got up in her big sister's dress. Carley looks a dream with her ethereal, fragile appearance and even Sarah appears sophisticated and soignée with her wild hair pinned up in a classic chignon and her black sleeves falling back in folds from her skinny arms.

Sammy, sitting hunched up with his fiddle talking to Willie Bode, looked more like a vulture than ever as we filed past him onto the stage. Not by so much as a flicker of his drooping eyelids did he acknowledge that we had anything to do with him. The hall was packed and as the news of Adrian's death had got around there was a certain prurient excitement present in the audience that manifested itself in noise and restlessness. They gave Sammy an enthusiastic ovation as he walked across the stage and took his place and when Willie strode on, resplendant in his tails, they outdid themselves.

The first work in our programme was Ravel's 'La Valse'. As we swung into the opening bars, audience and musicians alike relaxed and settled into the music. For me it was an unfortunate choice as it echoed the disquiet I was feeling. As the music swelled into the hectic rhythm that surges out of control, I had a sense of being swept along helplessly with it, and as the beat disintegrated and changed from a ballroom measure to a sinister parody of the opening melody it emphasised the bizarre sense of everything being out of kilter. When the music whirled to its final frenzied conclusion I felt shaken and quite wrung out.

Ivo was equally affected. Twice he missed the page turnover and his bowing was so disjointed that I feared he would call down Sammy's wrath in the interval. But when the interval came Ivo disappeared. The Stravinsky had been well received and it was several minutes before the audience would release us from its adulation. As we trooped backstage I turned to speak to Ivo, who I thought was following me, and caught sight of him vanishing down the stairs. He took his place for the second half at the very last moment, to the bemusement of the audience who was poised to acknowledge the return of the leader, and a spatter of applause followed his first steps across the stage before petering out.

'Where have you . . .? Ivo! What's the matter?'

He was very pale and his skin had a sickly sheen that contrasted baldly with his black glittering eyes. He settled on his chair and gave me a travesty of a smile that was meant to be reassuring but had quite the opposite effect.

'I . . . nothing, Kate. I'll tell you afterwards. I . . .'

Whatever he was going to say was drowned by the applause that finally located Sammy. Then we were into the Beethoven 7th and I was caught up in the discipline and magnificence of the work. But even that didn't get my usual one hundred per cent attention. I was aware of the tension emanating from the man beside me. Ivo was there in the flesh but certainly not in the spirit. Never had that symphony seemed so long, and when the finale thundered to its conclusion the audience went wild.

They demanded an encore and got it, the Rakoczy March in the Liszt arrangement, and when that was over they still would not let us go. Willie got us all to our feet. All, that is, except Ivo who positively cringed in his seat and looked round wildly as if planning to sidle off unnoticed, an impossibility on an apron-stage.

At last we were back stage and Ivo made a great business of casing his instrument. I demanded his attention.

'Well? Would it be too much to ask why you are behaving like a paranoic?'

'Sorry Kate. It's difficult to explain.'

'It's perfectly obvious.' He looked alarmed and I continued: 'There was someone in the audience you didn't want to see, or rather, someone who you didn't want to see *you*. Who was it? An ex-girl friend who's caught up with you at long last?'

'Would that it were. I'll try and explain but the truth of the matter is that I've got to get out.'

'What do you mean?'

'Look, we can't talk here.' He grabbed my arm and propelled me round a pillar into a dark corner of the cavern-like room. 'You remember that I told you that I had to leave my home and family – that there had been trouble with the police? Well, it was a bit more complicated than that.'

'I don't understand.'

'Someone was killed.' He saw my face and hurried on. 'There was a fracas amongst two rival gangs of youths. Feelings ran high and it turned nasty. We were half-stoned and – and the truth of the matter is, someone got knifed.'

'You killed someone?' It was a bald statement but I felt quite numb.

'No – yes. I mean, it was an accident, not a cold-blooded killing.'

57

'So you *are* wanted by the police?' I said feeling my way cautiously.

'No. I tell you, it was an accident. I was exonerated by the police.' He paused and looked at me helplessly. 'It was the dead youth's family. They held me responsible, they still do. In their eyes I owe them a debt.'

'You mean, like an eye for an eye, a tooth for a tooth?'

'A family feud. It is very binding. Their honour is at stake; the family honour has to be vindicated.'

'Are you trying to tell me that things like that still go on? Like the Mafia, Sicily, Corsica? It's preposterous.'

'It may seem so to your Western eyes but I can assure you it really happens in my part of the country. It is not just an Italian or Corsican prerogative. I'm as good as dead if they get their hands on me.'

'And one of the family was out there tonight? And saw you?'

'An uncle. I don't know if I was recognised but my name is in the programme.'

'But can't you claim police protection?'

'Don't be ridiculous. I've got to get out. I'll go to Baosic, to Mija's sister's place. We'll both go. You will come with me now, won't you Kate? I need you.'

'Yes, I'll come, but you can't run away for ever.'

'It's only for a couple of weeks. it will have blown over by then.'

I am grudging in my affections. I wanted to go with him. I *was* going with him. He needed me, and this appeal clinched things as far as I was concerned, but even as I made my decision a part of me queried whether he was emotionally blackmailing me, manipulating events to get his own way. I was immediately ashamed of my thoughts.

'Come on, or we'll miss the coach.'

'We must go now – tonight.'

'We can't possibly go tonight! Look, no one's going to be able to get at you on a private coach in full view of the entire orchestra. We've got to make arrangements, we can't just up and leave or it will begin to look like the ten little niggers.'

'Ten little niggers? What do you mean?'

'Oh nothing. Surely you've got to get in touch with Mija? How do we get to this place? What do we take?'

'Yes, you're right Kate. We'll leave it till the morning. I will ring Mija and arrange for her to get the key and find out the best way of getting there. Don't pack a lot. We can leave the bulk of our stuff at the hotel, we shall need very little. We'll go native, and I'll show you how the other half lives.'

He had recovered his usual aplomb and he was firing me with his enthusiasm. We grabbed our things and rushed after the others and only just made it to the coach in time.

Sarah was going to Greece. With the prospect of fourteen days' holiday before them, about a dozen members of the orchestra had decided to hire a mini-bus and press south to Greece and there was some talk of them eventually taking the ferry to Corfu. I had toyed with the idea of joining them but now I had to tell Sarah I had made other arrangements. Ivo had insisted that I didn't mention to anyone exactly where we were going so I was deliberately vague about our destination.

'So this is it, is it?' she said cramming clothes into a case. 'You're deserting your friends and throwing in your lot with our wicked Serbian Romeo.'

'Ha, ha, very funny! We're just going off for a couple of weeks' holiday and I for one won't be sorry to get away from everyone here and the present atmosphere – you excluded, of course.' The authorities had withdrawn satisfied after their enquiries into Adrian's death and everyone was eager to get away for a break.

'I know what you mean.' She became serious. 'This business of Adrian's death: I just can't believe it. It must have really knocked Ivo, they were such friends. Well, you must do your best to console him. And have fun. I must say though, you don't look exactly overjoyed at the prospect.'

'Some of us can control our emotions,' I said stiffly.

'Oh Kate, don't go all huffy on me. I didn't mean to offend you. I'm sure you'll have a fantastic time, and don't take any notice of me – I'm just green-eyed with jealousy deep down inside.' She smiled at me and we spent the next half-hour discussing what I should take with me in the way of clothes.

It was then that I remembered the wooden box in my case. Sarah couldn't understand why I wouldn't pack that night.

The Adriatic Highway runs from north to south of Yugoslavia, for the most part hugging the coastline as the name suggests; from Trieste in the north to the Albanian border, before swinging inland to Titograd and the scanty network that dissects the interior of the country. It is a main artery, *the* main artery serving the coastal resorts and it is narrow, congested, scenically fantastic and can be hair-raising to drive along. We travelled along part of it the next day, and Mija came with us to show us the way.

But first I had an encounter with Peter Brownstone that left a nasty taste in my mouth. I had risen very early, too early for breakfast in fact, and was waiting on the patio for Ivo to put in an appearance and breakfast service to start, in that order, when Peter appeared through the swing doors, blinking in the sunshine and cleaning his glasses with a large handkerchief. He put them back on his nose, saw me and sauntered over.

'Hallo Kate, couldn't you sleep?'

'I could ask the same of you.' I hoped he wouldn't stay around but he eased himself into a nearby chair and seemed disposed for conversation.

'One wakes so early in this climate. I suppose the only thing to do is to follow the natives; burn the candle at both ends and sleep in the middle.' He had got his metaphors beautifully mixed but I knew what he meant. There was the distant clink of crockery and cutlery and he raised his brows and continued: 'Are you going into breakfast? Shall we go together.'

'I am waiting for Ivo.'

'Ah yes, Ivo. I suppose he will be going back to England?'

'Why should he be doing that?' I asked in surprise.

'I presume he'll be attending Adrian Palmer's funeral. We can't all fly back, but as his closest friend Ivo will be able to represent those members of the orchestra who can't make it.'

The idea hadn't crossed my mind and I was pretty certain it hadn't occurred to Ivo either, but of course Peter was right; it was the natural assumption to make and I felt guilty on Ivo's behalf.

'We've made other plans,' I said shortly, hoping he wouldn't pursue the subject, but no such luck.

'You mean he's *not* going? I find that quite extraordinary. Whatever must Adrian's parents think?'

'You've changed your tune from yesterday,' I was goaded to reply.

'There are proprieties to be observed when these things unfortunately happen. I have spoken with his parents; they are very distressed.'

'I expect they are. If you're so concerned with proprieties why aren't you flying back to attend the funeral?'

'It is hardly my place to,' he said smugly, 'I intend staying here and seeing something of the country. It is too good a chance to miss.'

'Still the culture-vulture?' I enquired nastily.

It is a standing joke that when you first join an orchestra and go on tour you spend all your precious free time, and precious little there is of it usually, rushing round and 'doing' all the local sights; museums, art galleries etc. This soon palls and you quickly get culture indigestion. One museum looks very much like another, this historic monument the replica of that one and so on. All too quickly the memory of one place merges with the memory of another until you can hardly remember what place you are in, and any spare time is spent in relaxing and unwinding and not chasing the culture trail. Peter is an exception and is still an assiduous sightseer, as likely to be seen perusing a guidebook as a musical score. I decided I had had enough of his company for the time being and I got to my feet.

'I've just remembered, I'm supposed to be meeting Ivo in the dining room. Have fun.'

As I made my way indoors I thought about all the places in Dubrovnik I had intended revisiting: the Rector's Palace, the Church of St Blaise, the Dominican and Franciscan churches, the Collegium Ragusinum, the picture galleries. So far I had only made it back to Lokrum and the City Walls. But my mind shied away from thoughts of the City Walls. My memories of the Old City would always now be spoilt for me. Perhaps it was as well that I was moving on and exploring new places.

The coach station is situated at Gruz, not far from the New Harbour. It swarms with activity, long-haul coaches mingling with the local buses. We boarded a coach to Herceg-Novi where we would have to change. Mija sat beside Ivo and as they chatted away in Serbian I relaxed behind them and soaked up the scenery. After a short, steep climb out of the city we were upon the Adriatic Highway and bowling along the busy, winding road. To the right of us the ground fell away precipitously down to the sea and there was a fantastic view of the Old City below, lapped by the sparkling water, crowned by the island of Lokrum floating off-shore.

To the left of us the hillside rose up in a series of pleats and tucks, bare rockface intermingling with scrub and gnarled olives and pines; wherever there was a dwelling, whether a simple peasant cottage or a modern hotel complex, it was hung about with vines and figs and the burgeoning oleanders in their full pink and white glory.

A proliferation of erect, slender pines, darkly green against the bleached, dusty soil, announced that we were approaching Cilipi and the airport which serves Dubrovnik and the surrounding district. These Cyprus pines grow only in this area of the Dalmation coast and they cluster round the airport environment like a phalanx of sentries. Beyond Cilipi we passed vineyards which Mija said produced a very famous red wine.

Herceg-Novi was a bitter disappointment to me when we eventually arrived. We tumbled out of the coach into the glaring sunshine and as far as I could see the only building of any importance was the bus station itself, with its name AUTOBUSNA STANICA in crooked letters across the front façade and benches outside housing a motley collection of travellers and their luggage.

'This is Herceg-Novi?' I couldn't keep the surprise out of my voice and Mija patted my arm and smiled.

'It is very beautiful town, down there,' she gestured to behind the bus station where presumably somewhere the sea was hidden. 'It is long way down. Herceg-Novi is built on . . . *tri sprata*?' She appealed to Ivo.

'Three levels,' said Ivo.

'*Da*, three levels. Here is just the bus terminus, a garage, café, new buildings. You go down many steps, there is the town; many beautiful buildings, shops, gardens. Then down many more steps and is the sea.'

'And we haven't got time to have a look around today,' said Ivo. 'I think that's the bus we want over there.'

We threaded our way through the waiting buses and I tried to read the destination boards.

'What's the matter now?' Ivo saw the expression on my face.

'Some of them are in Cyrillic,' I said.

'Of course,' he replied with a quick grin. 'You're leaving the tourist trail now you know.'

'And I suppose Cyrillic or Roman – it's all the same to you?'

'We're brought up from the cradle knowing both. Do you want me to teach you the Cyrillic alphabet?'

'Serbo-Croatian in the Roman alphabet is enough to grapple with at the moment. I think I'll forgo the other pleasure for the time being,' I said hurriedly.

The blue-grey bus was built on strictly utilitarian lines. We entered by the door at the back, paid our fares to the conductor who sat behind a little desk near the rear and took our places on the hard, wooden benches that served instead of upholstered seats. The Adriatic Highway turns away from the sea here and follows that unique string of fiords, the Boka Kotorska. We spun along the road through places with fairy-tale names: Zelenika, Denovici, and as we got nearer to our destination I noticed that the houses and buildings seemed humbler and more tumbledown, apart from the odd roadside café or hotel that stood out like a bright scab on the scrubby hillside. I was fascinated by the hayricks that marked each little farmstead. They were cylindrical in shape, like elongated igloos, and had a pole sticking out of the top and some had little canvas hats.

The bus swung round another bend and Mija got to her feet. 'We are here.'

We struggled off the bus with our luggage and I looked around with interest. The road ran along literally on a ledge of the hillside. On one side the ground climbed up sheer to the skyline and on the other it fell away down to the shore which was hidden from sight by the mean little stone buildings perched crudely amongst the stunted trees and seared grass. It all looked very inauspicious and I glanced helplessly at Ivo who shrugged his shoulders and plunged after Mija down the rough concrete road that led downwards off the Adriatic Highway. The verges were dotted with blue-starred chicory and a rather attractive white umbellifer, and as we progressed downwards we left behind the barren landscape and entered a green tunnel, flamboyant with semi-tropical vegetation. Palm trees of many varieties arched above our heads, mixed in with sycamores, aspens, walnuts, olives and figs and through the trees there was a glimpse of vivid blue water. Little avenues led off the road and scattered haphazardly along these, amongst the trees, were the holiday chalets, many with their own small gardens bright with dahlias, cannas and other flowers I could put no name to.

Mija stopped in front of a chalet. It had a patio threaded with vines and was set out with table and chairs, and there was a sink with a tap and a primitive stove with double burners built into a unit near the door. The chalet itself looked hardly bigger or grander than the average English beach-hut but Mija unlocked the

65

door and threw it open with a flourish of pride. Inside it was larger than it looked from the outside. There was a kitchen with an ancient electric oven, work-tops and cupboards and a large collection of brightly coloured pots and pans; and three bedrooms led off this, each with built-in bunk beds and cupboards. It was pleasantly cool inside with the canopy of branches overhead.

'Where's the bathroom?' I hissed to Ivo and Mija heard me and burst into a fit of giggles. She was looking very pretty in a vivid yellow tee-shirt dress that showed off her smooth sunburnt arms and legs to perfection. I couldn't think how Ivo could possibly be interested in me when faced with such an attractive compatriot. She fished about on a ledge above the door and handed me a key with mirth sparking in her tawny eyes.

'I think it is a communal one,' said Ivo gently. 'Well, what do you think of it?' he gestured round the chalet.

'It's not quite what I expected,' I admitted cautiously.

Ivo started firing a fusilage of questions at Mija in Serbian and I left them to it and set out to reconnoitre the sanitary arrangements. I returned a short while later considerably chastened. Mija was inside checking the contents of the kitchen cupboards and Ivo lolled on the patio and watched my return with the same malicious amusement in his eyes that Mija had shown.

'Is everything all right?' He asked politely.

'This is primitive, not simple,' I retorted, stung by the smug look on his face. 'Do you realise exactly what the toilet facilities are? A HOLE in the ground!'

He nearly fell off the chair laughing. 'Oh Kati, you do sound so English and middle class. This will be good for your education – I told you, you'll see how the other half lives.'

I gave up in disgust.

Later, the three of us explored the village and I began

to appreciate its attractions. The beach was formed of shale and broken up by several little jetties that thrust out into the clear water. At the back of the beach ran a concrete and rock promenade bordered by hedges and a fringe of trees with feathery leaves that dipped their fronds into the very water itself in places. I found out later that these were mimosa trees and wished that I could see them in the spring when they would be covered with their yellow, fluffy blossoms. There were a couple of restaurants along the front and a shop and a small supermarket.

'They are open every morning and evening and closed all afternoon,' said Mija. 'You should be able to buy here all the food you need.'

The supermarket certainly seemed well-stocked but I eyed the meat counter with misgivings. There were slabs of dark, almost purple-coloured meat that resembled no cut with which I was familiar and chicken carcasses that all too obviously still housed their quota of innards and were distinguished by enormous pale yellow, scaly feet that seemed far too large for the birds they had once supported.

We retraced our steps and walked in the other direction along the edge of the bay and I bit back an exclamation of horror at the sight that faced us. A cascade of tumbledown houses, wrecked and dilapidated and spilling into the water, barred our way.

'The earthquake,' said Mija simply.

'How long ago was it?' I asked.

'1979.'

'And the damage hasn't been repaired?'

'There is no money.'

The buildings were torn open and leaning at crazy angles as if a giant had been playing skittles with them. Huge cracks split those walls still standing and pines that had been uprooted and submerged in the sea stuck up like ghost trees out of their watery graves. There were crude red crosses painted on the devastated buildings.

'Were many people killed?'

'It is very lucky here. No peoples killed on land, but one fisherman out in his boat – big wave drown him. One day they will repair.' She shrugged. 'Other places much worse. Kotor, inside the walls, all destroyed and farther down coast at Budva the old city is all knocked down. There is . . . was the epicentar.'

'The epicentre of the earthquake,' put in Ivo.

'Many peoples lose their homes in the earthquake,' continued Mija. 'Those buildings with red cross must be *srušene su* – pull down, those with green marks to be mended before peoples live in again. Those with zut – yellow mark, can be live in but to be mended.'

It was the first time I had seen earthquake damage in the flesh, so to speak, and I was devastated myself. The people here must live with this threat continually hanging over their heads; a phenomenon completely alien to me and my fellow countrymen.

'Don't worry, it won't happen again whilst we're here,' said Ivo. 'These quakes occur at well-spaced, plotted intervals and we're not due for another one yet.'

'I wish I had your confidence,' I murmured, still unable to tear my eyes away from the scene before me.

We walked back to the little kafana that shared a terrace with the local tourist bureau. This bureau had a board outside proudly announcing in English that it was an 'Informtion Bureau'. This statement set the pattern for all my subsequent transactions with this office. The girl clerk who insisted that she spoke English, was almost completely unintelligible and any information she gave me, such as local bus times, turned out to be totally inaccurate. I don't think Baošić had seen many

English visitors: it was a Yugoslavian resort built up over the years for and by Yugoslavians and it had a certain charm that already, after only a couple of hours, was casting its spell over me. It was a place to be lazy in and I felt myself relaxing as we sat under lemon trees bearing tiny green fruit and sipped limunadus.

Mija was spending the night with friends at Herceg-Novi before returning to Dubrovnik and after a meal at the restaurant we walked back up the hill out of the village and Ivo and I saw her off on the bus. We spent the rest of the afternoon swimming and lazing on the beach. The water was refreshingly cool and myriads of tiny fish shared our aquatics, streaking through the translucent water and curving in silvery shoals through the leaf-dappled shallows. Later we shopped and stocked up with food and wine, but Ivo insisted that I forgo grappling with the chalet's cooking facilities until the next day, so we went back to the shore-side restaurant and sat at a table under a gigantic palm tree and ate the national dish of mixed, grilled meat called cevapacici and drank the local wine. As we ate we were entertained by a group of youths playing the Yugoslavian equivalent of current pop music. As pop music it was banal and repetitious but the Western tones were overlaid by Eastern influence and gypsy airs and the result was curiously haunting.

We sat enchanted, watching what seemed to be the entire population of Baošić, strolling along the promenade and congregating in the restaurant garden, and the limpid night air was warm with the scent of charcoal grills and the music threaded its way through the still branches over our heads. We both drank too much; I, because I was overwhelmed by the thought of the night ahead, and Ivo – well, possibly for the same reason.

Later we strolled back to the chalet with our arms around each other and after a lot of fumbling in the dark managed to unlock the door. Ivo half carried, half dragged me through to my bedroom and proceeded to kiss me very thoroughly. I responded eagerly but as his demands grew more insistent I felt I was being swept along too fast. I pushed him away and sat up.

'What's the matter?'

'Nothing. I – I just want a few minutes to get ready.'

'OK,' he shrugged. 'I don't want to rush you. We're both going to enjoy this. I left my things in the other bedroom – I'll go through.' He disappeared through the doorway and, feeling more than a little mean, I swung my case onto the bed and unlocked it. I rifled through the contents seeking my nightie and my hand struck against the wooden box. I lifted it out and stared at it with misgivings, then clutching it to my bosom I walked through to Ivo's bedroom.

He was standing by the window looking out into the night and the sight of his magnificent male torso gleaming in the dim light made me feel quite weak. He turned and when he saw what I was carrying a look of exasperation passed fleetingly across his face.

'What are we going to do with this?' I asked, holding it out.

'You do choose your moments. Nothing for the time being.'

'Can't we just drop it into the water, somewhere it's deep and forget about it?'

'Forget about it? Are you crazy? That box contains a small fortune.'

'Whatever do you mean?'

'You still don't understand, do you Kate?'

'No I don't.' Suddenly I was cold sober and trepidation fluttered along my nerve endings. 'I don't understand – but I think I should. What is this all about?'

# Chapter 4

Ivo's answer was to sweep me into his arms. 'Leave it for now. I shall reveal all to you later, I promise. Right now we have more important things to do.'

As he picked me up the box slide from my nerveless fingers and fell to the floor. Ivo kicked it under the bed and began his assault on my willing body. As a lover he was demanding and dominating. After the initial shock my inexperienced flesh strove to match his, but although I was carried along on a wave of passion I ended up feeling more like a victim than a participant.

This was to become the pattern in the days that followed. His lovemaking was exciting and arousing but there was none of the tenderness that I had been led to expect when two people loved and gave themselves to each other. I felt used and oddly unsatisfied; there was something missing, and when I dared to try and analyse my feelings I realised that I had enjoyed Ivo better as a friend than I did now as a lover.

Yet they were happy days, carefree days, as long as I accepted things on a surface level and did not delve too deep into my and Ivo's emotions, did not try to read more into our relationship than actually existed. I was very fond of him, fond enough to sleep with him, but the

71

complete commitment was not there on either side. How the affair would progress I did not know and strangely enough I did not care. I was content to live from day to day, to enjoy myself and forget about the future.

We were lazy. Whoever woke first would walk down to the shop and buy bread and we would breakfast on the verandah on bread, jam, fruit and lemon tea. I could not bear the Turkish coffee which was all one could get locally. To me it was like drinking hot, nauseatingly sweet sand. Ivo teased me and quoted the old saw about 'hot as hell, black as the devil and sweet as a woman' and occasionally brewed up for himself; but although the smell was tantalising, the finished product continued to be a disappointment. But I was developing a liking for the tea, drunk out of a glass with fresh squeezed lemon and, again, very sweet. It was very refreshing but I boggled at the habit of eating spoonfuls of plum jam with it; a combination we were offered on several occasions when socialising with our neighbours. They were a gregarious lot, the other chalet occupants around us. They delighted in passing the time of day and inviting us to sample their cooking. Ivo warned me that they would be hurt and insulted if I refused, but whilst I was happy to indulge in as much social chit-chat as was possible, with my limited Serbian and their almost total lack of English, he held aloof and did not encourage any curiosity on their part.

Many of them came from the big cities, Zagreb and Belgrade, and these were their holiday homes where they spend weeks or months each year; but I gathered that some families, mostly elderly couples, lived here all the year round and even kept their own chickens. I had seen a few scrawny hens scratching around and once or twice had caught sight of a skinny kitten slinking between the chalet walls.

We would spend the mornings on the beach and when we were not swimming Ivo would stretch out in the sun, acquiring a mahogany tan and I would lie beneath a tree, grateful for the canopy of shade, and watch the patterns of serrated leaves chasing each other above my head in the delicate breeze. We lunched off more bread and fruit with salami and cheese and perhaps some tomatoes or sweet peppers. In the afternoons we either had a siesta or spent more time on the beach and as it grew cooler we would stroll along the shore or wander up the hillside amongst the seared grasses and dessicated trees. I exercised my culinary skills very little. Most evenings we ate in the restaurant, which was cheap and wholesome, but one night we cooked fish which we had bought from a local fisherman who had spilled his catch in the bottom of his boat where it lay like a cascade of silver coins, catching fire with an irridescent lustre in the sunshine.

One night we went to the little open-air cinema which was situated to the rear of the local supermarket. It consisted of a long, narrow enclosure, rather like an elongated squash court, with high walls all round and hard, uncomfortable seats, joined together in rows. The screen was the whitewashed wall at the end and was frequently partly obscured by enormous bats hurtling across the line of vision. Hordes of little boys colonised the trees surrounding the cinema. Whether they actually saw anything from their precarious tree-top perches I don't know but they certainly heard the sound-track; much good it did them. The film showing was an English one with Yugoslavian sub-titles. It was a comedy thriller and the rest of the audience could not understand why we always seemed to grasp the jokes and laugh a few seconds before everyone else.

We paced ourselves to match our neighbours and wallowed in sloth. The word '*Mañana*' is of Spanish origin but the concept has surely been pre-empted by the natives of these shores. '*Sutra*', or tomorrow, is the dictum by which they live and I was happy to fall in with this. The orchestra and my music seemed a world away. On Ivo's insistence we had not brought our violins with us and I felt not a twinge of conscience. I flexed my fingers of my left hand idly as we lay stretched out on the beach one day and murmured to Ivo, 'We are becoming Lotus Eaters. Even my fingers are becoming limp and decadent.'

He gently caressed the inside of my wrist. 'This could be for keeps.'

'What do you mean?' I yawned and rolled over.

'We don't have to go back.'

'Are you crazy? Are you suggesting we just stay here forever and vegetate? What about our music?'

'The orchestra isn't everything. There's a big world out there Kate; you haven't started to live yet.' He was propped up on one elbow regarding me seriously but I was in a flippant mood and disregarded what he was saying.

'You do talk a lot of nonsense sometimes. Are you going to get the ices or shall I?'

'I shall. I've got a phone-call to make first.' He shook some dinars out of his shorts' pocket and strolled along the promenade to where one of the only two telephones in Baošić stood at the base of the jetty. He was on the phone for quite a time and I could see him gesticulating from where I lay. To keep my curiosity in check I turned over onto my stomach and buried my face in my arms, and then I felt icy drips cascading between my shoulder blades and I sat up and snatched the cone from him. He made no attempt to enlighten me about his mysterious phone call but there was a gleam of excitement in his eyes. I could contain myself no longer.

'Good news?'

'Mmm.' He sat down beside me and polished off his ice and I evinced a sudden interest in a group of children who were paddling a canoe off-shore. Eventually he decided to put me out of my misery.

He snapped his fingers and said casually, 'I have to go to Herceg-Novi tomorrow.'

'Oh good, it's a place I've wanted to visit.'

'This is on business.'

'Oh? Are you trying to tell me that I shall be *persona non grata*?'

He flicked a piece of shale along the beach and squinted down at me. 'I'm sorry Kate, this is private business.'

'Well, thanks for telling me.' I turned my back on him and glared out over the water.

'Look, we can go to Herceg-Novi together as long as you don't mind if I go off and leave you for a while to look around by yourself. There are some attractive shops and the seafront is very pleasant.'

I allowed myself to be placated. 'I need some more money; is there a bank where I can change some travellers' cheques?'

'Yes, in the main street. Look, I'm sorry about this Kate, but you do understand?'

'Not at all. The more I get to know you the less I understand you. But don't let it worry you. I dare say I can manage to put in a couple of hours without the delights of your company. In fact, it might make a welcome break.'

He stared at me suspiciously for a few seconds, then laughed and rumpled my hair. 'You'd better go and sample our tourist agent's English and find out what time the buses run in the morning. I'll be getting back to the chalet – I need a shave.' He was rubbing his jaw as he loped off and I watched him thoughtfully before walking along to the 'Informtion Bureau'.

75

Early the next morning found us up on the highway waiting for the bus. Even at 6.30 am the heat was intense, away from the sea breeze and the trees. I tried to shelter from the sun beneath a miniscule sapling, and around me, in the parched grass, the crickets chirruped and hummed in a throbbing monotony. The bus was late, or pehaps wasn't running, or maybe the later one was early. Anyway, we eventually arrived in Herceg-Novi where the same confusion of travellers greeted us as before.

'I have to leave you now,' said Ivo. 'I don't know how long I'll be, but probably some time.' He pointed out the flight of steps leading downwards to the left of the bus station. 'If you go down there you'll come to the main shopping centre and when you're fed up with that you can go down the next flight and you'll come to the beach. There's a little café at the very bottom of the steps with a lovely vine canopy. I'll meet you there . . .' he glanced at his watch '. . . at about 4 pm.'

I wondered what business he could have that was going to take practically all day to execute, but I was determined not to ask. I slung my bag over my shoulder and started for the steps. 'See you later then – 'bye.'

'I'm not sure I should let you out of my sight with all these virile young men about.'

'If they are anything like you then you *have* got something to worry about, haven't you? Still, you've only yourself to blame.' I gave him a flippant wave and started my assault on the steps.

The first flight was comparatively short and brought me out onto a roadway which I presumed must wind down to the shore and I followed it for a few yards before coming to the second flight. By the time I reached the bottom and found myself in the town proper I was decidedly out of breath with aching calves. I spent a pleasant hour or so exploring on that level. I found the bank and changed my travellers' cheques and wandered in and out of shops, some of them silversmiths displaying a fantastic range of silver filigree work. I discovered a little municipal park ablaze with colour and, beyond that, a well-stocked supermarket where I purchased food for a picnic lunch. I determined to return to it later in the day to buy some delicacies so that I could cook a meal for us that evening. I photographed the quaint cobbled square and the Bell Tower and other buildings of architectural interest and then started on the descent to shore level.

I lost count of the number of steps I traversed but at the back of my mind was the thought that they all had to be climbed again to get back to the Adriatic Highway. I caught tantalising glimpses of the sea swimming between rooftops and palm crowns and then it was spread before me in a glorious blue sheet and I ran down the last few steps eagerly, my tired legs and gasping lungs forgotten.

There was an esplanade backed by a stretch of grass dotted with pine trees and I threw myself down under one of these to get my breath back. The cliffs rose up behind me, encased by stone walls overhung by giant cacti and agaves, behind which canna lilies and bougain-villaea fought for space amongst the dark, leathery palms. I swam several times between short, sun-bathing sessions, ate my picnic lunch and fell asleep beneath my allotted pine.

I awoke to the prickly feeling that I was under surveill-ance. I opened my eyes slowly and found myself staring into the yellow basilisk orbs of a little lizard that was perched on the edge of my sunhat about a foot from my head. I blinked and when I focussed again he had gone, but several times during the afternoon I caught glimpses of him darting through the grass and dead pine needles.

77

The day passed quickly and I managed to retain my privacy and fight off the local romeos who thought an unaccompanied girl was fair game. Just before 4 I gathered up my belongings and padded along to the *rendez-vous* at the café. I was delighted to spot a swallowtail butterfly spiralling above the sea. It dipped and swayed, a fragment of yellow and black mosaic, before soaring up out of sight.

Ivo was late but he came laden with apologies and a gift for me. It was a silver filigree bracelet; lacy medallions threaded together by a delicate mesh of chain. He snapped it round my wrist and held my hand away from him to admire it.

'It's beautiful Ivo, thank you. I see you've bought yourself a present too.' As he leaned forward a chain he was wearing round his neck slid out of his shirt exposing a black ebony cross. 'Why a crucifix?'

Although Yugoslavia is officially a non-Christian Communist country I had noticed several of the younger generation sporting chains and crosses, and icons and crucifixes were openly displayed in many of the houses. Ivo looked momentarily disconcerted. He fingered the cross, then tucked it back out of sight.

'I'll explain later. Have you had a good day? What do you think of Herceg-Novi?'

'It's a very attractive place and being built on three levels like this means it's unspoilt and can't be over exploited.'

'Yes, all the new developments are up at the top near the highway and the old town is left in peace; and of course, the new hotel complexes are further round in the bay.'

We had a drink before starting on our marathon climb and made it back to the bus station in time to catch the bus.

When we arrived back in Baošić clouds were piling up behind the mountains and the air was still and humid. As we walked down to the village the colour seemed to drain out of the water before our very eyes, leaving it leaden and opaque, and a faint mist hovered over the trees so that they looked as if they were gently smoking.

'I think we are going to have an almighty thunderstorm before long,' said Ivo. 'I gather they are quite a phenomenon in this area.'

I hate thunderstorms – the noise offends my ears – and I scanned the sky anxiously, fearing that he was correct in his forecast. I busied myself cooking the evening meal and tried to ignore the ominous signals from outside. I cooked veal escalopes in a sauce of peppers, onions and tomatoes which we ate with a green salad and afterwards we had fresh fruit with the local yoghurt.

Ivo praised the meal but I was on edge and I think the approaching storm was affecting him also; he was keyed-up and I had the feeling he was bracing himself to tell me something. I didn't want to hear. I suddenly knew that whatever he was going to divulge was somehow connected with his visit to Herceg-Novi, that he was about to force me to face something that I was trying to avoid and I wanted to go on living the carefree life, not think about the immediate future. Once it was out in the open nothing would be the same again.

I gathered up the plates and busied myself rinsing them in the outside sink and Ivo went indoors. In the distance I could hear music drifting through the trees from the shore restaurant. With it came the aroma of charcoal fires and grilling meat, but I could also smell a sweet, elusive scent from nearer home. I dropped the tea-towel and plunged through the doorway. Ivo was sitting on the bed propped up against the wall; his eyes were half-closed and a cigarette hung limply from his

79

fingers, the smoke curling in a damp whisp up to the ceiling.

'Ivo!'

He blinked open his eyes and smiled lazily at me.

'Ivo, you promised!'

'I didn't you know. Sit down.' He pulled me down beside him. 'Have a drag.' I shot away from him as if I had been stung.

'Relax Katerina, don't be such a prude. Don't tell me you've never even tried acid?'

'No,' I said emphatically, and as he looked at me in disbelief, I continued, 'and I'll tell you why. I shared a flat with a girl when I was a student. She went on a trip once and freaked out. She tried to throw herself out of an attic window.'

'A real bummer. How unfortunate. You can't go wrong with this stuff. Why shouldn't we have our dreams and get rich on it too?.

'I don't know what you mean. I thought it was Adrian's, that you were getting rid of it.' The black box was lying on top of the counterpane and I looked at it askance.

'Look in it, Kate. Have a good look and then you'll know what I mean.' He nipped out the joint and gestured to the box. There was an air of febrile excitement about him and his movements were disjointed. I gingerly opened the lid. There was a shallow tray which lay across the top fitted out with a collection of reeds, each slotted snugly into the framework which covered half the tray. In the other half were several small packets of white powder. Ivo nodded his head impatiently and I lifted out the tray. Underneath, stacked in tight bundles were what looked like banknotes. I eased a wad out. The notes were dollar bills held together by elastic bands.

'But there's hundreds of pounds here! Thousands of pounds!'

'Are you really as innocent as you pretend? This is our passport to a new world, a new life. Don't you see Kate, we're in the big money!'

I did see. With a sudden horrible clarity. 'You're a pusher! A drug-trafficker!' I dropped the bundle of notes as if they had been red hot and stared at him in horror.

'You make it sound as if I'm the devil and the head of the Mafia rolled into one. This is not the hard stuff. You've read too many sordid tales in the press. This is clean, enjoyable, a social cult. It's not snorted or fixed, you don't die from it.'

'It's a crazy habit and one thing leads to another. How did you get involved in the first place?'

'We'd both experimented . . .'

'Of course, Adrian was in on this too, wasn't he?' I cut in.

'And we were approached, offered money to do a little smuggling ourselves. Don't you see, we're in a unique position. Members of an orchestra that goes regularly on tour, travelling the world, moving effortlessly across borders from one country to another.'

'But we're pulled up quite rigorously by customs. Things are checked. Why, I believe the pantechnicon was practically taken to pieces on our last tour.'

'Yes, but there are ways and means. It's a real cinch if you know what you're doing.'

'How long has this been going on? How long have you been involved?'

'A while, but we're breaking into the big time now.'

'We? Who's we?'

'It was Adrian and I,' a spasm crossed his face, 'but now it's you and me.'

'You must be mad. I want nothing to do with it.'

'Just listen first. Please Kate, let me explain.'

'There's a lot of explaining to do. This money – where

81

did it come from? It doesn't belong to you?'

He leaned back and regarded the room through half-closed eyes and then began talking in a monotone.

'Adrian and I were recruited as couriers. We've never known who our contact is, who masterminds it. But I think it is someone connected with the orchestra.'

'You mean, there is someone else involved? Some other member of the orchestra?'

'It's not necessarily a musician. It could be anyone who has dealings with the orchestra. Whoever it is has organised a nice little network, but we were getting fed up with our side of the deal. We were carrying the stuff, taking the risks and only getting a small percentage of the rake-off so we decided to muscle in on it. That's when things started to go wrong.'

'How do you mean?'

'The set-up was this. We were supplied with the money and enough grass for our own use as a bonus, and we were given instructions how to make contact with our opposite number and make the drop.'

'But who gave you your instructions and the money? You must have known who it was.'

'No. It was done by anonymous phone-calls or an unsigned letter. We were told where the money would be left for collection – places like an empty house or even a laundrette were used. At the other end we would go to the *rendez-vous* and identify ourselves and an exchange would be made. We handed over the money or left it in some arranged place and collected the stuff. When we got back to England the same procedure went into action.'

'How did you identify your contacts?'

He put his hand into the neck of his shirt and pulled out the chain revealing the black cross. 'By wearing these. Anyway, we decided that this time we were going to hang onto the stuff and run our own show. Adrian had a *rendez-vous* on the Old City walls that evening. He didn't take the money – he went with an ultimatum.'

'But he had an accident and fell.'

'He didn't fall; he was pushed,' said Ivo grimly.

'You mean – he was murdered? But surely not – how do you know? I mean, he slipped whilst taking photos – didn't he?' I was desperately trying to deny what he was telling me.

'His camera still had the lens cap on. He wasn't taking photos.'

'Did Miles Bretherton know this?'

'*He* told me. Besides the cross was missing from his neck. I saw his effects so I know it was missing and he had definitely been wearing it when he left the hotel. I also knew that its removal was a warning to me.'

'But if there were suspicions about his death why was it covered up? Why did the police . . . ?'

'I certainly didn't want doubts aired, and our precious Miles Bretherton was only concerned with his beautifully arranged tour going ahead as planned. He obviously duped the police over the camera and lulled any suspicions they may have had. We both kept quiet for different reasons. Anyway, I realised our little scheme was not going to be so easy to carry out – they would be gunning for me too.'

'You didn't consider dropping it? Getting out altogether?'

'Certainly not. I was more determined than ever that they weren't going to get away with it, especially as the profits would all be mine now.'

As the tale unfolded from his lips I was feeling more and more uncomfortable and deluded. I was horrified by his apparent callousness about Adrian's fate. How could I have lived and shared my life with him without discovering these flaws in his character? I felt contaminated and I shifted away from him and gazed accusingly at his bent head.

Without being aware of my revulsion he continued:

'I knew they were after me at the concert the following evening. I saw someone in the audience who gave me a sign there was no mistaking.'

'So that's why you were in such a state,' I retorted, and then, as what he was saying sunk in, 'So all that talk about a feud was all lies?'

'Actually it was the truth and although it happened a long while ago if I set foot in my home town again my life wouldn't be worth a para; but it has nothing to do with the present situation – I had to give you some explanation. I managed to get word to my contact and convince him that Adrian's little hiccough was nothing to do with me and that I was willing to go along with the original plan. I was given a date and place and then . . . ,' he looked up at me with a crooked smile, '. . . and then, I disappeared. No one will have traced us here to Baošić and if my absence is noted they will just think I am lying low somewhere until it is time to make the drop.'

'And what are you going to do now?' I whispered.

'Today I contacted one of my own friends, a colleague from the old days. He is joining forces with me and tomorrow we go to Sveti-Stefan. Just think Kate, the millionaires' paradise is being used as a drug run.'

I had read about and seen pictures of Sveti-Stefan, the beautiful little island further down the coast, beyond Budva, that is joined to the mainland by a causeway. The entire island, which used to house a monastic establishment, is now a holiday complex owned by an hotel group and it is supposed to be one of the priciest places in which to stay in the entire country.

'But even supposing you get away with it this time, what then? You'll be a wanted man, you'll never be able to go back to the orchestra . . .'

'I intend running my own set-up from now on. I tell you, Kate, this game is where the big money is. We'll be as rich as Croesus, and who cares about the orchestra? Who wants to be a second violin in a little tin-pot orchestra for the rest of their lives? We'll go to America. Now I've got the contacts we can open up new lines – set up our own network in the States.'

'But if you leave the orchestra your travelling bona fides are finished.' I was desperately trying to think up any reason, however flimsy, to stop his flow of fantasy.

'But don't you understand? Up till now I've just been a courier, a small fish in a very big pond; now I shall be my own master. I shall be the boss and have people working for me, taking the risks.'

I could suddenly stand the atmosphere in the room no longer. I blundered to the door.

'Where are you going?'

'Out to get some fresh air.'

I slammed the door behind me and headed for the shore. It was pitch dark by now and tonight there were no moon or stars. I stood on the jetty and stared over the black water. Across the fiord a few distant lights pinpointed a village on the opposite side, and away to my left, facing down the Boka Kotorska a myriad of twinkling lights marked the town of Tivat. It was hot and still and then, as I stood and mused, a gust of wind snaked down through the trees rustling the branches and disturbing the quiet. I was standing beneath an unknown tree. It had feathery leaves and huge clusters of dried pods and these pods rattled like miniature castanets as the freak gust spiralled past. Then all was still again. Every leaf and twig and branch, every blade of grass and trailing vine hung motionless as if holding its breath and waiting. From the hillside behind me a dog barked and it was as if this were the signal the heavens were waiting for. There was an angry rumble in the distance followed almost immediately by a vivid flash of lightning and a loud clap of thunder right overhead. I turned and fled back to the chalet.

Ivo was waiting for me and as I bolted through the door he grabbed me in his arms. I struggled to break free and we tumbled onto the bed.

'Steady on, the storm can't hurt you. I've got you.'

'It's *you* I'm trying to get away from.' I pulled free of his importunate arms. 'Please Ivo, leave me alone.'

'What's the matter? There's no need to be so frightened just of a storm.'

'I'm not frightened. Don't you understand? I don't want you to touch me.'

I had got through to him at last. He rolled away from me and glared at me through slit eyes. There was an ugly expression on his face and I suddenly began to feel afraid.

'You've changed your tune. You weren't so reluctant a few days ago.'

'I made a mistake. It's no good Ivo, I don't go along with you at all. I want out.'

'Well, I want you, so stop fooling around and come here.'

He lunged at me and we fell back across the bed again and his lips clamped down on my mouth in a hard, brutal kiss. I could smell again the sweet odour of cannabis and in revulsion I renewed my struggle. I got my teeth into his bottom lip and hung on and he jerked back and gave me an almighty blow on the side of my face that carried me to the floor.

'You little bitch! This is not the time to start playing hard to get!'

He threw himself on me and then his hands were round my throat and I was fighting for my life. I could feel the blood beating behind my eyes and a red hot pain gathering in my chest as my lungs laboured to draw breath. My head struck a leg of the bed and I felt myself slipping into darkness. The next thing I knew I was being picked up and I choked and gasped as I was laid on the bed.

'God Kate! I'm sorry, I didn't mean to hurt you. Are you all right?' His face loomed over me and I cringed away.

'Please go away,' I croaked. He cradled me in his arms and I strained away from him.

'It's all right Kate, I promise I won't touch you, but can I get you a drink or something?'

'Just go away.' I turned my face away from him.

'I'll sleep in the other room tonight. I'm really sorry – I don't know what came over me. But I love you Kate – I can't let you go.' He was pleading now, but I hung my head and refused to answer and after a little pause he went out of the room, closing the door behind him, and I was alone.

I crouched on the bed nursing my injuries. My head throbbed, I had a bruise on my cheekbone, and my neck and throat were bruised outside and sore within. As I huddled there the storm broke in earnest. Lightning ripped across the sky, thunder cracked and the first drops of rain fell, heavy drops rebounding like teaplates off the roof. The rain gained momentum and was soon drumming down in a solid sheet, and as most of the chalets had corrugated iron roofs the noise was deafening; a cacophony that vied with the thunder in its assault on the eardrums. The storm seemed to last for hours. I lay on the bed with my hands over my ears and my eyes tightly shut and my tortured mind went over what Ivo

87

had told me, again and again.

My orchestra was not the one big happy family I had always imagined. It had been corrupted. There were alien forces working beneath the surface exploiting greed and human weaknesses. My Ivo was caught up in it – but no, he was my Ivo no longer. I had made a horrible, almost fatal mistake, but thank God, I hadn't been really in love with him. I felt shattered, betrayed, hurt, but at least I had never been completely, irretrievably committed to him. Some part of me had always recognised the flaw in him and had held me aloof. I had been infatuated but I would recover.

I could not bear to think any more of Ivo and instead I concentrated on what he had said about someone else being involved. I believed him and I wondered who could be the mastermind behind the drug running. Like a mouse in a wheel my thoughts ran round and round, considering and rejecting my fellow associates. It must be someone who had joined the orchestra in the last few years; that let out the older members like Sammy and Harris Fordham. Could it be Sven Larsen, the deputy leader, or Sylvester, our coloured joker? It might be an ordinary rank-and-file member of the strings, hiding in anonymity; I even considered Willie Bode; but the person who really seemed to fit the bill, as far as I was concerned was Peter Brownstone. He was bossy and always trying to manoeuvre events to his advantage. But surely, if he were indeed the guilty one, he wouldn't draw attention to himself in the way that he did?

The one person I refused at first to contemplate was Miles Bretherton; but as I weighed up the pros and cons of each person I was forced to the conclusion that the case against Miles Bretherton was blackest. He had the best opportunity; in fact, he had the perfect cover. He actually arranged the tours, or at least, had a big say in their planning. He visited locations beforehand to work out iteneraries and he came and went with no questions asked. I don't know why I was so reluctant to condemn him rather than one of my fellow musicians. Perhaps it was because there had always been an uneasy atmosphere between us and I was ashamed to damn him through personal prejudice, but the more I thought about it the more the evidence pointed to him. The very fact that he had been the one at the scene when Ivo and Adrian had smoked that night in the hotel seemed to prove that he was *au fait* with their doings and had been quick to pounce on them and suppress their careless act.

As the storm rolled and crashed around me I tried desperately to recall whether he had been present at the rehearsal that evening Adrian had met his death. Try as I might I could not remember. But why had he told Ivo about the business with the camera if he was guilty of murdering him, unless it was as a warning? I could not bring myself to believe he was a criminal and murderer. I could not believe it of anyone else either.

I eventually fell asleep as the first streaks of dawn were striating the sky and the final distant rumble of thunder rolled back over the mountains.

# Chapter 5

I slept deeply and woke to find Ivo by my bed bearing a tray. So heavily had I slept that I felt completely disorientated for a few minutes and the events of the night before were forgotten.

'Madam, your breakfast.' Ivo bowed and clicked his heels together. He was fully dressed and looked as if he had been up for hours. I sat up with an effort, yawning and rubbing my eyes and my fingers strayed against my bruised face. At that instant he dumped the tray on my bed and carried on, 'Buck up Kate. We have to leave for Sveti-Stefan soon.'

I was immediately shocked back to reality and fully awake. 'I'm not leaving for anywhere – with you!'

'Don't be an idiot. Eat your breakfast and hurry up and get dressed.' He went out whistling and I stared after him and wondered if I was suffering hallucinations. Had I imagined or dreamed the events of last night? In the light of day with a normal, cheerful Ivo clattering in the background I couldn't believe that he had actually attempted to rape and kill me. Then I remembered my bruised cheek and I fingered my sore neck and shuddered. Someone who suffered from such violent swings of temperament was verging on the paranoid, or was it just the effect of cannabis? I ate a few mouthfuls of bread and sipped at the scalding tea but I had no appetite and pushed it away and started to dress.

I washed under the running tap. After the storm the water pressure was high and I splashed the cold, gushing water over my head and shoulders and ran a comb through my damp curls. There was a freshness outside that was already being sapped by the burgeoning sun. I expected to find every path a quagmire after the deluge of last night, but already the earth had dried out and only the odd glistening drop sparkling from twig and stalk reminded one of the night's saturation. These violent storms, which are a feature of the geographical fault which is the Boka Kotorska, account for the lush semi-tropical vegetation that clothes the shelf between the water and the bare mountains.

Ivo had gone off somewhere and I wondered where he was and how long he would be gone. Had I got time to disappear before he returned? It would be so much simpler to present him with a *fait accompli* than risk another round of arguments and possible violence. I hurriedly finished dressing, pulling on a cotton blouse and skirt and thrusting my feet into a pair of sandals; then I pulled my case out of the cupboard and started throwing my belongings into it.

'What do you think you're doing?'

I started violently. Ivo lounged against the door jamb looking the picture of indolence but there was a nasty glint in his eyes and he was obviously spoiling for trouble. I tried to keep it all sweetness and light.

'I'm packing. I'm going back to Dubrovnik.'

'You're not, you know, you're coming with me.'

'And how do you propose getting to Sveti-Stefan?' I asked, playing for time as I went on stuffing clothes into my case.

'I – we are being picked up by boat. We go by water as far as Lepetane on the other side and then we continue by car. Just you wait Kate; you'll enjoy the boat trip and the scenery is fantastic.'

There it was again, that frightening swing of mood so that he now sounded as if he were propounding a Sunday school trip for a favourite child.

'Ivo, I'm not coming with you. It's all over between us, I'm going back to the hotel and I'm going to try and forget all this ever happened.'

He slammed down the lid of my case, narrowly missing my hands and pulled me towards him; but there was no ardour in his gesture, only animosity.

'You wouldn't be going to shop me, would you Kate?' He spoke softly, caressingly, but he ran his fingers hard down my bruised face making me flinch.

'Look Ivo, I don't agree with your mad plans. You ought to be stopped but I won't be the one to grass on you. I promise.'

'You don't trust me do you? Well, I don't trust you either. I've shot my mouth off to you, told you far too much and I daren't risk you getting a touch of conscience and babbling to the authorities. You're coming with me. We're in this together whether you like it or not.'

He picked up my handbag and rifled through it extracting my passport, travellers' cheques and loose change which he pocketed and then he tossed the handbag up on top of the cupboard far out of my reach.

'You don't want that anymore – I'm looking after you.'

He zipped the black box into a canvas bag with a shoulder strap which I noticed also held his passport and personal documents then he grabbed my hand and pulled me out of the door.

'You haven't locked up,' I said weakly.

92

'There's no need. Surely you've noticed that most Yugoslavians are transparently honest.'

'You being the exception?'

'I'm glad you haven't lost your sense of humour. Now get going.' He gave me a push and I nearly fell off the edge of the verandah. I steadied myself, backed away from him and sat down at the table, bracing myself against the vine trellis.

'I'm not coming with you.'

His answer was to sit down beside me and press my left hand palm upwards onto the table.

'Suppose I were to slice through the tendons of each finger? Your fiddle wouldn't be of much use to you then.'

Shockingly, his right hand had darted into his pocket and was now holding a knife. I recognised it as one of the kitchen knives we had used for slicing up meat and vegetables. It glinted in his hand in a very business-like manner and I watched mesmerised as he deftly carved a cross on the table top a fraction away from my imprisoned hand. I chose that moment to remember that he had already knifed someone to death, if his tales were to be believed, and I gulped and strained away from him.

'Well, are you going to be sensible? Come with me and we'll make it together. Refuse, and you won't live to enjoy it.'

He jerked me to my feet, clasped me firmly by the elbows and frog-marched me down the path.

I was helpless. Our neighbours and the occupants of other nearby chalets sat around leisurely eating their breakfasts or relaxing in the sun and they could have been in another world as far as I was concerned. I could not appeal to them for help; they would not understand and they certainly would not take my word against Ivo's. Yugoslavia is very much a man's country. The woman is

93

still the underdog and I had actually seen women give up their seats to men on the buses. I looked round despairingly as I was hustled along, but I managed to quell my panic enough to ask: 'Where are we going?'

'Where we won't have an audience to witness our departure.'

He led me along a path that I hadn't noticed before that ran amongst the trees parallel to the shore, and we came out at the far end of the village near the earthquake-damaged buildings.

Ivo edged quietly forward under their shadow moving down towards the water while keeping his grip on my arm so that I was propelled sideways along the uneven terrain. As we neared the water's edge I heard the phut-phut of an engine and through the jagged walls that barred our way I saw a small boat with an outboard motor nosing its way towards the shore, trying to pick a channel through the broken masonry that stuck up like dragon's teeth out of the water.

'Come on!' said Ivo savagely, dragging me down to a gap in the tumbledown buildings where we could, by wading, get through to the other side. I stumbled and floundered and banged my legs against unseen, submerged slabs of stone, and I heard the engine cut out and saw the boat snake deftly in to rest close by. The occupant was a dark, swarthy man about Ivo's age and build and I noticed the black cross hanging amongst the matted hair of his chest as he leaned forward and fiddled with the engine. When he looked up and saw us he called out sharply, '*Ko je ona*?'

'*Prijateljica, ona dolazi snama, ne brini.*'

We had reached the boat by then and the man stared at me suspiciously before moving forward to help us on board. Ivo let go of my arm in order to hand his bag over and as he swung it forward he slipped and half fell back into the water. I seized my opportunity. Step by step I moved backwards, cautiously feeling my way through knee-deep water and sunken debris whilst Ivo cursed and floundered. When he regained his balance he was so engrossed in getting his precious cargo stowed on board that he did not at first notice my defection. I knew I only had precious seconds before he spotted what I was up to and came after me. I knew it was hopeless to go back the way we had come, he would have no difficulty in catching me; instead, I turned and started to climb up through the ruins with the crazy idea of hiding in some dark corner.

He saw what I was doing before I had got more than a few yards.

'Where do you think you're going? Come back you stupid fool!'

He started in pursuit and I quickened my pace and blundered onwards scraping knees and ankles. I lost a sandal and wasted precious seconds retrieving it and a strap snapped as I thrust it back on my foot. The man in the boat shouted something after us; Ivo replied angrily and I heard him toiling behind me and the scrape of shoe on stone as he shortened the distance between us. I reached the first sizeable building still standing and squeezed through a slit in the shattered walls. The roof had gone and it was open to the sky. The walls leaned precariously inward and I bolted through what had once been a doorway and found myself in a positive maze of wrecked houses.

I tunnelled like a mole frantically through broken masonry and behind me Ivo cursed and threatened. I was gasping for breath by now and my heart was beating so violently that I thought it would burst out of my rib-cage. Ahead of me was the remains of a staircase and in the stairwell was a pile of debris. I crawled behind this pile hoping he hadn't seen me go to ground. Dust hung in the air and then, close at hand, I heard an ominous grating noise. The building I was in was shifting and I realised that my stampede through the ruins had been an imbecilic move. The whole structure was likely to come tumbling about my ears at any second. Even as I crouched low hardly daring to breathe I felt the wall behind me shift.

His voice reached me from outside. 'Come out Kate – the whole lot's going!' He was silhouetted in the doorway, the dark outline of his body framed by sunlight. I stood up slowly and we faced each other across the rubble-strewn floor.

'Come here Kate.' His voice was a seductive whisper. I shook my head and backed against the wall. I saw him throw up his arm and I caught the glint of metal and instinctively I dived for the floor.

The knife struck the wall just where I had been standing. I saw the cracks splinter outwards like a crazed star, then the cracks turned to fissures and the whole wall came tumbling down starting up a chain reaction. I rolled desperately away and just before the blinding dust cut off my vision I saw him jump back to safety. I clawed my way towards where I thought I had seen a window aperture, miraculously dodging the falling masonry, and more by luck than judgement I found a gaping hole and dragged myself outside before the entire building collapsed. I made it to the shelter of an oleander hedge before I collapsed myself.

The dust was in my eyes, up my nostrils and down my throat and I choked and retched. Much as I wanted to lay there and give way to my exhaustion I knew I must get away. Ivo might believe that I was buried beneath stone but if he suspected that I had got clear he would be after me again and my life-span could be counted in seconds. I sat up and tried to shake the dust from my clothes and hair. The filigree bracelet shone dully on my dust-streaked wrist. I clawed at it and broke the clasp and threw it with all my might into the bushes; then on all fours I crawled upwards through the fawn grass beneath the grey twisted branches of ancient olives. Ahead, presuming I got up the hill, was the Adriatic Highway and safety.

I heard voices behind me and I got to my feet and bolted, scurrying between the gnarled trunks. I could hear the distant hum of traffic and I made a superhuman effort to reach the top. My one idea as to flag down a bus or car or any vehicle and get a lift back to Dubrovnik and sanity. I broke from cover and raced across the open ground, slipping and sliding on the loose shale. It was so hot I could feel the stones burning through the thin soles of my sandals and I was gasping for breath. I reached the road and heard the sound of a car approaching. Without thinking I leapt out into its path as it roared round the bend, forgetting in my panic that traffic travelled on the right side of the road.

There was the shriek of brakes and it went into a skid, ending up on the hard shoulder several yards away facing the direction from which it had come. A door slammed and a very angry English voice bellowed: 'What the hell do you think you're doing!'

It was one of those mad, incredible coincidences that can only happen in real life. I scrambled back to the side of the road and stared in disbelief at the figure that emerged from the passenger door. It was Miles Bretherton. For a few seconds I think he was as dumbfounded as I was, then he swung across the road towards me.

'Kate! What on earth are you doing?'

'I forgot the traffic travels on the right-hand side.'

'I mean, what are you doing *here*? Where's Tomasic?'

'He tried to kill me. He's a pusher. He's going to

97

Sveti-Stefan.' It came out in a gabbled rush. Reaction was setting in.

'Very succinct,' he drawled. 'Suppose you try and explain?'

'I . . . Oh Miles, I must sit down.' My legs were trembling so that I thought I would collapse and I started to subside to the ground. He grabbed my arm.

'Not here. Not that it would make much difference,' he said looking from me to the dust bowl at my feet. 'You look as if you've been buried alive.'

'I almost have.' The driver of the car had got out and was making violent gestures in our direction. 'Your companion seems a bit upset. My God, he does look official. He's not going to arrest me for being a traffic hazard is he?'

'It would only be what you deserve.' Miles had got his hand under my elbow and was helping me across the road. 'Do you realise you could have been killed?'

'I think I must bear a charmed life. I've survived an attempted strangulation, a knifing, an earthquake spin-off and now this.'

He looked at me oddly as if he thought I was totally deranged. 'Get in the car and you can explain as we're going along. We're in a hurry so we can't stop. This is Kapetan Pero Njavro. He speaks very good English.'

The Kapetan was formally dressed in black trousers and tie and a military-style grey shirt and he had the most gorgeous drooping Zapata moustache. He greeted me gravely and shook hands as if it were an everyday occurance to pick up an hysterical English woman.

'This is Gospodica Kate Bracegirdle,' said Miles, equally formal. 'She is the girl who is involved, so we're in luck.'

I stared at him suspiciously but he looked back blandly and helped me into the back of the car before climbing in beside me.

'Are you all right?' he asked as the car swung round and headed off towards Kotor.

'I . . . I think so.' I felt far from all right. I was shaking like a leaf and my teeth were chattering. He put his arm round me and I tried to pull myself together. 'I feel an absolute wreck. Oh Miles, I've made a mess of your beautiful clean shirt.' There were smudges of dirt streaked across the pristine whiteness of his shirt, whose only concession to casualness and the climate were the open neck and rolled-up sleeves.

'That's not important.' He produced a comb and a large handkerchief and waited with admirable patience whilst I scrubbed and dabbed at my face and hands and dust-powdered hair.

'Now can you tell me what's happened?'

And I did. It all came pouring out; my involvement and disillusionment with Ivo, his part in the drug-running and his mad plans, his claims that another member of the Europa was involved, his personal attack on me when I wouldn't go along with him, my lucky escape from the collapsing buildings and his boat trip to Sveti-Stefan.

'He's completely unbalanced,' I muttered as I finally ground to a halt and dabbed at my sore cheek.

'Did he do this?' snapped Miles, examining my face and drawing a gentle finger round my bruised neck. I think that until that moment he had thought that I was wildly exaggerating but now that he was staring the evidence in the face he was quite shaken.

I nodded. 'I suppose you're going to say "I told you so". You must think I'm very gullible, the complete idiot.'

'I think many things about you, Kate Bracegirdle, but not that. You've had a very lucky escape, thank God.'

'Was Adrian Palmer really murdered?'

'I fear so, but we had our reasons for hushing it up. The young fools have nearly spoilt everything.'

It wasn't until he said that that I suddenly remembered he was my chief suspect; that he was in all probability the mastermind that Ivo had referred to and I had blurted out everything and was virtually a prisoner in this car being carried to God knows where. I stared at him in horror and pressed back against the upholstery.

'What's the matter now? You're looking at me as if you thought *I* was going to knock you off.'

'Aren't you?' I whispered, unable to tear my eyes away from his throat where I expected to catch a glimpse of a black chain and cross. 'You're the one in charge, aren't you? The one who is running the drugs circle. You killed Adrian Palmer!'

He looked completely taken aback, then he leant forward and said urgently: 'I didn't. I promise you Kate his death was nothing to do with me. I am involved – but not in the way you think. How can I convince you?'

'By stopping this car for a start and letting me go. Where are you taking me?'

'We're going to Sveti-Stefan. Kapetan Njavro has had a tip-off about the drugs drop there. I am helping him.'

'Helping him officially in his enquiries?'

'I suppose you could put it like that. We know Ivo's involved and we want to get there first. What you have just told us makes it even more imperative that we don't lose any time. That's why I can't stop and escort you safely back to Dubrovnik. I don't want you involved any more but you'll have to come with us for now.' And being me I believed him.

'Whereabouts in Sveti-Stefan?'

'We don't know – do you?'

'I've told you all I know, or do you still suspect me of being involved?'

100

'I never really suspected you Kate. You're one of the world's innocents.'

I glared at him suspiciously suspecting sarcasm, but his next words re-assured me.

'As I've said, we know Ivo is connected with this drugs drop but I was sure you couldn't be involved, however unwittingly. I knew you had gone off with him, but I imagined he had left you tucked away somewhere whilst he pursued his dangerous pastime.'

'I knew nothing about it until yesterday evening; he had completely duped me. But he expected me to go along with him, couldn't understand my scruples. I just wanted to get away from him – to put as much distance as possible between us. It just seems incredible that you should be the person to pick me up – rescue me.'

'I couldn't believe my eyes when you burst in front of us. I had been wondering about your whereabouts and I thought I must be hallucinating, too much sun etc. It's the old long arm of coincidence at work again, fact being stranger than fiction and all that.'

Then the car flashed round a bend and I was thrown against him. He gently disentangled himself and appeared to be deep in thought and I studied him out of the corner of my eye. To my chagrin his fair skin had developed a beautiful tan and his hair was bleached almost white in the front.

'How do we find it then?'

He drew his attention back to me. 'Not "we" Kate. Just Pero and I. You are going to wait in the car whilst we go and investigate.'

'You just said that I was going to Sveti-Stefan with you.'

'That was a figure of speech. You will stay safely on the mainland whilst we go across to the island.' He spoke firmly expecting no resistance; but although I said nothing and let him think I acquiesced to his plans, privately I had other ideas.

We flashed through the village of Bjela and the miles fell away as the car sped steadily inland following the curving lines of the Boka Kotorska.

'Don't you think *you* owe *me* an explanation?' I asked, as Miles appeared to clam up on me. '*How* exactly are you involved?'

'I'm trying to stop the orchestra becoming mixed up in a drugs scandal. Captain Njavro is a member of the Yugoslavian Drugs Squad. We think Adrian and Ivo are very small fry but they are the link in the chain and can possibly lead us to the identification of others more deeply involved.'

'Did I tell you about a black cross worn round the neck being a means of identification?'

'Yes, and there was definitely no cross on Adrian's body when he was found.' I pondered on this and wondered where Ivo now was. The thought of meeting up with him again filled me with dread. His behaviour of last night could just about be put down to emotion, temperament, frustration, but the calculated attempt on me this morning could not be explained away on these terms. He had deliberately, in cold blood, tried to kill me, and when I thought of how intimate we had been my blood ran cold. I made a little inarticulate sound and Miles cocked an eyebrow at me questioningly.

'How . . . how do we get to Sveti-Stefan? Is it far?' I was damned if I was going to let him know how sick and betrayed I felt.

'At Kamenari we go on the car ferry across to the other side and then through Tivat and down to Budva and the coastal road.'

But when we reached Kamenari there was a hitch to these plans. A long tail-back of traffic greeted us; cars, lorries and buses were nose to tail along the ferry lay-by and spilled back onto the highway itself. Pero Njavro pulled the car into the side of the road, jumped out and went into the office. I could see him waving a card around and gesticulating angrily. He came back again almost immediately, his spaniel-brown eyes gleaming with annoyance as he slammed back into the car.

'There is a hold-up – a big traffic jam each side. We shall be delayed here for hours if we wait for the ferry. Even with authority to go out of turn it is impossible to get round the waiting vehicles.'

I could see what he meant; unless the car could jump or fly, there was no way we could push in front of the queue.

'We shall have to go the long way round via Kotor,' he continued, starting up the engine.

'How long will that take?' asked Miles.

'Two . . . three hours,' he shrugged; 'there is no other way. We get these hold-ups here in the summer months.'

As we edged back onto the road and pulled away from Kamenari I saw the two ferries approaching each other across the glassy water. The two massive black, red and white leviathans, packed fore and aft with an assortment of vehicles, dipped and swayed towards each other like some gigantic participants in a marine ballet. Somewhere in the centre of the strait they would slide past, assigned forever to sail their set, solitary course.

The car swung round a ninety degree left-angled bend and we were facing a vast expanse of water which Pero Njavro told us was the Bay of Risan. He pointed out the two tiny islands nestling near the far shore, each supporting a church. The larger one was Sveti Dorde and the Benedictine Abbey rose above a frieze of pines; the smaller one was an artificial isle called Gospa od Skrpjela, a bare rock on which the baroque-style church with its cupola and bell-tower reminded one of an Eastern mosque. On the long haul round the Bay of Risan we saw these two churches from every conceivable angle; sometimes looming close at hand, a stone's throw across the water; and at other times, twin mirages floating white and ethereal above and below the mirrored lake.

Afterwards, I could remember very little of that long drive to Sveti-Stefan. I suppose I was in a state of shock and I have only jumbled recollections of the journey. We must have passed through the towns of Risan and Perast but they did not register with me. We just seemed to drive for hours along an interminable road that wound alongside the water's edge, a ribbon that divided the sheet of water from the bare mountains that towered up on our left-hand side. Kotor was a blur of modern concrete by the harbour, thickly dotted with palm trees, the old city being tucked away behind the walls that clung to the foot of the hills in defiance of gravity.

'The old city was razed to the ground by the earthquake,' explained Pero as we flashed through. 'Inside the walls it is kaput. The people are rehoused in the new part of the town.'

We were at the far end of the Boka Kotorska and, in the valley at the head of the waterway, new skyscraper apartment blocks were being built amongst the industrial development of factories, garages and workshops. Once through Kotor the road wound up the side of the massive Mount Lovcen, a seemingly insurmountable object and I settled back and closed my eyes. But I could not relax. We crawled along to the accompaniment of grinding gear changes and every few minutes the car seemd to turn back on itself and I felt myself sliding from the protection of Miles's shoulder to be jammed against the door. I opened my eyes.

'I hope you don't suffer from vertigo,' said Miles's

voice in my ear. I looked out of the window and then wished I hadn't.

'My God! How have we got this far without going over the edge?' I clutched him as we lurched round another sharp bend and stared with horror at the chain of zig-zags falling away down the steep mountainside. The road hugged the very edge of the cliff and Kotor was now a minute huddle in the valley far below, a sheer drop of hundreds of feet.

'Don't worry, we are nearly at the top,' said Pero Njavro over his shoulder as he skilfully manoeuvred the car round yet another hair-pin bend.

'But we have to go down the other side?'

'It is not so bad, you will see.'

It was not. We were soon in the Valley of Tivat which was barren looking and little cultivated, due to the fact, said Pero, that there was very little fresh water; but farther down in the next valley there were vineyards and stands of sweet corn.

'I presume you are going to have to search all over Sveti-Stefan aren't you?' I said as we slipped down the road to Budva. 'That's going to be impossible, surely, without a lead of some sort – I mean it's a private hotel complex, isn't it?'

'The public are allowed on it on payment of an entrance fee. We must just hope we strike lucky.'

'You're not really bothered about getting there before Ivo, are you?' I said, a suspicion that had been simmering in the back of my mind for some time floating to the surface. 'You just want to be around when he's there.'

'He could save us a difficult search.'

'You mean you'll confront him? Shouldn't the Kapetan have a posse of men at his side?'

'There'll be no confrontation. I don't want him alerted or arrested yet. We'll just stick around and see where he goes.' He looked at me thoughtfully. 'He really got you all screwed up, didn't he? If you'll pardon the expression.'

'If you'd been attacked twice within a few hours, wouldn't you be wary of your attacker? Not to mention attempted rape.'

I saw the look on his face and muttered: 'Yes, I didn't tell you that, did I, but it's true. It was before he half-strangled me.'

'I assumed you were lovers.'

'And that gave him the right to . . . to . . . My God! You men are all alike, you . . .!'

'Steady on, I'm not trying to get at you. As far as you and I are concerned comrade Tomasic has more things to answer for than drug-running. I hope I do come face to face with him in the near future.' It was a comforting reply and I managed a wan smile. 'That's better. I was beginning to think our old Kate had totally fled.'

'The girl with a wisecrack a minute; the fall guy for the entire orchestra?'

'Nonsense. You're a breath of fresh air in what is a somewhat rarefied atmosphere, and you're transparently honest, if you'll excuse the clichés.'

'And I got myself mixed up with a guy who's a complete stranger to the truth. Who tells so many different tales that I don't think he himself knows any more which are fact and which are fiction. How gullible can you get?'

'We all make mistakes,' he said gently. 'Don't let it tear you to pieces.' This was a new Miles and one I would never have suspected existed. He sounded almost human and there was real concern in his eyes. For the first time I realised that behind that sophisticated exterior a warm-blooded man lurked.

'Look, we've almost reached the coast.' He pointed

out of the window. Sure enough, ahead of us a deep blue line snared the horizon and at Budva the road met the sea and curved round the bay on a little verdant plateau that gave one marvellous views of the coastline and the island of St Nicholas that is, insisted Pero Njavro, the last island off the Dalmatian coast before the Albanian border.

Then Sveti-Stefan was below us, a little humpbacked appendage sticking out into the sea, tightly packed with white stone buildings whose terracotta roofs gleamed floridly in the overhead sun. There was a car park at the bottom of the zig-zag leading down to the resort and we parked on a stretch of concrete that was positively shimmering in the heat.

'You don't seriously expect me to stay here in the car do you?' I asked. 'I'd definitely be a corpse by the time you returned.'

'There is a café just over there where you can sit and wait for us,' Pero Njavro flashed me a quick smile. 'It is very modern and you can even buy English newspapers.'

The café, when we reached it, was indeed very up-market with a marvellous display of cakes and snacks, with prices to match. My stomach gave an anguished rumble.

'Oh Miles, I'm so hungry. I've had practically nothing to eat today.'

'Well, you can sit here and charge up.'

'But I've got no money,' I wailed.

'I can soon remedy that.' He put his hand in his pocket and pulled out a handful of notes and coins which he handed to me. 'This should be enough to stave off the pangs.'

'Do you think I'm too disreputable to grace these surroundings?'

He eyed me up and down. 'If you sit quietly over there

in the corner I think they might manage to ignore you.'

I watched them out of sight as they walked briskly away from the café through smart, bright gardens set out with displays of canna lilies and expanses of grass so incredibly green that they made one wince. With amazing patience I gave them time to get across the causeway. I even treated myself to a limunadu, ignoring with great difficulty the mouth-watering delicacies arrayed before me. Then I padded after them, padded being the operative word as my broken sandal was inter-ferring with my walking.

It was a good job I had managed such a magnificent sample of self control in the café; I had just enough money to pay the entrance fee. I scuttled through the archway and started on my exploration of the island kingdom feeling that my transparent honesty was getting just a little opaque.

There were no signs of Miles and Pero Njavro or Ivo and his accomplice, though there were plenty of tourists wandering up and down the narrow alleyways and flights of steps. There were hedges of oleanders, pomegranate trees bearing half-grown fruit and a couple of trees with enormous leaves and clusters of brown, nut-like pods which I discovered later were foxglove trees. The entire place was a warren of cottage-type buildings, paths and terraces, all set on a steep gradient; but it was an ordered warren. Each stone cottage was spick and span and housed an enviable first-class suite for the discerning and rich holidaymaker. The paintwork gleamed, the terraces were spotless and set out with modern garden furniture; even the flowers looked polished. The overall picture was one of charm, beauty and elegance but there was an artificial air about the whole set-up. One began to long for a little natural clutter; a garden run riot instead of contrived perfection everywhere, even some litter, like the odd discarded sweet wrapper, would have helped to combat the feeling that one had somehow wandered onto a stage set. It seemed inconceivable that a sophisticated setting like this was being used for a drugs drop. Where did one start looking?

Plodding ever upwards I reached the little stone chapel that is set on the summit of the isle and found that it was locked. I dipped down to the south-western side that faced out to sea and discovered a swimming pool; a blinding flash of blue tucked away in a fold of land that provided a level shelf with a terrace and an array of shady pines. At one point the path petered out on the cliff edge and from a gap in the rock, seedheads of allium and maritime cinneraria hung out like bleached skeletons over the vivid viridian and ultramarine sea burning far below.

I retraced my steps and plunged along another maze of interlocking paths and alleyways and found myself in a little paved courtyard. In the centre was a large ornate stone urn beneath an arch canopied by a trailing vine with sprays of orange trumpet-shaped flowers. I thought at first it was a wellhead and wandered over for a closer look. There was a wooden lid and I lifted this expecting to see the gleam of water somewhere down in the dim recesses. Instead, I found a metal grille firmly fixed across the top of the vessel and through this mesh I could see the glint of coins piled up inside.

'Kate! What are you doing here?' I started violently. It was the second time in a few hours that he had shouted at me and this time I felt far more guilty.

'I thought it was a well,' I said inconsequently.

'What, up here?'

'You have a point. Miles, have you found anything?'

'No, and you haven't answered my question.'

'You didn't really think I was just going to sit there

and miss all the action, did you?' From the look on his face that was just what he had thought. 'I decided that three searchers were better than two. Look, this stone pot thing is stuffed full of coins. It must be a sort of wishing well – you know, like the Trevi fountain in Rome.'

Miles joined me under my arbor. He was on his own and he looked as hot and ruffled as one of his mien could be expected to look under the circumstances.

'This is not a game you know, Kate. These people are dangerous.'

'You don't have to tell me that.'

'Sorry, but I've got enough to concentrate on at the moment without having to worry about you as well.'

'You're not responsible for me, Miles. I'm quite capable of looking after myself.' This was the mis-statement of the century. With admirable restraint he said nothing and I turned back to the treasure trove. 'There are coins of all nationalities as far as I can see and paper notes too. Do you think it's sorted out and counted up at the end of the season and given to charity?'

'Possibly. Kate please go back and wait on the mainland.'

I sought to distract him.

'Look, there's even a billet-doux been left.' The crumpled envelope had been stuck to the side of the grill with a piece of sticking plaster. It came away and I held it up and painstakingly read out the message:

'*Za mog dragog snovo-stvaralaca*. That means "to my darling" something or other. It's even got kisses all over it.' There were crosses all over the front of the envelope and one large one on the back.

'Here, let me look at that!' He snatched it out of my hands and examined it closely, tilting it this way and that. 'This so called "kiss" on the back could be a black cross.'

'You mean . . .?'

110

He inserted a pen under the flap of the envelope and rolled it open and lifted out the folded sheet of paper it contained. There were a few words scribbled on it:

## СВЕТИ ТРИПУН МАДОНА

'It's in Cyrillic!' I cried in frustration and we both glared at it in bafflement. Miles examined it more closely. There were traces of a white deposit on one corner and he ran his finger carefully round inside the envelope. It came away with white dust particles clinging to it and with a thoughtful look on his face he sniffed at it and then delicately tasted it with the tip of his tongue.

'It's hash all right. Let's find Pero Njavro and get him to translate.'

We didn't have to look far. Pero had heard our voices and appeared up a flight of steps at the side of the courtyard.

'You have found something?' He came towards us looking expectant. Miles handed him the envelope and he read out carefully, '"To my darling dream-maker."' He raised his eyebrows and took the sheet of paper and a slight smile flashed across his face. 'It says "Svetac Tripun mdona", that is to say, "St Tripun Madonna".'

Miles and I looked at each other blankly. 'Does it mean anything to you?' he asked Pero.

'St Tripun is the name of the cathedral in Kotor,' he said slowly. 'I do not think there is an English name for this saint. The cathedral is the only building inside the old city that was not badly damaged by the earthquake. There are many statues of the Madonna there.'

'So this could be a message spelling out the information that the stuff is hidden in this cathedral?'

'It could be. We've drawn a blank here. The only places we haven't searched are inside the individual

111

suites and in the holidaymakers' personal luggage. I think that is most unlikely and I need higher authority and a sniffer dog for that.'

'Then what are we waiting for? Back to Kotor!'

Before we left Miles folded the paper back in the envelope, re-sealed it and taped it back into place at the side of the grille. It really didn't look as if it had been touched.

# Chapter 6

I joined the rush to leave Sveti-Stefan and scrambled down to the exit in their wake, slipping and stumbling in my broken sandal. Half-way across the causeway I gave up the struggle and took off both sandals. I regretted it immediately as the burning concrete scorched my bare feet.

Surprisingly enough the journey back to Kotor seemed to take less time than the outward one and even the descent from the Lovcen massif was not quite so terrifying although the car seemed frequently to be standing on its nose. Back in Kotor, Pero parked the car on the wide esplanade and led the way past palm trees and market stalls. These stalls were a feast of colour, piled high with mountains of tomatoes, peppers, peaches and melons and their accompanying swarms of wasps and flies. There were also souvenir stalls hung about with brightly woven rugs displaying embroidery, leather goods and hand-carved wood. I noticed small black-edged cards pinned to tree trunks, some of them bearing photographs and realised they were obituary notices. My presence had apparently been accepted by the two men. There were no more attempts to get me to wait in the car, but I kept a deliberately low profile and slunk at their heels.

As we approached the city walls there was the sound of pumps and rushing water and when we reached the gateway a torrent of water greeted us, gushing out through the arch on its way to the harbour. A precarious catwalk of planks had been laid across the network of hoses and pulsating water, along which tourists, trying to enter the old city, were teetering awkwardly.

'Floods?' asked Miles.

'The after-effects of the earthquake,' said Pero. 'The old city was built on top of a series of caves. The main earthquake that caused the devastation happened at 7.20 am but there was an earlier one that broke through the foundations and flooded the caves. They are still trying to pump them out.'

'After all this time?'

'Shortage of money,' Pero shrugged. 'Repair work is now being sponsored by UNESCO but the finance doesn't always get channelled in the right direction.'

He led the way through the gateway. Minus my sandals I waded happily through the surging water; Miles, after only a few steps along a slimy plank, slipped and splashed up to his ankles. He swore under his breath.

'Why don't you take off your shoes and socks and roll up your trousers, or are your feet not used to the light of day?' I enquired sweetly. He ignored me.

Once inside the old city we were high and dry but it was a melancholy sight and, after my recent experiences at Baošić, one that struck terror into me. Those buildings still standing leaned at drunken angles; broken edifices clawed the sky, shattered walls and windowless façades propped up by girders mocked the splendours that had once been and the air was rent with the noise of pumps and drills. Pero had been right about the time of the earthquake. The clock tower, though heavily damaged, was standing – just – and the clock had stopped at 7.20. I wondered how Pero came to be so well-informed about the tragedy and as if he could read my thoughts he said, 'This is my home town. My family have lived in Kotor for many generations, fortunately now in the new section, and our house escaped damage.'

I caught sight of movement in the top storey of one of the delapidated buildings, figures moving behind a shattered window.

'There are people up there – surely they're not still living in these places?'

'Everyone is supposed to be re-housed in the new apartment blocks but some of the old people refused to move. They have lived here all their lives and they wish to die here. The government refuses to take any responsibility for them, but it turns a blind eye.'

He led us across what had been the main square and we turned a corner and had to pick our way along an alley strewn with rubble, the buildings on either side of which leaned precariously towards each other. A dust-smeared fig tree leaned out of a crack and snatched at us as we passed.

'Are you all right?' Miles was regarding me anxiously.

'Are you sure we should be here? It looks highly unsafe.'

'Hundreds of tourists come in and out every day. This part is perfectly safe or no one would be allowed entrance.'

'Of course, I'm being silly. It's just that I've already been through my own private earthquake today.'

'I wonder if there is a penalty for bringing about the collapse of a building. "Defacing public property?" "Causing a public danger?" "Causing danger to human life?" "Causing a public nuisance?" It would be interesting to find out.'

'If I didn't know you better I would almost say you were joking.'

The cathedral has a Roman Basilica fronted by a twin-towered façade. Pero had explained that it had escaped serious damage because it was situated at the back of the old city and built on solid foundations. There were a lot of other people besides ourselves converging on the entrance and a German guide was shouting out information to his flock of tourists as he shepherded them inside.

'This is all we need,' groaned Miles. 'A public audience.'

'Don't worry, I will see to it,' said Pero and disappeared into the cathedral. He returned almost immediately with an elderly, emaciated man in tow. He was wearing a dark suit several sizes too large for him and his thin, wizened neck emerged from his collar like a tortoise from its shell. He possessed a pair of brilliant blue eyes, very rare in this part of Yugoslavia. I never did find out who he was – priest, official guide or verger – but he spoke a stilted English and insisted on taking us on a comprehensive tour of the cathedral and its treasures.

'Is this necessary?' Miles was getting fidgety.

'Please, it is the best way to search,' said Pero. 'We can approach the Madonnas without drawing attention to ourselves and he has promised he will let no more visitors in once this lot has gone.'

It was dim and cool inside the building and my eyes were drawn at once to the magnificent silver screen backing the altar. Nearby was a *pietà* in stone. Our guide led us round, pointing out the features of interest but I took in very little. We went up the stairs to the left of the north aisle to the Reliquary which was an octagonal room stuffed with treasures including a lot of gold work and paintings and an ancient sarcophagus. I was fidgeting by this time, Miles having transmitted his impatience to me, but our loitering in the Reliquary paid off. By the time we descended the stairs the other sightseers had left and we had the cathedral to ourselves.

Even then we didn't immediately investigate the Madonnas, of which there were several, but continued our traipse in the steps of the guide. On the left of the altar, about halfway down the nave, there was a glass case containing a figure lying on its back, dressed in a black habit, almost lifesize. I wasn't sure whether it was meant to be a monk or a nun but it hardly fitted my idea of a Madonna. On the same side of the nave, but nearer the door, was another glass case. This one was upright and inside was a very ornate figure, resplendent in silver and gold and topped by a towering Byzantine crown. Beneath the crown, where the face should have been, was a black hollow. The guide beckoned us closer and flashed his torch into the aperture. I felt the hairs rise on the back of my neck but I needn't have worried. In the glow of light a most beautiful face swam into view, a magnificent example of *trompe l'oeil*.

'Just a moment. Shine that torch again!' Miles voice was sharp and the guide obligingly flashed the light onto the figure.

'No, behind the case.'

Pero Njavro produced his own torch and shone it where Miles was pointing. Behind the case was a niche between two square pillars and a little shelf curved between the pillars and the wall and disappeared into the shadows. I could see it then; a darker mass to one side, some object wedged in the corner.

Miles edged carefully behind the case and reached forward to get at the object. Beside me the guide said nothing but he was positively radiating disapproval. Pero gave an appreciative grunt as Miles handed the package to him. It was about the size of a bag of sugar, wrapped in dark polythene.

117

'Is that it?' I couldn't keep the excitement out of my voice and Miles flashed me a warning look, but Pero's voice was warm as he answered me.

'Almost certainly.' He moved back to the centre of the nave where the light was better and we all followed him. I craned my neck to see what was inside as he carefully peeled back the outer covering.

'Kate, get the guide to take you round the Reliquary again,' said Miles urgently.

'But . . .'

'Don't argue. Get him out of the way.'

Mutinously I obeyed, so for the second time in less than half an hour I ascended the stairs with the guide in tow. I professed an interest in the triptych which had place of honour against one wall. It had been executed by a local Renaissance artist and I tried to look fascinated as the guide gave me a potted history of this artist and his school of painting. With heroic effort I managed to ask intelligent questions about the other *objets d'art* and insisted on examining in great detail many of the paintings. Eventually both I and the guide were exhausted and we returned to the nave in time to see Pero replacing what looked like the original package in its hiding place.

'You're not putting it back are you?' I hissed at Miles.

'That's a substitute.'

'Which the Kapetan just happened to have on him?

'Which the Kapetan happened to have on him,' he agreed solemnly. Then, seeing the look on my face he said, 'Yes, it was cannabis, good quality stuff, about a kilo.'

'How much is it worth? What will happen to it now?'

'About two and a half thousand pounds. The Kapetan's department will deal with it. I believe it is usually burnt. If the substitute is collected and passed on no harm will be done.'

118

'What is the substitute?'

'Probably talc or some such substance.' I looked at him in disbelief.

'But suppose Ivo or someone along the line tries it?'

'I don't think they are experienced enough to think of testing it and anyway, you said Ivo had his own supply, didn't you, so he is hardly likely to break into this?'

'Mmm. Are you – are we going to hang around to see if he turns up?' I could not keep the apprehension out of my voice.

'No, there's no point and the Kapetan will follow it up from here. Do you think you could wait in here a little while whilst I go with him to sort out some details?'

It was politely put but I knew he had no intention of letting me in on their little *tête-à-tête* so I acquiesced. I sat in a pew at the back of the nave, Miles and Pero left and the guide opened the big west doors and a new spate of tourists flooded in.

I think I must have dozed. I had no idea how long I sat there but suddenly they were back at my side.

'Have you completed all your business?' I asked sarcastically.

'Yes, the Kapetan is staying here in Kotor but he is lending me his car and we'll hie back to Dubrovnik. Are you ready?'

The heat hit me like a wall when we got outside and I screwed up my eyes against the blinding rays of sunlight. As we made our way out of the old city and back to the car I limped and stumbled across the burning pavements.

'A moment please,' said Pero. He beckoned a young boy of about ten or eleven and fired a fusilade of instructions at him. The boy gave me a startled look and then scurried off. 'Just a short wait,' said Pero turning back to me. 'Why don't you sit here and rest.' He gave me a melting smile. 'Here' was a low bench tucked in the shade of a palm and I gratefully sank down on it whilst he and Miles went into another huddle. I was feeling quite faint with hunger by now and my concentration was wandering.

The boy returned from his errand and handed something to Pero who presented it to me with a flourish. It was a pair of the little white canvas boots which all the female workers in Yugoslavia seem to wear. The heel and toe are cut out and they lace up the front. I had seen them on the feet of waitresses and shopgirls and had been intrigued by this article of what seemed to be national uniform.

'They are very comfortable,' Pero assured me and I played the part, kicking off my broken sandals for the last time and wriggling my bruised feet into the boots. They were extremely comfortable.

'They do something for you but I'm not sure what,' said Miles laconically.

I thanked Pero profusely and he walked us back to the car, shook hands with both of us and helped me into the passenger seat. At the last moment he slapped Miles on the shoulder and said something in Serbian whilst giving me a look that I can only describe as lecherous. Miles gave a guffaw of laughter and started up the engine.

'How much Serbian did you say you know?' I asked crossly, waving to Pero as we drove out of Kotor.

'Some phrases are universal.'

'Are you sure you can drive this thing?' A van overtook us honking furiously and Miles swerved further over to the right.

'Of course; it's not so very different but I'll keep our speed down. There's no hurry now.'

My stomach gave an angry roar and I clasped my hands over it. 'Can one die of hunger in just one day?'

120

'We'll stop soon and have a meal. The Kapetan has recommended a restaurant between Perast and Risan. Didn't those cakes at Sveti-Stefan do the trick?'

'How do you think I paid the entrance fee?'

'Oh the perfidy of woman! I won't say you deserve it. Never mind, we shall wine and dine in style if you can hang on for a few more minutes.'

'I haven't any money.'

'Be my guest. I think I can run to that. I can probably put it down to expenses anyway.'

'You have a winning way with you, Miles Bretherton, I don't know how any woman can resist you.'

'Most don't try.' But he grinned as he said it and I resisted the urge to make the obvious reply. Conversation lapsed after this. Miles was concentrating on his driving and I was too tired to bother.

We nearly missed the restaurant. The turn-off to it was situated on a bend and we were half way round before we saw the sign. Miles braked suddenly and reversed cautiously off the highway and a bus thundering round behind us narrowly missed clipping our bonnet. A gaggle of schoolboys gesticulated rudely from the rear of the bus and a cascade of empty crisp bags and sweet wrappers swept onto our car roof and dribbled down the windows.

'I think they are trying to tell us something,' I said. Miles grinned lopsidedly and manoeuvered into a parking space.

It was an attractive restaurant. One could either eat outside on the vast terrace or in the dining room, which featured a lot of folk pottery and bare wood, the Yugoslavian answer to stripped pine.

'Miles dear, do you think I could possibly borrow your comb again?' He handed it over and I spent an industrious fifteen minutes in the cloakroom. By the

121

time I was ready to join him again I was at least clean, but that was about all that could be said for my appearance. My hair was a jungle of damp curls and a new layer of freckles blossomed across my face. I had no make-up on me; not that I needed any further colouring, rather, something to tone down my fiery cheeks and the livid bruise disfiguring one of them. My skirt and shirt were dirty and torn, there was nothing I could do about them; and my feet oh my feet! I wriggled my toes in their little white boots and regarded them ruefully. They really were extremely comfortable, but . . . I had noticed a couple of waitresses wearing identical ones as we came in and I wondered what they thought about my choice of footgear. They probably thought I was an eccentric English tourist; they might even be flattered by my apeing their peasant attire. Miles was a different kettle of fish. There could hardly be a greater contrast between me and the sophisticated dolly birds he usually squired around but he was lumbered with me for now and I, for one, did not intend to let this reflection inhibit me or spoil my enjoyment of the coming meal. I swept out of the cloakroom in style and was disappointed to find that I had no audience.

Miles was lounging out on the terrace. He eyed me with twisting lips. 'You look very . . .'

'Don't tell me.'

'. . . very wholesome and *au naturel*, I was going to say. I have ordered. Shall we wander around out here whilst they're preparing it. I have been promised some very special apple juice whilst we wait.'

A stream ran through the grounds and the very special apple juice was dredged up out of this. The home-made cordial was bottled and the bottles were suspended in clusters beneath the surface of the water for cooling. It was delicious. We followed the stream and a little farther down a miniature waterwheel turned the handle of a spit on which a suckling pig was revolving over a charcoal fire. The aroma was nearly my undoing.

'Oh Miles, I could tear it off with my bare hands and devour the lot.'

'Not long to wait now. Come and inspect your fish course.'

Part of the stream had been dammed and a large pool opened before us edged with rosemary bushes and other aromatic shrubs. It was positively heaving with fish; large grey forms undulated and coiled in a seething mass in the shallow depths.

'I think they are some kinds of trout. I've chosen ours and they have been extricated and bashed over the head.'

I refused to rise. 'I hope you picked large ones.'

We ate at a table on the terrace. I had difficulty in restraining my appetite and not making an obvious pig of myself.

'When have you last eaten today?'

'I haven't. It was yesterday evening, apart from a couple of mouthfuls this morning.'

'You poor girl, I didn't realise it was as bad as that. You must be starving.'

'I am. Just try and not look if it upsets you.'

'Talk about looking, is it my imagination or are those two waitresses over there giving me rather odd looks? Now, if it were you I could understand . . .'

'You displaying your usual sartorial elegance but me being a little frayed at the edges you mean?'

'I wouldn't have put it quite like that.'

'I shouldn't worry.' I concentrated on extracting the bones from my fish. 'They probably think you're a wife beater.'

'They what?' He looked at me in astonishment then

started to grin. 'I see what you mean. Not the traditional black eye but quite a nice decoration.'

'You've probably gone up in their estimation and they're secretly feeling rather tickled that one of their Western sisters is not as emancipated as they have been led to believe. The Yugoslavian male likes to be seen as master in his household and the Yugoslavian youths are very macho, hadn't you noticed?'

'I can't say I have. And does that turn you on?'

'No, it certainly does not. You wouldn't be trying to suggest that I'm a natural victim? That I graduate to that type of man, get a kick from masochism?'

'No, that doesn't figure. Are you ready for the next course?'

We ate Duveč, which is a goulash of pork and peppers; very spicy and apt to take the roof off your mouth unless you wash it down with wine and apply yourself diligently to the side salad. By this time we had a feline audience. A grey tabby insinuated itself under our table and wove in and out of our legs, mewing soundlessly and fixing us with piteous stares from its yellow eyes. As native cats went, it wasn't too badly emaciated. It probably did quite well for itself with customers' leavings but in England it would definitely be a candidate for the RSPCA. I offered some pieces of meat from my plate and it bolted them ravenously and pleaded for more.

'For God's sake be careful,' said Miles. 'A rabid second violin is all I need.'

'It's starving,' I protested. 'How can you be so cruel?'

'If you must feed the damn thing at least put the food on the ground – don't let it lick your fingers.'

'Oh my, have I discovered another nasty trait in your character, indifference to the sufferings of our dumb friends?'

'I just happen to have a healthy regard for the anti-

124

rabies precautions. Do you want a coffee?'

'I don't think so thanks, not if it's the usual Turkish.'

'Haven't you acquired a taste for it yet? Hot as hell, black as . . .' He saw the expression on my face. '. . . what's the matter? Have I said something wrong?'

'It's just . . . just a phrase that Ivo used to trot out a lot.'

'I'm sorry if I touched a raw nerve. You must try and forget the whole ghastly experience. Put it behind you and start again.'

'Stop behaving like an agony aunt and treating me as if I were a hung-up teenager. How old do you think I am, for God's sake?'

'I know how old you are, and I am not talking down to you. Now, do you want a *cappuccino* if I can get one?'

The restaurant manager was very obliging and used to Western European palates and, wonder of wonders, he produced two *cappuccino*. Business was hotting up inside the building and a coach had just disgorged a large party of tourists, but out here, on the edge of the terrace, we were in a world of our own. The restaurant and its grounds were situated in a lush little rift between the highway and the mountains, and the sinking sun painted the nearby rockface in a technicolour display of crimson, scarlet and orange. It reminded me of a picture I had seen of the Grand Canyon; there was something primitive and savage about the molten light flooding the escarpment and splashing the rocks like gobbets of blood.

I sipped my coffee and studied Miles. The sun behind him turned his hair to strawberry blond and his eyes looked almost silver in the tanned planes of his face. I decided he had some explaining to do.

'How old are you Miles?'

'Too old for you.'

'And far too young to be the business manager of a world-famous orchestra.'

He looked at me warily. 'What's age got to do with it?'

'Come clean, you're a phoney.'

He sighed but there was a glint of amusement in his eyes. 'That damned Battle Symphony I suppose. You set me up didn't you. I looked it up afterwards. But I still don't see why a business manager should be expected to know every obscure piece of music in the classical repertoire.'

'No, but if you were genuine you would have admitted your ignorance, instead . . .'

'Of trying to cover up?' he broke in. 'I always said you were a very astute woman. I hope you are unique in your perception and nobody else has rumbled me.' He leaned forward and crumbled up a piece of bread and flicked the pieces onto the ground. The cat streaked out of the shadows and pounced before slinking back in disappointment.

'Well, who or what are you? You really can't hold out on me any longer.'

'What do you think?' he countered, looking as if he would rather be a thousand miles away.

'Well, I've finally and rather regretfully come to the conclusion that you're not the villain of the piece.'

'Me?' He was righteously indignant.

'You must admit you occupy the perfect position for being the mastermind behind a drugs ring. You travel abroad, you have contacts in masses of countries, no one queries your comings and goings and you seem to know an awful lot about drugs. You were the obvious candidate.'

'And what made you change your mind?'

'You fraternise too much with the authorities. You're one of them. What are you exactly – a policeman? A member of M15?'

'I'm a customs officer.'

'You're never?' I stared at him in disbelief. That was something I had certainly not contemplated, but it figured. In fact, the more I thought about it the more everything clicked into place. He pulled a card out of his hip pocket and flashed it under my eyes. It was a warrant card, complete with photograph, that established his identity as an officer with HM Customs and Excise.

'But the orchestra – Richard Godbold – I mean . . .' Then I came out with the stupidest remark. '. . . you're not in uniform.'

'I'm an officer in the Investigation Division, plain clothes, cloak-and-dagger stuff and all that. I can see I shall have to fill you in a little but don't forget I've signed the Official Secrets Act.'

'Miles, I'm flabbergasted. You really will have to explain you know.'

'You realise this is highly confidential? I could jeopardise the entire operation involving you, an outsider.'

'But I *am* involved already and surely I've been a great help to you today.'

'Yes,' he admitted grudgingly. 'You must know what the score is because you are involved, however unwittingly, and you could be in some personal danger.'

'You mean Ivo . . . ? His words brought the morning's events horribly to my mind again and I had visions of Ivo peering over his shoulder.

'I don't think you'll have any more trouble from Ivo himself. It's who is behind him. Narcotics are big business, you know, involving thousands, millions of pounds, and the brains behind this ring are not going to let anyone stand in their way. Do you want a brandy?' He asked inconsequently.

'No, I want to keep my wits about me and be sure I don't miss anything, so stop prevaricating, mister, and lay it on the line.'

He sighed. 'This is serious Kate.'

'Do you think I don't know that?'

'I'm sorry. All right, I'll try and make it as brief as possible.

'As I said, drugs are big business and getting bigger every day. We track down and confiscate hundreds of kilos of the stuff each year but it's just the tip of the iceberg. Sometimes we strike lucky – we get a tip-off or someone's activities arouse our suspicions, or . . .', there was a far-away look in his eyes and I felt that now we were getting to the nitty-gritty, '. . . or we plot supply and flow. We always know when a new consignment of drugs floods the market and we balance it against the movements of suspicious parties.' I must have looked blank because he leaned forward and spoke urgently. 'Look, we always have our eyes on those sectors of the population who travel regularly, and quite legitimately, in and out of the country. When the movements, of say, a certain group always seem to coincide with renewed activity on the drugs scene, we get suspicious and follow it up. Itinerant musicians are always prime suspects – pop groups, bands and orchestras.

'It was noted some time ago that after each foreign tour of the Europa, the drugs scene hotted up. Supplies, large supplies, were getting in and filtering through the various middlemen, many of them known to us and under surveillance. So it was decided that the Europa needed looking into. I was chosen for the job. I'm not the complete phoney, you see; my father is a musical administrator, currently with an Australian orchestra, and I really did intend to become a musician myself. I grew up with that background and I *do* know quite a bit about music and orchestras and how they are run', he gave me a sly grin, 'so I was the obvious choice for the job.'

'But how did you manage to walk in just like that? I mean, Richard Godbold really is ill, isn't he? The Board . . . ?'

'The Chairman of the Trustees was told and we had his full co-operation. Apart from him only Richard Godbold knows the true facts. He is under the weather at the moment and was only too glad to take a temporary break from the orchestra. He showed me the ropes when I went as his assistant on the Benelux tour last year and gradually eased me in. No one had any reason to doubt my bona fides and I can tell you I've been working very hard on behalf of the Europa Management Committee since I took up the job.'

'And has it paid off? Is the Europa a cover for a big drugs syndicate?'

'It is.' He sounded grim. 'Some member or associate of the orchestra is using his status to promote narcotics smuggling on a large scale.'

'And you don't know who it is, just as Ivo didn't know.'

'This has nothing to do with Ivo. A consignment of drugs came back with the orchestra from Amsterdam. We discovered it, or rather I did, hidden in the pantechnicon the instruments travel in, and I alerted the authorities at Harwich when we got back and a very discreet search was carried out by sniffer dogs when all the orchestra personnel were safely out of the way. It was only a small cache, obviously more was getting through in some other way, but we confiscated it, substituted a harmless alternative, as the Kapetan has done in Kotor, and followed it through. We now know the people involved in the UK ring.'

'But didn't you arrest them?'

'Most certainly not. They are just a very small part of the organisation. It is a network spreading right across

129

Europe and we want to find the mastermind and all his Continental contacts before we move in and do anything to make them suspicious that we are on to them.'

'These sniffer dogs, are they really competent?'

'Oh yes. They are trained by the RAF to sniff out any trace of narcotics. Very little fools them though they have been known to go on the blink occasionally and they work much shorter hours than your average Customs Officer! We are also experimenting with electronic equipment. A new electronic surveyor is being developed for use at airports which is capable of detecting drugs by smell and bleeping accordingly. Unfortunately, orange squash seems to have the same effect!'

'Orange squash! You mean it smells the same?'

'Hardly, but there's obviously some obscure connection which we are working on.'

'How fascinating, but what about the police – aren't they involved too?'

'Not directly. We co-operate when possible but we work independently. We don't tell each other what we are doing.'

'That sounds as if you are rivals.'

'No, I mustn't give that impression. We just have different methods of working but this can sometimes lead to misunderstandings; such as when the police get a tip-off and move in on a drugs run we are monitoring. They can queer our pitch by making a premature arrest when we were following a policy of watch and wait to discover identities further down the chain. By the way, we have the same powers of arrest and prosecution as the police.'

'Miles, you keep mentioning narcotics. But surely that's heroin and all the hard stuff, not hash like Ivo was handling.'

'Yes, hadn't I made that clear? We wouldn't go to all this trouble just to nobble a small-time marijuana smuggler. The man we are after deals in the hard stuff and how Ivo and Adrian Palmer got tied in with him I don't know and can't understand. I can only think that their ability was being tested first on a relatively harmless drug run before they were let in on the big thing. But they were smokers – that makes it even more incomprehensible. Drug takers are unreliable to say the least, and drug runners do not indulge in the vice they are promoting, or not in any significant way. Yet it is too much of a coincidence to suppose that there are two separate drugs rings operating within the Europa, one pushing the hard stuff, the other dabbling in hash.'

'Are you sure it is a man? There are a lot of women in the orchestra; is it at all possible that the person you are after could be a woman?'

'That can't be ruled out altogether of course, but I think it is highly improbable.'

'And have you no lead at all?'

'Let's put it like this; some people have been eliminated from my enquiry. I have my own short list but no proof.'

'Which you are not going to reveal to me?'

'I've told you all I know.' I was sure he was not levelling with me but I could understand his attitude.

'So what happens now? Why have you been so keen to follow up Ivo and Adrian if you think they are not important in the scheme?'

'Don't you see, they were behaving in a thoroughly foolhardy manner and were likely to bring the local police down on our heads and an enquiry and possibly an international incident, which would jeopardise both my objective and our quarry's. I don't want this whole thing to blow up in my face now I am so close to nailing it. I am

131

sure that any day now the drop is going to be made. It hasn't happened so far, that I know, but it is only logical to suppose that it is here on the coast that it will take place. You know what the coastline is like – hundreds of islands and inlets. It is impossible for the Yugoslavians to patrol it properly; all too easy for a boat to slip in and out unobserved.'

'So what can you possibly do?'

'Don't worry, I'm not on my own. I have the full support of the Yugoslavian Customs Service and Drug Squad behind me. We know what we are looking for; I don't think our fish will slip through the net this time. In the meantime, we haven't found the money.'

'Money?'

'The money that is going to be handed over in exchange for the stuff. None has travelled over here in the hiding place where we found the last cache of drugs.'

'Where exactly was that?'

'I suppose I can tell you. You know the framework inside the pantechnicon built to hold the instruments? Each instrument is slotted into its own niche; well, we discovered that part of the framework had a false section underneath, which, when opened, revealed the hiding place. Of course, it doesn't really mean anything – that there is no money there; it could be stashed away with someone's personal belongings or, again, no money need be involved. All transactions could be done through a numbered Swiss bank account, especially if the organisation is big enough.'

'Where does the heroin come from?'

'Most of it originates form Asia – the Far East – or Africa. But here you've also got Turkey on the doorstep and the Arab States. We think the ring we're interested in get their supplies through North Africa.'

'I still can't believe that one of my friends or associates

is involved in this filthy trade. What will happen to the orchestra when he is caught? The scandal . . .'

'I can promise you the orchestra will not be compromised. Now, are you happy with my explanation? My career would be short lived if my superiors knew how I'd shot my mouth off.' He smiled as he said this and didn't seem too concerned.

'I appreciate your confidences and I promise you no one will discover your guilty secret through any fault of mine. There's just one thing; you said earlier that I could be in danger – what do you mean?'

'Yes.' He suddenly looked very serious and leant towards me across the table. 'Don't you see, you're known to be involved with Ivo, you went off with him. If Ivo now defects, our man may wonder how much you know, how deeply you are involved. He may decide you are too dangerous and try to eliminate you. That's why you're not going back to the hotel.'

'I'm not?'

'Pero Njavro and I discussed this – it is too dangerous. I don't want you to meet up with anyone from the orchestra in the next few days.'

'But . . .'

'He has arranged for you to stay with a family in Dubrovnik. They take in paying guests, especially during the Festival season, and you can live quietly with them until the last concert.'

'Oh can I? What about Sarah and . . .'

'Sarah is still in Greece. I shall let it be known nearer the time that Ivo has ditched you and gone off and you're so upset that you can't bear to face anyone yet. You won't put in an appearance until the concert rehearsal.'

'You've got it all worked out, haven't you?'

'I don't want to appear high-handed Kate, but it is your safety I'm concerned about. Your getting mixed up in this is a complication I hadn't anticipated but I'm not taking any chances. You are keeping safely out of the way from now on. I'm sorry if your pride is going to take a blow from this tale but better that than you personally coming to danger.'

'Do you really think I'm in danger?' This on top of everything else was almost too much.

'I hope not. I hope we can get across the picture of you as an innocent bystander but I'm making doubly sure.'

'Whereabouts in Dubrovnik am I staying?'

'On the Lapad Peninsular.' He fished a piece of paper out of his pocket. 'Your hosts' names are Zuber, Milan and Veshna. The Kapetan phoned them and they are expecting you tonight.'

'That is very close to the hotel.'

'Yes, but no one from the hotel is likely to leave the private beach and stray down to Sumatrim. You should be perfectly safe mingling with the local holidaymakers.' I forebore to point out that I had done just that when staying in the hotel, and he had obviously forgotten the incident. 'If you are ready,' he continued, 'I think we should be on our way. It will be dark by the time we get back.'

'My things are all at the chalet in Baošić.'

'Then we shall have to make a stop and collect them.'

I didn't fancy the prospect at all but it wasn't until we were in the car and bowling along the highway that I remembered. I clutched his arm.

'Miles!'

The car swerved and he threw me a furious look. 'For God's sake, what are you trying to do?'

'Miles, he took my passport and my travellers' cheques and money. I've got nothing!'

He pulled into the side of the road. 'Now try and explain coherently.'

So I told him how Ivo had ransacked my handbag.

'Was there much money? Have you got the numbers of the travellers' cheques?'

'There were only a few 500 dinar notes and there is a note of my travellers' cheques' numbers back with my stuff at the hotel.'

'Well we can stop them and don't worry about paying for your accommodation. I'll deal with that and lend you some money for the time being.'

'My passport?'

'I'll sort that out with the Consulate. You're not going to need it immediately. Stop worrying.'

At Baošić he stopped the car once more. I felt panic surging through me. I did not want to go back to the chalet – anything but that. He must have sensed my withdrawal.

'There's no need for you to come with me, you can stay in the car,' he said gently. 'Just tell me where the chalet is and what I've got to pick up.'

'It's number 39. You turn off to the right from the road near the bottom. It's not locked. My stuff is all in the middle bedroom with my case. Suppose Ivo has come back?'

'I don't think he will have, but it would give me great pleasure to meet up with him.' He suddenly sounded very formidable and I was glad he was on the same side as myself.

'Miles, have you got a gun?'

He looked startled. 'No, customs officers are never armed, but do you know, I'm beginning to think that's not such a good idea.'

He got out of the car and started down the concrete road and I opened the door and yelled after him: 'Miles, my handbag – it's on top of the cupboard, probably right at the back.' He raised his eyebrows but said nothing and in a few minutes he had disappeared from view.

Dusk was falling rapidly and I settled back in my seat prepared for a long wait. I fell asleep.

The sound of approaching footsteps woke me a little later. I came to with a start and glanced apprehensively out of the window, but it was only Miles returning laden with my case and handbag.

'I couldn't find your fiddle,' he shouted as he neared the car.

'I didn't bring it with me.'

Then suddenly everything caught up with me. I hadn't handled my beloved violin for over a week. I had cut myself off from my musical lifeline and I was bereft. I burst into tears. Miles hurriedly thrust my belongings onto the back seat and gathered me into his arms.

'Now what is the matter?'

'Oh Miles, I haven't played for ages, my fingers have seized up, I've betrayed my . . . my . . .'

'Steady on, here . . . .' He produced his handkerchief again and I blew my nose loudly and tried to stem the tears pouring down my face.

'I'm sorry, I don't normally do this sort of thing. I'm not the crying sort. I don't know . . .'

'It's reaction. You've had one hell of a day. Don't mind me, I'm getting used to mopping you up.'

I gave him a watery smile and he gently kissed my bruised cheek. This nearly produced another paroxysm but I managed to control myself.

'Try and sleep again. We've still got a long way to go.'

The next thing I knew, the car was stationery again and Miles's voice was in my ear: 'Just take a look at that.'

We had pulled up in a lay-by on the outskirts of Dubrovnik, near where the Adriatic Highway started the descent down to the town. Below us lay the Old City and poised above it, like an enormous canteloupe melon, was the moon. It drifted gently above the rooftops, a child's apricot-coloured balloon that at any moment would impale itself upon a pinnacle and be no more. It was huge, completely out of proportion to the huddled buildings it illuminated, and below the water-line another city glowed redly back. Truly 'A rose-red city, half as old as time'.

I caught my breath. 'It's completely unreal. If you painted it no one would believe you; Surrealism out of Bosch.'

'With a touch of Byzantium thrown in. It makes our harvest moons at home pale into insignificance. How are you feeling?'

'Battered but not completely overthrown.'

'Good girl. Now hang on whilst I find my way through the Dubrovnik road system.'

He must have had an unerring sense of direction because in a very short while we were down from the hillside and speeding along the perimeter of the New Harbour which glittered darkly beneath the street lamps and reflected light from the many moored vessels. High above us now, the moon spun away, a fraction of its former self. We left the harbour behind and climbed the hill that divided that part of the suburbs from the Lapad Peninsular. Miles squinted down at the piece of paper on which he had written the address.

'We want the Bulevar Leninja. It's just off there.'

'I think that is the main road where all the buses stop.'
I was right. Miles parked the car at the side of the wide avenue and we eventually found our way to the alley that led to the apartment block. It was an austere modern building and once inside the entrance we found oursel-ves confronted with a setting of bare walls, concrete stairs and stark iron bannisters that seemed horribly like

137

a prison complex. There was a list of names just inside the doorway, each with a bellpush and a series of post lockers bearing identical names.

'Here we are,' said Miles. 'Zuber, Milan – it's on the fourth floor. I suppose we just ring and go up.'

He pressed the bell and we started up the stone stairs. Our footsteps echoed round the dark stairwell.

'Are you sure we've come to the right place?' Above us a door opened and a shaft of light splintered down the stairs. There was the smell of cooking and the muted sound of music. Milan Zuber was a small, brisk, voluble man whose mish-mash of languages rivalled Willie Bode's. He was clearly expecting us and drew us inside the flat where his wife Veshna welcomed us with a beautiful smile and a total lack of verbal communication. After the insalubrious exterior I was prepared for the worst but I was pleasantly surprised. The rooms were bright and airy and tastefully furnished with modern pieces and spotlessly clean.

The room I was shown to had ample cupboard and storage space and neat twin beds with crisp white linen. The sight of those pristine sheets and downy pillows drew me like a magnet. I left Miles to deal with the Zubers whilst I slowly unpacked my few belongings. He appeared in the doorway a short while later and handed me a roll of notes.

'I must go now. Are you sure you'll be all right?'

'Yes, all I want to do is get into bed. I think I could sleep for a week. What's this money for?'

'In case you get overcome with pangs of hunger between meals or need to buy a few bits and pieces. I'll collect your belongings from the hotel and bring them here tomorrow. Now remember, you're not to communicate with anyone from the Europa. You've gone to ground and I shall be your only link with that world.

138

Have you got all you need for now?'

'Yes Miles, and thank you for everything.'

'I'm only following my course of duty.' But he smiled crookedly and drew me into his arms and gently kissed me. I was about to ask whether that too came under his terms of reference but I managed to bite back the remark. Actually, I rather enjoyed it. In fact, for one mad second I had almost responded with passion, reacting as if he were my lover and not Miles Bretherton, your suave man-about-town who is not my type at all. It just showed how pole-axed with exhaustion I was.

At the door, I listened to his footsteps clattering down the stairs and turned back into the flat. The Zubers were quite willing to prepare a meal for me but I managed to persuade them that I had already eaten and all I wanted was to retire for the night. With old-world courtesy they showed me the bathroom and explained about breakfast arrangements. I don't know what Pero Njavro had told them over the phone; my bedraggled appearance must have puzzled them, but they showed no curiosity and accepted me at face value.

I managed a shower before collapsing into that welcoming bed and I was out like a light. Strangely enough, I had no dreams.

# Chapter 7

I practically slept the clock round and woke not knowing where I was for a few seconds. I could hear voices in the background and I jumped out of bed and made a sortie to the bathroom, I was almost inside when Miles poked his head out of the living room.

'Go away!' I hissed. 'I haven't repaired the damage yet and I am not ready to meet my public. Give me ten minutes.'

It took me nearer twenty minutes to achieve a satisfactory toilette but it was worth it for the expression on Miles's face when I finally made my entrance. I had combed my damp curls back into a tight helmet and donned one of my best dresses; a white silky affair with cowl neckline and a gold chain belt. I was sorely tempted to put on my little white boots for sheer devilment but decided I had offended Miles's aesthetic susceptibilities too much already. I settled for a pair of high-heeled strip sandals and screwed gold dangly earrings into my lobes.

'No need to ask if you slept well,' said Miles. 'You look positively radiant.'

Veshna Zuber was hovering anxiously in the background and I indicated that I was ready for my breakfast. She served it on the little balcony and Miles joined me at the table. There was a very hard-boiled, lukewarm egg, some salami, plenty of freshly-cut bread, butter and jam and lemon tea. I tucked in with gusto and Miles leaned back and watched me.

'I always seem to have you as an audience when I'm eating,' I said crossly as I tackled my egg.

'It appears to be an occupational hazard.'

'Why don't you join me. I'm sure our hostess wouldn't grudge you a crust.'

'Don't worry, she's already given me a slivovic'.

'God, you're really going native on me. No, don't come any nearer, I can smell it from here.'

'I've brought your things from the hotel. If you'll just give me the numbers of your travellers' cheques I'll stop them and arrange for you to get some more.'

'Are there many of my colleagues around?' I asked, trying to sound casual.

'The Greek party are not back yet. Willie is in Frankfurt and a large number of brass are bumming around on Korcula.'

'Peter Brownstone?'

'He's at the hotel. I had quite a job explaining away why I was leaving the hotel carrying a case *and* violin. By the way, it is quite OK for you to practice here; you won't disturb anybody. You must get those strong, capable fingers working again.'

'You mean I've got large, ugly hands.'

'I mean you've got musician's hands. You're a second violin; the harmonies, not the melodies; all that stretching.'

'My, you are learning. Fancy you knowing that! But you're right about the shape of musician's hands. The best pianist I ever met had very broad hands and short stubby fingers. Breadth and strength are what counts.'

'I remember seeing a film about the life of Chopin

once, and there he was, draped over the piano with long, white, languid hands.'

'I do believe I saw the same film. He was certainly limp and languid. He wouldn't have had enough strength in those fingers to play chopsticks. By the way, what are we doing today?'

'*You* are spending the day quietly here. Perhaps a trip to the Sumatrim beach is permitted. I . . . I am furthering my enquiries.'

'Which you are not going to tell me about.'

'Which I am not going to tell you about,' he agreed.

'Don't you think I should be *au fait* with every current aspect of this case? To be forewarned would surely be helpful if you really think I am in danger.'

'The less you know the better. Remember, we agreed on that yesterday evening.'

'You may have done. I don't think my wishes were actually taken in consideration. All right, I'm not going to argue with you. I've had enough drama and trauma over the last few days to last me a lifetime. I am quite content to lie on a beach and vegetate.'

The balcony overlooked a stretch of individual gardens, each one packed with flowers and vines, and beyond these were further blocks of flats. In the distance, peeping between the trees was the blue of Sumatrim Bay. From some nearby construction site came the sound of hammering and the distant traffic was a muted roar. A little breeze reached us up here, rustling the venetian blind and unwinding my curls.

'Miles, what about my passport?'

'Don't worry, I shall be working on that.'

'I hope you're keeping account of all the money you've given me and spent on me.'

'If it will keep you happy, I promise to present you with a bill when it is all over. In the meanwhile you'll

142

have to look on yourself as a kept woman.'

He left soon after this and the day stretched in front of me. I took stock of my surroundings. The flat was small but was so neatly laid out that it appeared much larger. A crucifix hung on one of the living-room walls and the sight of it sent a *frisson* through me. The other walls contained garish prints of mountain scenes and in the place of honour on the sideboard was a coffee set in beaten brass. The curtains, table-runner and chairbacks were attractively embroidered in the traditional needlepoint. Veshna saw me admiring them and drew a fold of curtain towards me so that I could see it better. I pointed at her to ask if she had done the work and she nodded shyly.

'*Dobra, dobra,*' I said, and she beamed and gestured to me to wait whilst she went out of the room. She returned with a large cardboard box which she opened to display a collection of embroidered articles which I gathered were for sale. The stitching, in vibrant shades of dark red and blue, was exquisite and I knew I must buy some for souvenirs. I was going to be in even greater debt to Miles. There was no sign of her husband and I guessed he had another job during the day. I knew that they had two married daughters who lived nearby.

I found my way down to the beach and spent the rest of the day swimming and relaxing with a book under an olive tree. Late in the afternoon I returned to the flat and the delicious smells of cooking. I sat on the bed and carefully lifted my violin out of its case, savouring the moment. I flexed my fingers and picked up my bow and tuned the instrument as well as I could.

Then I was away. I don't know how long I played. All the frustrations and pent-up emotions and fears of the last couple of days went into my music and were soothed away as the notes spiralled up into the still air. I played

143

until I was exhausted, and when I paused there was a knock at my door and an announcement that my dinner was ready.

After I had eaten I felt strangely restless and I gathered up my handbag and wandered down to the shore again. The evening was in full swing. From the many restaurants came the smell of charcoal barbecues, and they were doing good business, filling up with customers whilst white-shirted waiters darted amongst the tables and chairs. There were strings of coloured lights threaded amongst the trees and the insistent beat of pop music mingled with the haunting tunes of a folk group over to the left of the bay. I felt intensely alone and immensely sad. Everyone had their own friends and companions; convivial groups spilled out along the pavement and families walked arm-in-arm. I was the only one alone. I sat down on a low wall and stared out over the black sea.

What was Miles doing this evening? But why think of Miles? Anyone was better to focus on than letting my thoughts drift back to Ivo. But how could I think of any man after what had happened with Ivo? I was finished with men. From now on men were strictly *verboten* as far as I was concerned. But I could not stop thinking of the two men, one tall and dark, one tall and fair. The former had treated me badly, the latter I disliked. Or did I? I was beginning to feel very mixed up about Miles. Perhaps the sophisticated veneer he sported was as much a pose as his business-manager front, and I had been privileged yesterday to catch glimpses of the real Miles Bretherton. But this was ridiculous. I was so shot-up about Ivo, I was ready to rebound onto the nearest male within my orbit. I couldn't possibly fall for someone like him; he exasperated me intensely, to say the least – and as for what he felt about me, I was an encumbrance and a

144

liability he could well do without, though he had been very good about my precipitation into his affairs.

These sorts of thoughts would get me nowhere. I slowly retraced my steps and froze in horror at one point as a tall, dark silhouette, momentarily resembling Ivo, crossed my path.

Both Zuber daughters, plus their husbands and respective children, were gathered at the flat when I got back. In fact, quite a party was going on and I was quickly drawn into the scene. The inevitable bottle of slivovic was in evidence and also vinjak, a local grape brandy. I managed to refuse these but agreed that a little vino would be welcome. Veshna handed round a dish of sweet peppers and Milan clapped his arms round her shoulder and told me:

'Mama speak no English, only a little Italian. You speak Italian?'

'*Un poco*,' I suggested tentatively, thinking of my music.

'*Si, si,*' said Veshna eagerly, but we progressed little further. The wine flowed and I struck up a conversation with the Zuber daughters, Irina and Maria, who both spoke very good English. One of them worked for the local tourist bureau and the other was a teacher. Their children, who ranged in age from five or eleven, were all learning English at school and were eager to try out their vocabulary. Milan sat proudly at the head of table, his balding head shining under the light, and manipulated the evening with a patriarchal air.

'Madame Katerina, you play your violin,' he commanded when there was a lull in the proceedings. Well, that was all right with me though I thought I had better keep off the heavy classical stuff. I fetched my fiddle from my bedroom and I had hardly got going before one of the Zuber grandsons produced what looked like a penny whistle and joined in. Soon the entire family were clapping their hands and stomping their feet to the music.

There was a knock at the door and the neighbours from the flat below were ranged on the doorstep. I thought how in England a knock at the door would have heralded an irate neighbour complaining about the noise; here, they just wanted to join in. Someone had a guitar, and to my delight, there was also a one-stringed mandolin. We played away together, throwing and catching the melody between us. I do not know what we played but afterwards I was convinced that 'The Yellow Rose of Texas' figured largely.

Suddenly Milan clapped his hands to his head and pointed at me. 'My head, my silly old head, I almost forget. I have message for you, Madame Katerina. Your Mister Milan telephone for you. He say to tell you he come for you tomorrow morning at 8 o'clock.'

Well, I suppose Miles – Milan – it was all the same. I wondered what Miles wanted, but I was soon drawn back into the music-making. The wine flowed and at some point during the evening I vaguely remember being shown how to play the one-stringed mandoline and making a complete hash of it. At the back of my mind was the thought that I should make an early night of it if I was hoping to rise early, but there seemed no point in opting out of the party; I should never be able to sleep with all this noise going on.

The festivities ended abruptly not long after midnight. Goodbyes were said and sleepy children whisked off home. Yawning but wonderfully relaxed, I tumbled into my bed and for the second night running fell immediately into a deep, dreamless sleep.

Amazingly enough, I was up and ready when Miles called the following morning, and not too hung-over.

Trying to read the expression on his face, I asked first if all was well.

'Yes, completely. We're going to have a day off; I've arranged an excursion. The only proviso is that you enjoy yourself and put all thoughts of drugs, customs officials and Ivo Tomasic aside for the day. They are not to be dwelt on or mentioned.'

'That's fine by me. You're looking mighty pleased with yourself; where are you taking me?'

'Why shouldn't I – a beautiful day, a beautiful woman and a boat trip to the Elaphite Islands. What more could I ask? What did you do with yourself yesterday?'

'Well, there was this terrific party last night . . .'

'Party?' He looked absolutely horrified so I put him out of his misery and explained about the family gathering.

'We had a fantastic time indulging in our music,' I finished up.

'That wasn't the only thing you indulged in,' he said darkly. 'Come on, we've got be down at Sumatrim by 8.30. The boat is leaving from the jetty outside the Kompass Hotel.'

We hurried down the slope leading to the bay. The beach was almost deserted at this hour of the morning and had a cleanness and freshness about it that would soon be overlaid by hordes of holidaymakers. Under the trees a solitary pair of collared doves strutted amongst the bleached grass, rooting out the crumbs from yesterday's picnics.

I had expected a large modern cruiser like the ones that featured in the Atlas adverts, but the boat that swung gently at her moorings was ramshackle looking and only about twelve feet in length. Our captain was as ramshackle as his boat. He was in his late fifties and dressed in a dirty singlet and shorts; he had a pair of the wickedest brown eyes I have ever seen and sported an impressive belly. As in Greece, a corporation in middle age is seen as a sign of prosperity and well-being and is carried proudly. He helped us aboard and waved us to a seat. There was a small cabin near the bows but the well of the boat, which housed the passengers, was covered by a canopy and the seating was a plank of wood that ran all the way round the inside of the gunwhale. The rest of the passengers consisted of a party of Germans from the nearby Kompass Hotel. They were large and voluble and obviously intended enjoying themselves.

Our captain started up the engine and cast off and we were hardly out of Sumatrim Bay before he left the wheel and dived into the cabin to come up clutching a basket full of glasses and some bottles which he dumped on the engine casing.

'Schnapps,' he announced for the benefit of his German guests as he lifted out a bottle of slivovic. 'Help yourselves.' And he rolled his eyes and beamed round at us all. Miles leaned forward and took a glass and helped himself out of the bottle.

'Miles, you're never! It's only 8.30 in the morning.'

'I'm acquiring a taste for it, and it's quite true what they say; it helps to settle your stomach.'

There was a bottle of home-made wine and a bottle of mineral water and I cautiously poured myself a slug of wine and topped up with the mineral water. Even watered down the wine nearly made me choke.

'*Ziveli*!' said the captain toasting us solemnly.

'*Ziveli*!' we all replied and downed our drinks.

After that the ice was broken and I settled back to enjoy the trip. The sun scintillated off a halcyon sea and I was glad to shelter under the awning and hide behind a pair of sunglasses. We chugged past rocks and little nameless islands and set course for Kolocep, which is the

nearest of the Elaphite Islands lying north of Dubrovnik. A solitary seagull drifted past the boat and I
watched it idly and remembered something that had
been puzzling me.

'I can't understand why there aren't more birds about.
There are the pigeons and swallows in the city and a few
sparrows and I thought I heard a blackbird at Baošić,
though I never actually saw it, and the odd seagull, but
that's all. I mean, the sea is stuffed with fish, you'd think
there would be masses of seabirds, if nothing else.'

'Perhaps it's too hot.'

'Could be, but I seem to remember that in the Far East
fishermen train cormorants to dive and fish for them,
and it's surely hotter there?'

'You have a point. It would be interesting to find out.'

'Where are we stopping off?'

'Our main destination is Lopud, which is the largest
island in the group; it has a sizeable town and caters for
the tourist trade, but I believe we are calling at Kolocep
first on the way. Are you enjoying yourself?'

'Mmm, just what the doctor ordered.' I leaned over
the side and watched the viridian ripples curving away
from the boat.

'I've brought a picnic,' said Miles, tapping the small
rucksack at his feet. 'I hope there's enough food.'

'You make me sound like a glutton,' I protested.

'It's a pleasant change to be with someone who enjoys
her food and isn't always harping about her current diet.
Can you hear that noise?'

'Yes, whatever is it?' We were approaching a large
island and the captain announced roguishly: 'Kolocep'.
In front of us was a curving sandy beach backed by a
hillside covered in pine and scrub. A strange throbbing,
humming sound was coming from this backcloth and as
we got nearer the noise increased.

'It's crickets!' exclaimed Miles. 'The whole hillside must be alive with them, it's incredible!'

As we got closer inshore we could see a little jetty to the left of the beach and we headed that way.

'A moment,' said our captain and disappeared into the cabin leaving the boat unmanned, which seemed an extremely hazardous thing to do, as there were rocks jutting out of the water and other boats around. He reappeared a few seconds later triumphantly waving a pair of spectacles, which he rubbed on a corner of his singlet and slapped on his nose with a flourish.

'Now I see,' he announced triumphantly, re-possessing the wheel.

'Do I presume we've been running on automatic pilot up to now?' said Miles in a stage whisper. 'The phrase is assuming a new meaning for me.'

'I don't think he has donned them for navigational purposes. Do you see what I see?'

'Good God! They're starkers!'

'Naturist beach,' beamed our captain salaciously. 'We stop here for a swim.'

'Dirty old man,' said Miles. 'Is this likely to upset your susceptibilities?'

'I can't wait to get in the water, appropriately clothed, of course. Who we encounter on the way in is quite irrelevant.'

We moored at the jetty and scrambled ashore, having been warned that we only had an hour before sailing again. The sand was soft and burning and scattered with palm leaf umbrellas. We collapsed under an unoccupied one and stripped off our outer clothes. I was wearing my bikini underneath and Miles had on his bathing trunks.

'You're not going the whole hog?' I leered at him and pretended to be disappointed.

'What would I look like with the state of suntan I have

arrived at? If I removed anything more I should look piebald. Now, it wouldn't show so much on you . . .'

'Nothing doing.' I stood up and ran down the beach into the water. It was very shallow and you had to wade out a long way before it was deep enough to swim. The sand rippled under my feet. A sandy beach is very rare on this part of the Adriatic coast and I wondered if this one was man made. It looked very natural.

We swam and splashed each other and floated on our backs and altogether behaved like a couple of schoolkids. I felt a sense of well-being creeping over me and I gave myself up to the pleasures of the moment. Miles seemed equally relaxed and I felt that he was truly with me in body and spirit that day and not half-occupied with other matters, as was usual. We dried off in the sun and the wave of noise from the crickets was deafening, rising to a crescendo with the midday sun. When we got back to the boat the German party were already aboard and talking amongst themselves with great hilarity. I wished my German was better; by the look on Miles's face, he could understand much of the conversation.

We set sail again and behind us the wake splintered into a thousand crystal fragments seething against a green and blue backdrop. There were other boats sailing these waters, some of them large, expensive-looking cruisers that swept past rocking us as we chugged along low in the water. I was glad that Miles had chosen this means of transport and not booked for one of the luxury cruises. Our piratical looking captain was enjoying himself as much as his passengers and he seemed to have an inexhaustible supply of bottles. With this sort of hospitality his financial return must have been small; but he was happy in his occupation, that was plain to be seen; a round peg in a very round hole.

The town of Lopud on the west side of the island

bearing the same name was a charming place. There was a quaint, almost Edwardian feeling about the atmosphere. It catered for the tourists and all that meant in twentieth-century terms, but it hadn't been spoiled and retained an air of unhurried, pleasing elegance. Miles told me that in past times many important Dubrovnik officials had built summer residences here, and there were many gracious looking houses set in their own orange and lemon groves.

We picnicked on the beach, then explored the church perched high on the headland behind the harbour. Everywhere we went we were met with flamboyant hedges of oleander that ran the gamut of pinks and reds, with the occasional white thrown in for good measure. It was very hot and we were soon back on the beach and in the water again. Later we found a little grass patch behind the esplanade fringed with a variety of palm trees that shed spikey shade over us as we lay beneath.

'Do you come from a musical family?' asked Miles rolling over onto his stomach and raising himself on one elbow.

'No, not as much as you, it would appear. My father always declares he can't tell a major from a minor key, but my mother is a very good amateur pianist and one of my brothers used to play a cornet in his school's band.'

'Tell me about your family.' So I did. I told him about my father's and grandfather's connections with Yugoslavia and all about my brothers' activities and my musical training. I chatted away happily and he seemed very interested, but it suddenly struck me that maybe the initial enquiry had been a way of promoting idle conversation, a conversational *bon mot* that was not supposed to be taken at its face value. I was probably boring him to tears. I stopped abruptly, then seeing the enquiry on his face, I stumbled on:

152

'I'm sorry, I didn't mean to go on like that; boring you with details of my home life. You must wish you had never opened your mouth.'

'Don't be silly. I'm very interested in finding out what your background is, what makes you tick.'

'You're very good at drawing people out. I suppose that is one of your professional skills. I think I am very bad at understanding people's characters from short acquaintance. Look now mistaken I've been over you.'

'You have?' He looked apprehensive.

'I thought you were a very sophisticated, starchy, man-about-town who only patronised the fashionable scene and was up-to-date with every nuance.'

'Me?'

'Now don't pretend you don't know what I mean. You've been hiding behind a very carefully thought-out front.'

'I knew I could never fit in with the musical milieu so I thought the next best thing would be to stick out like a sore thumb. In that way, any obvious mistake I made could be put down as an eccentricity.

'Miles, how do you train for a job like this? Surely not all customs officers do this sort of thing?'

'Oh no. HM Customs and Excise is a very diverse organisation and the Investigation Division is just one of many sections. Officers are usually chosen for this branch initially if they show a flair for undercover work, and also, young graduates joining the service are often creamed off for this. It is the policy now for the Customs to try and infiltrate suspicious organisations by getting a man in on the inside. Someone who has a knowledge of accounting and commerce say, can be used successfully in a trading organisation, or if we want to get in on transportation and road haulage, it helps to have a man who can handle a lorry and knows the ropes.'

'But surely this sort of undercover work can be very dangerous?'

'It can be as we are rather out on a limb, cut off from our normal network. A colleague was shot dead in East Anglia recently in a fracas involving a drugs syndicate and Customs Officials, and one of our undercover men in South America has gone missing. Don't worry; these are exceptions, not the rule. We *are* well briefed. We even go on police courses and are trained in observation and following techniques and driving skills and so on. Would you believe, I have spent many hours crouched in a hedge toting a pair of binoculars?'

'I could believe anything of you now.'

'So now you've seen through me and understand the real me?'

'Oh no. My first impression was totally wrong but I'm no nearer understanding my second one. You must give me more time.'

'Will this help?' And he leaned over and kissed me very thoroughly. It was quite devastating. It was passionate and mixed in with the passion was the tenderness and good humour that had been missing in Ivo's kisses. This was the sort of embrace I had dreamed of receiving, but not from Miles Bretherton, oh no! I scrambled into a sitting position and he immediately withdrew and looked at me with a quizzical expression.

I turned away and he said lightly; 'If you've cooled down a little, shall we walk along the esplanade? We haven't got all that much longer left before we go back.'

How could he possibly ask that having raised my temperature with his kisses? I pulled on my sundress and gathered up my belongings.

'Come on then, and you'll have to buy me an extra large limunadu.' Keep it light, Kate, keep it light. Don't let him see how much he got to you.

154

We strolled along the esplanade and marvelled at the various shapes and sizes of the middle-aged matrons squeezed into bikinis and stretched out under the sun.

'I feel positively anorexic,' I said as we passed a particularly large, well-endowed woman, more out than in her swimsuit.

'You're fine. You don't have to worry about your shape.'

We stopped at a café and drank limunadus and Miles was amused when I refused a cake. As we walked back towards the jetty we passed a group of stalls sheltering under a pine tree, displaying various local craftwork. There were leather slippers and sandals and belts, embroidered blouses and shawls and table linen. We stopped and inspected the goods.

'These are very attractive,' said Miles, fingering the blouses and eagerly watched by a stallholder hovering nearby. 'I wonder if my daughter would like one.'

For a few seconds everything swung out of focus. I felt as if I had been doused in icy water and come up spluttering. The words beat into my head: my daughter, my daughter. But why shouldn't he have a daughter? It stood to reason that a man as attractive as him and in his thirties would be married with a family. Why hadn't I expected this? But why, if he was married, had he just kissed me like that? I felt anger battling with my confusion and I moved away. He didn't seem to notice my reaction.

'Which one should I get? I don't know her size.'

'How old is she?' I managed to get out, and I hoped it sounded casual.

'Seven, but she is tall for her age.'

I rooted blindly amongst the blouses and shook one out. 'I should think this one will do. Does she like blue?'

'She's fair, so I think it will suit her.'

He turned to pay the stallholder and, unable to stop myself, I said, 'What about one of those tablecloths for your wife? They are beautifully embroidered.'

'I haven't got a wife,' he said gently, 'only an ex. I am divorced.'

'I didn't know you were married – had been married.'

'Why should you. It was a long while ago.'

He wasn't going to get away as easily as that. He had just had a blow-by-blow account of my family; now it was his turn.

'Do you see much of your daughter?'

'Yes. Liz, that's my ex-wife, has never made any trouble about access. She is married again to a very nice chap, far better suited to her and we're all good friends.'

'How very civilised,' I said in a small voice.

'That's the best way to be.'

'What is your daughter's name?'

'The same as yours. She was christened Katherine but has always been called Katy.'

'And is she plain Kate, bonny Kate or Kate the curst like me?' He picked up my reference. 'She is the prettiest Kate in Christendom and you run her a good second. I think you would get on very well together – you are the same mental age.'

I looked at him aghast and he laughed. 'Don't look so stricken; that was meant as a compliment. You are both fresh and eager and questioning and have not yet lost your innocence.'

I looked at him suspiciously but he seemed to be perfectly serious. 'And you have not re-married?'

'No, so far I have never felt the need to.'

And I wondered just what he meant by that.

We called at Kolocep again on the way back, but this time we were put ashore on the other side of the island, at the main town. It turned out that our boatman lived on Kolocep and he gave us forty minutes to explore the waterfront whilst he paid a flying visit to hearth and family. Miles and I strolled along until we came to a very modern hotel, set back from the sea in a pleasant garden which had a public restaurant attached, and I agreed that lemon tea and a strudla would be very nice. I had been subdued on the return journey, turning over in my mind what Miles had told me about himself and his family, and he tackled me about it.

'You seem very quiet, Kate. Did I offend you when I kissed you?'

'Why should a simple kiss offend me?' I was determined to keep it light.

'Perhaps it was too soon after your débâcle with Ivo?'

'I thought we weren't going to talk about Ivo?'

'Perhaps it is time we cleared the air. You know, you weren't in love with Ivo.'

'I never said I was, and how dare you presume . . .'

'If you really had a thing going for him you would have gone with him.' As I was completely speechless by this time, he continued, 'Not as an accomplice, but to save him. You're a crusader, Kate. If you had really cared you would have gone with him to try and wean him off the filthy habit, to persuade him to give up his dangerous pastimes. Instead, you didn't want to know. So don't pretend you're heartbroken, don't go on holding a candle for him.'

'I am not holding a candle for him or any man. Now don't you think we ought to get back to the boat? I don't want to be marooned on Kolocep with only you for company.'

I gathered my scraps of scattered dignity about me but secretly I was amazed by his insight. Though I was loathe to admit it, what he had just said was basically true and I wondered if I really was as callous as Miles seemed to think me. Needless to say, the journey back to Dubrovnik was not so carefree as the outgoing one had been.

I thanked him politely for a lovely day as we stepped ashore at Sumatrim. Our German friends, looking very sunburnt and slightly tipsy, went off in a flurry of '*Auf Wiedersehen*'.

When they had gone, Miles burst out, 'Hell Kate; I didn't mean to spoil everything. Why did I have to bring up Ivo?'

I didn't enlighten him that it wasn't mention of Ivo that had set my thoughts in turmoil.

'Forget it. I've enjoyed myself today and I'm truly indebted to you.'

'It hasn't ended yet. Are you hungry?'

'You should know better than to ask a question like that.'

'Then we'll round off the day by having dinner in that restaurant in the Old City – the one we saw when we were walking the walls – you know, in that courtyard.'

'It's a lovely idea but the Zubers are expecting me to share their evening meal.'

'That's soon remedied. We can call in now – it's on the way – and tell them you don't want a meal this evening.'

'Supposing someone from the orchestra sees us. I'm supposed to be in hiding, remember?'

'I should think it highly unlikely we'll meet anyone we know. They'll all be holed up in the Splendid. My rosy-tinted picture of a higher life in the world of the Arts has taken quite a bashing since coming into contact with you lot. Most of you, with the exception of yourself of course, are absolute Philistines, positively moronic, not at all interested in sampling the splendours of the places in which you find yourselves.'

'You are now displaying your abysmal ignorance of orchestra life in general, and touring in particular. You should really get together with Peter Brownstone.'

'Should I now? And what vice is he into? As far as I can see, bridge and poker schools provide the entertainment for most of the male section of the orchestra. What about the women?'

'You should know,' I retorted before I could stop myself. 'You appear to have worked your way through most of them.' His eyes gleamed as he drawled back, 'I took a long while getting around to you, Kate.'

He was infuriating. I tried to ignore him as we walked up the road from the beach but he suddenly drew me aside and hurried me down a little alley behind one of the restaurants. I wondered if he were going to mount another amorous onslaught and how I would and should react, but my fears were very wide of the mark.

'It's Harris Fordham and Tom Meyer,' he said quietly, looking cautiously over the wall. 'I wonder what they are doing?'

'Look, I shall be perfectly all right if you want to go off chasing after them or sleuthing.'

'I still think you have strange ideas about my profession. It's not at all a James Bond role.'

'Maybe not, but I can't quite see you somehow, standing behind a table chalking crosses on travellers' cases. Though I suppose you must have had a stint at that during your training.

He smiled and changed the subject. 'Have you any more objections against having dinner with me. That's two I've disposed of.'

'Only that you're spending an awful lot of money on me.'

'And is that so terrible?'

'I'm not ungrateful, I just don't like being beholden to

you. It's bad for my ego – and don't make it worse by telling me it comes out of expenses. Do customs officials run up large expense accounts?'

'What a shocking idea. You'll get me shot at dawn if you go around mouthing sentiments like that.'

We walked the rest of the way in silence and when we reached the apartment block housing the Zubers' flat Miles said, 'Do you want to wait down here whilst I toil up the stairs and tell them?'

'I was hoping I'd have the opportunity to change and tidy up.'

'You look fine as you are, but OK, we'll both go up. I shall take the opportunity of practicing my Serbo-Croatian on the Zubers whilst you tart yourself up.'

'You're more likely to get tanked up on slivovic,' I said darkly.

The restaurant, when we eventually found it, was as attractive as our original glimpse had promised. It took some finding though. We knew that it was somewhere near the Pilé Gateway to the Old City but we made several false sorties down alleyways and through dark arches before we eventually located it, but the result was worth the effort. It lived up to our expectations, from the crisp linen napkins, almost as large as tablecloths, to the service and excellent food that was served to the accompaniment of a live band playing pop tunes of yesteryear. But though I enjoyed the meal I was very aware of the City Walls running along one side of the courtyard, way above our heads. They were closed now to the public and there were no figures to be seen silhouetted against the darkening sky, but my imagination ran riot. I made patterns in a little heap of salt that had spilt on the table and jumped when Miles reached over and took my hand.

'What's bugging you Kate?'

I sighed. 'Adrian Palmer.' I looked up and our eyes locked. 'He was a damn fine musician you know. To achieve the status of principal oboe at his age was quite something. What a waste! Just because he was led astray.'

'I'm glad you acknowledge that he was not the instigator of their little pastime.'

'I have no illusions left about Ivo. He's the original bad cookie in the barrel; but all that talent gone to waste, his and Adrian's. What do you think will happen to him?'

'The Ivo's of this world aways fall on their feet. He'll pop up again somewhere. He's totally amoral – one of those people who is literally incapable of telling right from wrong, but I think he's chosen the wrong people to tangle with this time.'

'His behaviour was quite psychotic at times,' I said slowly. 'I really wonder if he was a manic-depressive, or would hash have that effect?'

'Who knows,' Miles shrugged. 'Getting psyched up is not going to help any form of mental instability; but I don't know why you are still so concerned about him after the way he treated you.'

'I'm not concerned about him, I'm just terrified of coming face to face with him again.'

'I should think that is highly unlikely. He's probably thousands of miles away by now. Don't get uptight about him.'

'I'm not uptight about him, 'I said with dignity. 'In fact, I have no intention of getting uptight about any man again. I am eschewing the company of men from now on and concentrating on my music.'

'You are?' Miles looked amused. 'Then what are you doing sitting here with me?'

'I look on you as a father figure.' I was happy to note that didn't please him.

'You do?' He sounded quite indignant.

'Well, you are the one who said I reminded you of your daughter. How long have you been divorced?'

'Three years.'

'And your daughter is seven. How long were you married before she was born?'

'I married at twenty-two and she was born the following year, which makes me thirty-three,' said Miles blandly.

'All right, I can do my arithmetic.'

'Is there anything else you want to know,' he drawled, but there was a spark of annoyance in his eyes.

'What went wrong? Couldn't she stand your philandering?'

'That is a spiteful remark which sounds out of character, coming from you. I have never philandered in my life.'

I had the grace to look ashamed. 'Sorry Miles. Treat it as one of my infantile jokes. I just wondered how anyone could want to be shot of you.'

He eyed me with suspicion. 'You're compounding the insult now; flattery will get you nowhere. There's nothing really to tell. There was no sudden dramatic break up. We just grew apart. We had married very young, far too young. We hadn't even come to terms with ourselves, what we wanted out of life, how we felt about things, who we were; let along take on another person as a life-long partner. We drifted apart, my unsociable working hours didn't help, and we agreed to split up. As I've already told you, she eventually found someone else and they appear to be very happy and Katy is too. She finds it something of a cachet having two doting fathers.'

'I'll bet she's spoiled rotten. I'd like to meet this daughter of yours.'

'That could be arranged.' He spoke lightly but I sensed a deeper meaning in the casual words and I shied away'

'I'm a career girl, remember? I should be a bad influence on her.'

'I don't believe you, Kate. I know your music means a lot to you but I don't believe that all your *joie de vivre* and affectionate nature can be completely channelled into such a narrow activity. It would turn sterile, wouldn't fulfil you, and your music would suffer too in the end. You've been hurt but you'll get over it and there will be someone else.'

There is someone else. I almost said it aloud, so suddenly did it hit me. I felt clobbered by the knowledge that had suddenly forced itself onto my awareness; talk about the road to Damascus! As he faced me across the table I realised he was the someone else. I wanted Miles Bretherton. It was a shocking idea, especially as he obviously had no such reciprocal feelings about me; he was, even now, urging some, as yet unknown, man into my affections. I stared at him aghast.

'What have I said now?' He misinterpreted the look on my face. 'Are you afraid you couldn't combine your career with marriage?'

I eagerly accepted the carrot he held out. 'A lot of people seem to manage both successfully. What do you think?'

'I think it can be done,' he said slowly, 'but they couldn't be on an equal footing. One would have to take precedence. Which would mean most to you Kate?' He was challenging me. I took a long time replying and then I was not sure I had answered his question.

'When I was a little girl I used to have long talks about life with my grandmother. Very profound they were, even at that tender age, and we frequently discussed love

163

and marriage. I asked her once how you knew when you had met the right man, the man to be your partner for life and she said . . .' – I hesitated and frowned – ' . . . she said there was only one reason for getting married: because you couldn't bear not to. If you felt like that, everything would be resolved, wouldn't it?'

'My God, Kate,' he sounded quite shaken. 'Your grandmother was a wise woman. Let us hope you find someone you can be so whole-hearted about.'

'Don't be so damn patronising.' I glared at him. 'I don't see why my love life should be any more interesting to you than yours is to me.'

'You're the one who wanted to know,' he pointed out.

'Don't you think we've been here long enough?' I blundered to my feet and knocked the basket of bread off the table. In the ensuing mêlée I tried to pull myself together. I had managed to conceal my true feelings from him. Amazingly, he had no idea of the shattering discovery I had just made, and that was the way it was going to stay. Mr 'Bloody' Miles Bretherton was not going to learn I had conceived a yen for him, oh no.

Whilst he sorted out the bill I made a sortie to the Ladies, and when I emerged I was more or less my old self, or at least, on the surface. I thanked him for the meal, and when he took my arm and led me back to the Placa I managed not to tremble at his touch. I had got over Ivo, I could get over Miles Bretherton. It was only a temporary aberration brought about by the way we had been thrown together by events.

We did not linger in the Old City. The holiday atmosphere engendered by the jostling crowds seemed alien to me that evening and I think Miles felt the same way. He escorted me back to the Zuber's flat, as careful to avoid any contact with me as I was with him, and bade me a formal goodnight at the bottom of the stairs. He

164

made no attempt to kiss me, for which I was thankful. Any such move on his part and I might have completely lost control and blurted out my feelings for him – unthinkable. I scuttled up the stairs without a backward glance and was between the sheets in record time.

The next day I was quite frankly bored. I had recovered from my physical exertions of the previous days and I had more or less got my emotions under control; or rather I had swept them under the carpet, preferring not to try and analyse my present feelings as regards Ivo, Miles and the whole dubious business. Being gregarious by nature, the thought of another day spent entirely on my own was not appealing. I wondered if I dare return to the hotel to find out if Sarah and the others were back from Greece, but reluctantly decided that I had better not. I could not believe I was in any danger from any of my colleagues at the hotel; I was more afraid of coming face to face with Miles.

I bought postcards from a roadside kiosk and wrote them to my friends and relations in Scotland, giving no hint of recent events. I filled them with innocuous remarks about the weather and scenery and when I had posted them I wandered down to the beach for a swim. The heat drove me indoors at midday. I returned to the flat, stripped off and showered, closed the shutters, lay on my bed and closed my eyes.

I must have slept because the next thing I knew there was a tap on the door and Veshna Zuber was saying something about Gospodin Milan. I quickly donned some clothes and blundered into the living room. Veshna silently indicated the balcony and disappeared into her kitchen. Miles was standing, his back to me, staring out across the vista. I could tell by the way he held himself, the taut line of his back and the way he

165

gripped the rail, that something had happened.

'Miles?'

He swung round and when I saw his face I knew my foreboding had been correct. He didn't speak but held out to me the object he had been hiding in front of his body. It was my passport. The stiff cover was now softened and bent and vaguely soggy. In contrast, the leaves inside were stiff and dried up and the ink had run badly. It looked as if it had had a long immersion in water.

'But . . . ?'

'It was found on Ivo's body. He's dead.'

The walls spun round and the floor came up to meet me and I felt myself plummeting down a long, dark tunnel.

# Chapter 8

'For God's sake come away from the edge of the balcony!' Miles's voice had a ragged quality and he grabbed me by the shoulders and propelled me back into the room and down onto the settee. I fought back against the blackness that threatened to engulf me.

'How?' I managed to get out in a croak.

'He and his companion – their bodies were washed up near Tivat.'

'But how could they possibly have drowned? It was so calm.'

'They were both shot through the back of the head. I'm sorry to be so brutal, but you have to know. Your passport was found in Ivo's pocket.'

I dropped it on the floor and shuddered. 'I don't understand.'

'Neither do I.' He sounded very grim but he held me against his chest and chafed my hands tenderly. 'Are you OK? You're not going to pass out on me? I should have broken the news more gently.'

'There's no way you can soften news like this. What can have happened?'

'His plans to pervert the course of his master's drug ring didn't get very far – they were on to him very quickly.'

167

'Do you think they discovered the fake hash in the cathedral and acted in revenge?'

'I think he was shot before he got to Kotor, before we reached Sveti-Stefan, probably not long after he left Baošić.'

'So if I had gone with him . . .'

'Don't think like that,' he held me tightly. 'You're safe. It didn't happen. But I am afraid we have underestimated them. They are a frighteningly efficient organisation and quite ruthless in eliminating anyone who gets in their way.'

'If they have followed up the trail from Sveti-Stefan to Kotor and discovered the false hash, they'll know someone is onto them,'' I said slowly, working it out as I went along. 'It's not just me who is in danger, it's you and Pero Njavro also. They will put the finger on you.'

'I'm sure my cover is still complete – I've been very careful – and even the Mafia don't go around knocking off members of the Drug Squad indiscriminately. Pero was not working on his own, you know.'

'What about the black box Ivo had with him that contained the money?'

'Nothing else was found, not even a trace of the boat, just their two bodies; and, as I said, they had been shot through the head – there had been no attempt to make it appear an accident. They were killed quite callously, possibly as a warning, but from whom and to whom I don't know.

'Like Adrian Palmer?'

'Yes. They have a frightening disregard and contempt for people.'

'What will happen now? About Ivo and the orchestra and . . .' 'Nothing. It will be kept quiet for the time being.'

'But can you possibly hush up his death?'

'Thank God he kept his Yugoslavian nationality. He

didn't take up American citizenship so I shan't have the CIA breathing down my neck. This can be dealt with internally and for the time being kept under wraps. Eventually, of course, it will come out, but not for a few days. The official line is still that he ditched you and cleard out for places unknown. You have no idea where he is or what he intends doing. You are upset at his treatment of you and annoyed at the way he has let the orchestra down. You know nothing else, do you understand?'

'Miles, don't shout at me.'

'I'm sorry. I'm just worried about your safety. I'd rather blow the entire operation than risk you coming to any harm.'

'I'm very flattered, but you're talking nonsense. I take it this is a combined operation between the customs forces of many different nations. How could you possibly even think of putting the whole thing in jeopardy, especially when you are so close to bringing it to a successful conclusion? Quite apart from the damage it would do your career. Actually, shouldn't you be broadcasting my involvement instead of hushing it up? Couldn't I act as bait? Let it be known that I have things to divulge, and wait around to see who attempts to shut my mouth. That might be an easy way to find you man.'

'Absolutely nothing doing. Put the idea right out of your head. We don't work like that. You've been reading too many second-rate thrillers. We're going to crack this thing in the next few days and you are not going to be around.'

'What do I do in the meantime?'

'Stay holed up here. The rehearsal is called for 8 am tomorrow morning. You won't put in an appearance till then. You're performing in the open air this time, in the Poljana Marina Drzica, the square between the Rector's Palace and the cathedral.'

'And we're rehearsing out there in the morning?'

'Sammy wants to put the final touches to his seating arrangements. Willie is tearing his hair out about the whole thing. He is deeply suspicious of performing outside and fears his entire concert may be sabotaged. He just wants to have a try out – there won't be many tourists around at that hour of the day. There's a room nearby where you will actually rehearse. He wants to run through the concerto now that our soloist has arrived.'

We were to play the Dvorak Cello Concerto and a young Yugoslavian virtuoso cellist had been engaged as soloist. I dragged my mind away from thoughts of Ivo and tried to concentrate on the distraction Miles had provided.

'What is he like? I've heard he's a bright young thing with a great future and an ego to match.'

'He's very sure of himself and determined not to be thwarted. I engaged him and got him here. The ball is now in Willie's court.'

'Has Willie been told the sad tale of my fiasco with Ivo?'

'Yes. He looks on Ivo's departure as just one more drop in the cup of sorrow he has to bear. Sammy thinks one missing second violin is not going to make much difference.'

'That does cut one down to size.'

'No man is indispensible, only you Kate,' and he gave me a smile that made me sag at the knees. 'I have to go now. Will you be all right? Try not to brood.'

'His body?'

'It can't be released yet. There will be no public funeral for the time being, no mourning.'

'That makes it so much worse.'

'Don't get maudlin. Remember; he tried to kill you.'

On that thrust he departed.

I discovered that the top flight of stairs in the building led up to the roof. This was flat and had railings all round. I spent the rest of the day lying up there in the shade of a wall trying to read a book.

There was a reception committee waiting for me next morning when Miles and I arrived at the rehearsal. Sarah darted out from the crowd and plunged straight in, having never assimilated the old adage about angels fearing to tread.

'Kate, where have you been? I've been so worried about you. Where has that bastard Ivo gone?'

'Language, language. I'm sure you've heard the sorry tale. We had a row and Ivo cleared off. It didn't work out. It never would have, and now I just want to forget the whole thing.'

'And he's really walked out on his musical career too?'

'In so far as his commitment to the Europa is concerned. How have you been getting on?'

'Oh we had a fab time in Greece. It's a pity you didn't come with us, but you seem to be doing all right now. Off with the old and on with the new.'

'What do you mean?'

'Our renowned Miles Bretherton seems to have taken you under his wing. Some people have all the luck.'

'Don't be ridiculous.' I looked round hurriedly but Miles had disappeared. 'He just happened to be around and he's been very kind, a sort of father figure, you might say.'

'Don't give me that. If he casts many more such paternal looks in your direction you'll have several members of the orchestra trying to scratch your eyes out.'

I was saved from replying by the arrival of more of my friends. They jostled round dispensing pleasure at seeing me again, sympathy for my recent predicament and

171

censure over Ivo's behaviour. They were all on my side. No one had a kind word for Ivo, and it struck me suddenly that he had had no real friends in the orchestra apart from Adrian Palmer, and only I knew the truth about that friendship. He had never fitted in and no one was going to mourn his departure.

'He was no good for you Kate,' said Sylvester, his shiny black face for once serious. 'A hyped-up bully-boy. You're better off without him.'

My mouth dropped open. Sylvester knew about his activities? Surely he wasn't the person we were looking for, not Sylvester, my big coloured friend? But if he were involved, surely he wouldn't have brought it up casually like this? It looked as though he knew about Ivo's drug-taking. How many other members of the orchestra knew? The ramifications of this thought were too compli-cated to follow up at present. I pulled myself up with a jerk and listened to what Sylvester was saying.

'Do you realise how his name translated into English? Ivo is Serbian for John and Tomasic must be Thomas. John Thomas!' He gave a guffaw of laughter. 'What do you think of that?'

'That our nigger boy has actually read his *Lady C*,' I said coldly. 'D. H. would be gratified to think he had penetrated deepest Haarlem.'

'Shut up, Sylvester,' said Sarah, snapping her dark eyes at him. 'You're not helping matters at all.' She turned to me. 'You'll have to do your own page turns. Sammy insists on no re-organisation of the strings for this concert.'

'Oh God, I hadn't thought of that.'

I coped with the page turning but I was very much aware of the vacant place at my side. I was so used to playing in tandem with my partner; so aware of his proximity, the scrape of his chair, a caught breath, the

172

sighs and sweating, that when my eyes flickered sideways and he wasn't there it was like a physical blow jolting me back to reality.

Our soloist was tall and thin with a shock of light brown hair. He was temperamental with a big T and jumpy as a colt. I thought we were never going to get beyond the tuning stage, but when he started to play, all was forgiven. The sombre opening theme announced by the clarinets and bassoons shivered out into the still morning air and was taken up poignantly by the horns and swept into the minor key. By the time the cellist made his entry, stalking the original theme in A flat minor in a wonderful sweep of melody, I knew we had a winner. He produced magic from his wooden box and I lost myself in the music, died and was born again.

The other works in this concert were Schubert's Unfinished Symphony and Till Eulenspiegel by Strauss. I have never been very fond of the Schubert. It promises so much but never delivers, and this is not because it has no ending. The Strauss is a sprightly orchestral exercise with much virtuoso stuff for different sections and keeps one stretched, and by the time Willie pronounced himself satisfied with our efforts I felt quite wrung out. Sammy tackled me as I was putting my violin back in its case.

'What have you done with Tomasic?'

'I have done nothing with him. We split up and I have no idea where he is.' My voice wobbled. 'He's been very unsettled recently. Perhaps he wants to try new fields, chamber work or something in that line.' I was becoming quite a fluent liar.

'Young fool,' snapped Sammy blinking his reptilean eyes and I got the impression he was referring to me as much as to Ivo.

'You are coming back to the hotel with us, aren't you,'

173

asked Sarah shuffling her sheets of music.

'No, actually I'm not, not yet anyway.'

Her eyebrows shot up. 'What's this? Has Miles tucked you away in a little love-nest somewhere?'

'You're talking a lot of nonsense. He arranged for me to stay with this Yugoslavian family he knows. I'm enjoying it. There's nothing like mixing with the natives if you want to get the real feel of a country. There's a family party today – I've been invited – I can't just walk out now; it would be most rude and unkind. I'll see you tomorrow.'

She gave me a speculative look, then shrugged her shoulders. 'OK. See you tomorrow, if that's the way you want it.'

She went off in a huff and I watched her departure with the rest of my colleagues with a sinking heart.

I treated Miles to a ferocious scowl when he joined me a few minutes later.

'Did anyone display any curiosity, ask any questions?' he demanded ignoring my stormy looks.

'Just about everyone.'

'Yes, of course they would. You're a very popular person; I might have known.'

'Also, the general consensus of opinion is that you have caught me on the rebound and are having it off with me somewhere away from the public eye.'

'Is it really?' He gave me a bland look. 'It might be a good idea to play along with that.'

'For your benefit or mine?'

'To put our common enemy off the scent.'

'Have you discovered anything? Are you any nearer finding out who our man is?'

'My lips are sealed, but I promise you it will all be over in the next few days.'

'We leave for Belgrade then.'

174

'Yes, and I've got to find another oboeist for the final concert. By the way, Pero Njavro send you his regards.'

'He's rather dishy. I suppose he's happily married?'

'And with at least four kids.'

'Just my luck. Am I still under house arrest?'

'I'm afraid so. I'll take you back now. You can go to the local beach but nowhere else. Bear up, it's only for another day.'

After he had left me I found myself thinking of Mija Novakovic. Had she known about the nefarious trade that Ivo dabbled in? Had she discovered the deserted chalet at Baošić, and was she wondering what had happened to us? There had been an affinity between her and Ivo. Perhaps by now he had joined forces with her. God, what was I thinking about! Ivo was dead, and my solitary confinement was turning my head. Ivo was dead, Miles divorced with a daughter and Pero Njavro was a patriarchal figure. Only I, Kate Bracegirdle, was on my own, alone and frustrated and fearful of looking into the future.

The bouquet was delivered to me just before the start of the concert. We were all assembled in one of the reception rooms of the Rector's Palace waiting to file out into the square to take our places. We were crowded together and there was much jostling and manoeuvring for position and all the last-minute nerves and tension that preceed a public performance. The delivery boy looked official in his uniform and was almost lost behind the enormous bouquet he carried. He checked that I was indeed Miss Bracegirdle and thrust the flowers at me with a little bow. They were carnations, at least four dozen in garish pinks and reds, and I recoiled from the assault of their perfume.

'You've got another admirer,' squeaked Sarah. 'Who are they from?'

'How do I know?'

'There's an envelope attached – look.'

I was the focus of attention as I removed the envelope from amongst the foliage and slit it open. I declare every member of the orchestra was waiting with baited breath to see who had sent Kate Bracegirdle an armful of flowers large enough to fill a kettledrum.

I got the envelope open and tipped it up to extract the gift card. Instead, there was a jingle of metal and a gold chain slipped out into my palm. A gold chain attached to a black cross. For the second time in a couple of days I nearly fainted. I dropped the chain as if it had burnt me and felt the black clouds of nausea and dizziness swooping round my head.

'Kate, whatever is the matter? You've gone as white as a sheet!'

Somebody put an arm round me and someone else brought a chair up.

'The heat – it's made me feel a little faint.' I looked round wildly for Miles. Where was he? He should be here, but there was no sign of him.

'Doesn't it say who it's from?' demanded Sarah.

'No.'

'What about the cross and chain? The chain is broken – how odd. It must be a clue to the sender, must have some significance. Don't hold out on us Kate.'

'I've no idea what it means. It must be a stupid joke.'

'Well, there's no need to react as if someone has sent you a letter bomb. I declare now to all and sundry, that if anyone feels the urge to send me a super bouquet like this it will be received with proper appreciation.'

Someone blew stridently down their reed and I flinched and tried to pull myself together. We had been called and my fellow members started to file out through the door.

'Aren't you going to wear one of them as a corsage?' asked Sarah snapping off a slender stem.

'No. Whoever sent them doesn't know me very well. I loathe carnations. Always have done.'

This was quite true. I had always felt they were artificial looking with an overpowering sickly-sweet scent. They reminded me of funerals. I followed the rest of the second violins outside and took my place on the makeshift platform. The square was floodlit and it was very hot. The heat from hours of sunshine had accumulated in the walls and they acted as a storehouse, generating warm impulses from the ancient stone towards audience and orchestra alike. We tuned and settled and then the ominous opening chords of the Unfinished swelled out encompassing the whole square.

Willie had been right to fear obstruction, but the attack came from an unexpected quarter. The swallows took umbrage at the musical assault on their quarters and countered with an attack of their own. They swooped and shrieked and hurled avian abuse at full voice. The volume of the screaming and twittering was quite unbelievable and no doubt they distracted the audience as much as they did us. They were particularly bellicose during the Strauss. Perhaps they felt an affinity with the saga of Till.

As we filed back inside for the interval and the cool drinks awaiting us, Miles pounced on me.

'Come on, let's get out of here for a while.' He whisked me through a doorway, along a passage and under an arch, and we found ourselves in a back alley which boasted a small kafana. He sat me down at a table and fetched two beers from the interior.

'Now, what happened exactly?'

'You've heard about it?'

'I was there, across the other side of the room. I

177

couldn't get to you.'

'It was horrible, Miles. I opened the envelope expecting to find a gift card inside and this cross and chain fell out. It wouldn't have been so bad, only the chain has been snapped as if it had been torn from someone's neck.' I shuddered and he patted my hand.

'Where is it now?'

'I don't know. I dropped it and I think Sarah picked it up. It's probably still lying in the room.'

'It isn't, I've looked, but it isn't important now.'

'But what does it mean?'

'It means, my sweet, that you've been rumbled. Someone set a nice little trap and you've sprung it. In spy-thriller jargon, your cover is blown.'

'You mean, I've given myself away? I couldn't help it, Miles. I'm sure that chain had been taken from Ivo's body. For a few seconds I just went to pieces.'

'It was beautifully stage-managed. Just about every member of the orchestra was there and watching. Our man got the information he wanted without giving himself away. He now knows that you understand the significance of a chain and black cross, that you were probably fully in Ivo's confidence and could be a great danger to him, especially as you're not exactly known to be reticent.'

'Miles . . .' I protested.

'Look, he's probably also realised that you're frightened to death and not likely to shout your mouth off deliberately, but could let drop something incriminating quite innocently when you're babbling on. What are we going to do to ensure your safety?'

'But I don't know anything, do I?'

'No, but he doesn't know that.'

I gulped down the remainder of my pivo. 'I'm going back to the concert. My audience awaits me; the second bell must have gone.'

'I don't think you realise the danger you are in. Two people have been killed, three if we count Ivo's companion in the boat, in the last couple of weeks, for no very compelling reason except that they stepped out of line. They're not going to scruple at knocking off another, especially if they think she has information that could endanger their lucrative little game.'

'Are you deliberately trying to frighten me? Do you want me to shake so much that I can't draw my bow across the strings? Nothing can happen to me in front of an audience of hundreds, or do you think some member of the orchestra is going to draw a gun and shoot me in full view of everyone?'

'Of course not, but he's not in this on his own, is he? Our rogue musician didn't personally murder Adrian Palmer or Ivo. He may have arranged their demise but he didn't do his own dirty work. He's got a powerful organisation at his back.'

The buildings closed in on me. I could easily believe there was a ring of assassins around me, skulking in the shadows of this not very salubrious quarter of the city, waiting to pounce and finish me off. Even Miles looked sinister, his light hair gleaming silver under the lamplight, his tautly held body speaking of controlled violence. I pushed back the chair and got to my feet.

'I must go back. If anyone's watching my movements they will find it very suspicious that we two have gone off together. You are probably a marked man too.'

He shrugged this off and ushered me back to the concert arena rather in the manner of one who was carrying out an arrest.

'When the concert ends, sit tight. I can't come back with you but I'll arrange, somehow, for you to be escorted home.' From the way he spoke a posse of armed milicija would not have surprised me.

179

The second half of the concert started and the audience took our young cellist to heart. Crouched over his instrument, his hair falling romantically over his forehead, his face tense in ecstatic communion with his muse, the music pouring passionately and effortlessly from his bow, he resembled some medieval representation of St Sebastian, all agonised and suffering. They would never have believed what a cussed, egoistical individual he actually was.

By the time the concerto was over and the audience was clapping and stamping in appreciation, I had got over the intial shock engendered by the delivery of the bouquet and its sinister message. The euphoria that comes with a satisfactory performance had got me in its clutches and everyone was affected in the same way. We were elated and lighthearted as the audience finally let us go and we filed back inside the Rector's Palace. There was to be a reception given in our honour after this, our last concert in the current Dubrovnik Festival, and I wondered if I was going to be given the chance to participate or whether Miles had arranged for me to be secreted away beforehand. I didn't intend to go without an argument. I was not going to be denied a welcome meeting with my fellow *homo sapiens* if it were at all possible.

If there were safety in numbers I certainly had it that evening. The room was crowded with people; all the members of the orchestra, other visiting participants in the festival and a large scattering of local dignitaries; in fact, I think just about anyone who was anyone at all in the social stratum was there. Everyone was talking at once and I could hear at least half-a-dozen different languages bombarding me from all sides. Jammed up against a wall and trying not to slop my drink, it came to me how easy it would be for someone to slip a knife between my ribs. My assailant would never be identified in the scrum and I would probably still be wedged upright a long while after life had fled. With this chilling thought in my mind I edged my way towards the magnificent baroque table taking the place of honour in the middle of the room, on which were laid out the refreshments.

'They don't do very interesting nibbles, do they?' said Jenny Seaman, eyeing the plates of chopped peppers and sliced meats disdainfully.

'What do you expect, caviare and lobster? Try some of this raw ham,' I indicated the slivers of pink flesh nestling in their dish. 'It's a local delicacy.'

'No thanks,' she shuddered. 'Think of the salmonella, or is it botulism? Have you seen our revolting little cellist lording it over there with his admiring groupies?'

'This is probably the highspot of his career so far. Don't deny him his moment of glory.'

'It's only that I'm green with envy of the sounds he can coax out of his instrument. God, it's hot in here. These functions get more barbaric the farther East we travel.'

'Remember the time in Tokyo when Willie had to sit on the floor and eat raw fish?'

'And our Australian pianist said that the shrimps reminded him of the grubs the Aborigines favoured. Talking of our Aussie friends, I think Miles Bretherton is trying to establish eye contact with you.'

I looked across the sea of heads and met Miles's eyes. When he saw Jenny watching him with interest he nodded vaguely in our direction and disappeared behind a group of bodies.

'Playing hard to get, are you?' enquired Jenny with a nice mixture of malice and levity. 'I should think that's just about the way to snare Miles. You're learning Kate; play him along cannily. That is the expression you Scotch use, isn't it?'

'Scots, not Scotch, and if you're not careful your own wit will choke you.'

Someone rapped for silence and after a spattering of applause the speeches began. I had heard them all before in many different tongues and I shut off and went into a reverie in which thoughts of Ivo and Miles Bretherton chased themselves round my head. I came to at another louder burst of clapping and realised the reception was at an end. It was then that I saw him – the same delivery boy who had brought me my bouquet earlier in the evening. He wended his way through the crowds and made a beeline in my direction. I felt myself freeze. What did he want? What further mischief was he bringing?

It wasn't me he wanted this time. He homed in on Sammy who was standing a little way behind me and handed him an envelope. Why wasn't Miles around to see this transaction? He could follow the boy and tackle him about the sender of my bouquet. I edged close to Sammy and watched him open the envelope, then I pounced.

'Sammy dear, I thought for one absurd moment you were going to be the recipient of another bouquet. What is it? A billet-doux?'

'How sharp you are, Kate. It is an invitation from one of my admirers.'

'Male or female?' I asked and was rewarded with a baleful glare. 'Is he going to take you scuba diving, or is she going to whisk you off to her castle? Do tell.'

'There are no private estates here, they are all comrades, remember? I'm sorry to crush your romantic theories, but an acquaintance has asked me to meet for a swim on Lokrum tomorrow.'

'No secret assignation? I don't believe you.'

'It's perfectly true. Why don't you come with me, then you'll see for yourself.'

'Come with you?' my voice rose and Sammy gave one

of his special sardonic smiles.

'You can be my chaperone. You're at a loose end, aren't you? Enjoy a lazy day on Lokrum and meet my friend.'

Why not? I couldn't come to any harm on Lokrum in broad daylight in Sammy's company. It would be as good as having a guard dog in attendance. I was fed up with a hole-and-corner existence; this would be the perfect excuse for breaking out. Even Miles wouldn't be able to find fault with this proposed expedition.

'You're on. When do we go?'

'Meet me in the hotel foyer about 9 o'clock.' He turned to go and I suddenly remembered.

'You still haven't told me whether it's a man or a woman.'

'Wait and see.' He beetled off into the milling crowds.

I was sure that Miles couldn't object but somehow I didn't bring myself to mention it when he extricated me from the reception hall and frog-marched me down the Placa to the Pilé Gate.

'I'm putting you in a taxi which will take you straight back to the Zubers' flat.'

He was tense and preoccupied so I kept silent and wondered how he was going to commandeer a taxi with half the population of Dubrovnik pouring out over the drawbridge with the same idea in mind. I should have known. With the minimum of effort and gesture he secured a taxi, instructed the driver in what seemed to me to be perfect Serbo-Croatian, handed him a wad of notes and almost pushed me into the back seat. At the last minute he gave me a chaste peck on the forehead, avuncular in the extreme. I was dismissed.

I awoke the next morning feeling quite lighthearted. Sammy was taking me to Lokrum. He might joke about me acting as his chaperone but that was exactly his intention; not to keep him on the straight and narrow but to protect him from any untoward advances from this mysterious friend. He really was a fraud; all growly and sarcastic on the surface but soft and caring underneath, petrified of being stampeded into an impetuous relationship. He was a loner, an essentially selfish man who shied away from human contact, but beneath it all, vulnerable; a member of the wandering tribe, rootless and fearful of commitment. If his friend were a man I would flirt with him, if she were a woman I would flirt with Sammy; that should provide the protection he craved.

I really ought to let Miles know about this expedition in case he wanted to contact me during the day. I didn't feel capable of grappling with the local telephone system but I would probably run into him at the hotel when I went to meet Sammy. I was not sure I wanted to, he was certain to object through sheer bloody-mindedness. Ever since our trip to Lopud and that startling kiss he had seemed to distance himself from me, acting in a distinctly lordly manner and making me feel at times like a recalcitrant schoolgirl. I didn't want him to think of me on those terms. I wanted him, oh horror of horrors, to think of me as a woman, an attractive woman, a desirable woman. Heaven help me, I had fallen for Miles Bretherton, and it was a lost cause.

I did not eat my breakfast on the balcony that morning. A stiff breeze was rattling the shutters and snatching at the curtains and Veshna had laid my meal on a table in the living room, muttering something about a 'bura' which I took to mean wind. As I walked down the road to the hotel this wind had strengthened and was buffeting the tops of the pines so that they whipped about above my head in crazy patterns. It was a warm wind and not unpleasant. In fact, it was quite exhilarating and the crossing to Lokrum promised to be interesting.

It was as I crossed the road and entered the hotel grounds that the idea came to me. It was quite brilliant. Miles had dismissed my suggestion that I act as decoy but now I had the perfect situation for setting it up and he would reap the benefits of my sacrifice. Most of the Europa members would still be in the dining room. I would announce to all and sundry that I was going with Sammy to Lokrum. It would kill two birds with one stone; a way of letting Miles know where I was going without him being able to object in front of everyone; and the person gunning for me would know how and where he could get at me. All Miles had to do was follow him, and *voilà*, all would be resolved.

My plan received an immediate set-back. Neither Sammy nor Miles were in the dining room when I arrived, but my entrance didn't go unnoticed.

'Behold, the wanderer is returned!'

'Bring on the fatted calf.'

'To what do we owe this pleasure?'

They bombarded me from all quarters and I made the most of the limelight.

'I'm meeting Sammy. He's supposed to be taking me to Lokrum, or is it the other way round?' Did I hear an indrawn breath, a stifled exclamation, or did I imagine it?

'Watch it Kate. There's no dog like an old dog!'

'I didn't know you were into sugar daddies!'

'You've got your lines crossed. He isn't here.'

'He's not?' I looked round the room. I had netted just about everyone else. I had the ears and eyes of the entire orchestra; would my plan work?

'He left a message,' said Sven Larsen, looking up from the book propped against his cup. 'He'll meet you on the quay at the Old Harbour.'

'Well, I wish I'd known sooner. It would have saved me the slog down here.'

'But nobody knows where you've been hiding yourself,' said Peter Brownstone spitefully, his eyes gleaming behind his glasses.

'If you're looking for the other string to your bow, meaning Miles Bretherton, he's not here either,' said Sarah. 'Come and have some coffee.'

'No, I won't stay. You don't happen to know where he is?'

'Not being in his confidence I can't say I do, but I heard him tell the manager earlier that he would be back soon.'

'Thanks, I'd better keep my *rendez-vous* with Sammy. I'll see you later.'

'You know we leave for Belgrade tomorrow? You are coming with us I hope. You're not going to drop out too?'

'Of course not. Everything will be explained in due course.'

I stopped in the foyer to write a note to Miles. My whole plan would be in jeopardy if he were not around to follow it up. I was beginning to be a little scared at what I had set in motion. I had been relying on Miles to be hovering in the background whilst I made my grand gesture. What Sammy would be doing in all this I did not know. Being Sammy, he would probably go to ground at the first sign of any trouble. In my note I explained briefly what I had done and I hurriedly sealed it and handed it in to the girl in reception who assured me she would give it to Mr Bretherton as soon as he returned.

Nobody from the hotel followed me onto the bus which was, as usual, packed. At Pilé I alighted and threaded my way amongst the crowds converging on the Old City. I slipped across the bridge at the Pilé Gateway, past orange trees bearing fruit already turning golden, and hurried down the Placa. Nobody took any notice of me. Above my head the Festival banners streamed out like fiery tongues in the wind but within the shelter of the walls all was still and humid. I passed a poster advertising the exhibition of the Naïve School of Painters now being held as part of the Festival. I very much wanted to see this exhibition. Would I be able to fit it in before leaving for Belgrade, always supposing, of course, that I was still around to enjoy it? I almost got cold feet then, and contemplated turning round and fleeing back to Lapad and the Zubers with my tail between my legs, but I pulled myself together. Probably nothing would happen and I would enjoy my day on Lokrum with Sammy and his mysterious companion.

Sammy was waiting on the quayside complete with violin. He looked as miserable as sin and was hunched up, clutching his violin to his chest as if in protection against the cold. I hailed him as I hurried across the white flagstones.

'Sammy! You're never taking your fiddle with you.'

'It's safer with me.'

'It can't be. You might get mugged or drop it overboard.'

'There's been a lot of petty pilfering at the hotel, hadn't you heard? I feel safer with it under my eye all the time.'

'I'm sure this sun can't be doing it any good. You don't tote a Guarnerius about like a beachbag.'

'And you don't have to broadcast it to all and sundry. Keep your voice down Kate. You're a musician, not a cheer-leader.'

I must say the instrument in question didn't look like a priceless antique. Sammy kept it in an old leather case, scuffed and discoloured, and no one would have guessed from looking at it that it was other than a very second-rate instrument belonging to a down-at-heels itinerant musician.

We took our seats on the crowded boat and as it pulled away I scanned the quayside but could see no one acting in a suspicious manner. There were the usual flocks of tourists embarking and disembarking from the pleasure boats and ferries, mingling with the fishermen and harbour workforce who didn't look very work-orientated.

It wasn't until we were out of the harbour and crossing the strait that the full force of the wind struck us. Our boat, one of the smaller ferries, pitched and rolled like a trawler on the Dogger Bank. The sun blazed overhead, the wind roared and the waves were enormous, towering over our little vessel and meeting us broadside on. One moment we were perched on a pinnacle, the next we were hidden in a trough with another navy wall rearing up beside us. It was quite unbelievable and I felt as if we were caught up in the filming of a documentary about the RNLI. I secretly winged an apology to Richard the Lionheart. He had had every reason to run aground if he had encountered a hurricane like this.

A young woman beside us, an American who had lived in Dubrovnik for several years, explained that we were experiencing a 'bura', a tempest-like phenomenon that occurred about three of four times a year. The hot, violent winds that raged like a hurricane usually blew themselves out in a couple of days but the effects were spectacular whilst they lasted. Sammy was looking rather green and bent double over his precious instrument, trying to shield it from the worst of the elements. He muttered imprecations as we dipped sideways and a mighty wave smacked the gunwhale, drenching us with a deluge of water.

'I told you you shouldn't have brought it with you,' I

said, licking the salt off my lips and trying to look suitably subdued though actually I found it rather exciting. Sammy muttered some more and edged further into the middle of the boat.

Just as I was beginning to wonder whether we would make it or whether the next wave would swamp us, or the next, or the next, we rounded the shoulder of Lokrum and immediately were in calmer water. As we made landfall at the little jetty the sea was only mildly choppy.

'Where is the *rendez-vous*?' I enquired as we ambled off the ferry and took the path leading into the interior of the island.

'Not here and not yet,' said Sammy consulting the deceptively plain Cartier watch he wore on his wrist. A gift from another admirer? I didn't think even the Leader's salary ran to such collector's items. 'We shall swim a little and perhaps partake of some luncheon and later you shall meet my friend. I think a sheltered spot is called for today. We shall go to the little lake away from the sea.'

That was certainly a good idea. As we left the shelter of the trees and walked across the sward, the roar of the sea pounding the western shore was deafening. The waves broke in spectacular sheets of spray and spume and the rock slabs that usually displayed sun-baking bodies were today deserted. The pines that backed the shore were bent almost horizontal and cones and pine needles bombarded anyone that came within their range. By contrast, the lake, hidden deep in its rock setting, was an oasis of peace and stillness.

I changed and swam the lucid water and Sammy sat on a rock, still clutching his fiddle, and watched me.

'Come on in Sammy, it's glorious.'

'Later perhaps.' He didn't seem to be enjoying

himself and hadn't stripped off at all but was still tightly buttoned into his high-necked, long-sleeved shirt. He looked ill at ease and I think he was regretting the expedition. I guessed his 'friend' had stood him up and my company was no solace. When I had swum enough I waded out of the water and dropped down beside him.

'You're worried about that damn fiddle. I told you you were crazy to bring it. Look, you can go in now and I'll guard it.'

'I've changed my mind, I don't think I'll swim today.' His golden brown eyes gleamed at me beneath heavy lids. They reminded me of the lizard I had encountered at Herceg-Novi.

'The trouble with you Sammy is, you're getting old. The rot has set in. You'll soon be nodding off in the sun and boring everyone with your reminiscences.'

'You young people are so restless. *Now* where are you off to?. I had donned my sundress over my wet bikini and was preparing to scramble back up the path.

'I'm going back to the café to buy us a picnic snack.'

'Stay here Kate.' It was almost a command. 'I'll buy us both lunch at the restaurant. I'm not eating junk food outside and risk being pestered with flies and wasps.'

The old softie was petrified of being left on his own so I played along with him.

The sun was directly overhead when we made our way back to the restaurant and the wind was still doing its gale-force-ten thing. There is a self-service cafeteria in the old monastery building and I led the way to this. It was in a large, high-ceilinged room with a vaulted roof and white-washed pillars and was pleasantly cool. Sammy paused on the threshold and wrinkled his nose in disgust as he viewed the queue of people shuffling along past the counter and heard the clatter of trays and cutlery and hum of voices.

190

'We might as well be back in London and the studio cafeteria. There is a proper, decent restaurant here and we shall eat in that.'

It was an open-air restaurant, pricey and high-class but very attractive with tables and chairs set out on a terrace beneath trees with a large workforce of waiters and waitresses. We were sheltered from the worst of the wind and I didn't point out to him that we were just as likely to be pestered by flies and wasps here as down by the lake. He was buying me a meal so I held my tongue. As we ate, Sammy proceeded to interrogate me.

'I presume Ivo Tomasic freaked out. He hadn't moved onto the hard stuff, had he?'

'You knew about the drugs?'

'That he dabbled in marijuana? I should imagine that most people were aware of it.'

'Just that?'

'What more is there to know?' He leaned forward and fixed me with his reptilean gaze. Careful Kate, careful.

'Why nothing. I'd rather not discuss him, if you don't mind, but you must admit he was a gifted musician.'

'Was? You speak as if he were dead.'

'He is dead to me. I just want to forget him.'

Much more of this and I should give myself away. I hurriedly changed the subject but could not rid myself of my unease. Throughout our leisurely meal Sammy watched me closely and I felt that he was weighing me up. Perhaps he suspected that Ivo had initiated me into drug-taking and was looking for the signs in my demeanour and actions. I did not really enjoy my meal, which was a pity as it was an excellent one. Sammy is a finicky eater and he pushed food about his plate with a fastidious hand and left as much as he ate. I felt that the meal had been more a means of passing time for him than a natural slaking of appetite.

191

The restaurant was crowded. I think people were gravitating to it to avoid the bura which showed no signs of abating. Sammy muttered his disapproval of all the scantily clad, sun-bronzed bodies packed round the tables, though he was the one who looked out of place, being hopelessly overdressed. A sudden gust of wind blew eddies of dust across our table top and he snorted and pushed his plate aside.

'If you've finished, I suggest we leave. This place is getting like Clapham Junction.'

We left the restaurant by the archway that led through to what must have been the original cloisters and as we walked along the stone colonnaded path I marvelled at the variety of cacti and palms that graced the enclosed square and colonised the ancient stone walls.

Then I glimpsed him through another gateway over the other side. Peter Brownstone. He appeared fleetingly, framed by the lintel arch and then disappeared and I shot back behind an obliging palm and trod on Sammy's foot.

'*Do* look where you are going. What is the matter?'

'It's Peter Brownstone. He mustn't see me.'

'Don't tell me you've got yourself involved with yet another member of the orchestra.' Sammy sounded peeved.

'No, but it is imperative that he doesn't see me.'

'Then let us go the other way.' He led the way through yet another archway and we rounded a hedge and came to a gate bearing the legend 'Botanical Gardens'.

'Let's go in here; I've wanted to see these.' Sammy acquiesced good naturedly and I pushed open the gate and we walked down a path curving past a tall stand of dark pines. These pines surrounded the garden and provided privacy and a living wall. The tops whipped about in the wind but the space they enclosed was a sun-bowl, sheltered from the bura and sizzling in that heat. Everywhere were cacti: small ones nestling in the dusty, parched grass, bush-sized ones bristling with jade and grey spikes, the shaving-brush cacti and gigantic specimens that produced flower spikes at least ten feet tall. Mixed in with these were yuccas in full bloom and agaves and a variety of palms.

'This is not my idea of a Botanical Garden,' said Sammy disapprovingly.

'What did you expect – aubretia and bedding plants? Is that a prickly pear over there, do you think?' It looked as if it should be, but I really had no idea what a prickly pear looked like.

'I wouldn't know.'

As we wandered across the bleached sward amongst the desert-like flora I worried about the presence of Peter Brownstone on Lokrum. I was sure he had followed me across to the island and was even now spying on me. Now that I had set events in motion I was afraid. Almost as if he could sense my disquiet about Peter, Sammy said:

'Did you know that Peter is married?'

'He is?' I was startled. It was something I hadn't known. I had never suspected him of enjoying any other status than that of single bliss and I was sure that most other members of the orchestra were equally ignorant of this fact.

'Twice. The first marriage was a failure and his ex-wife took him to the cleaners. I believe the second one is proving equally disastrous.' He sounded smug. I suppose as Leader of the orchestra he made it his business to know about the private lives of his members.

'I can understand that. I should think he's not the easiest of people to live with. He's . . .' I hesitated, and for a second I was tempted to pour out all my fears and suspicions to Sammy, to bring him up to date with what was really happening in his beloved orchestra and to wipe the smug smile off his face, but I resisted the urge. If Peter Brownstone had alimony debts round his neck these provided a reason for his snatching at any means that produced a quick penny. It didn't excuse him but at least it was an explanation.

We wandered round the garden, our feet scuffing up little puffs of dust and I felt the sweat trickling down my neck and my thin dress sticking to my shoulder blades.

'Just look at that cactus over there.' I pointed to one that balanced fleshy segments in a tottering pyramid, heavily laced with lethal-looking prickles. 'It looks like something out of the Wild West. All it wants is a cowboy to come moseying along on his hoss swinging his lariat; to the accompaniment of Grofe, of course.'

But of course it wasn't a cowboy, only Peter Brownstone. He was looking for something or someone, peering short sightedly through his glasses and I felt panic spreading through me. I shot back behind cover, but this time I chose unwisely. I slashed my arm on the razor-sharp leaves of the yucca and cannoned into Sammy nearly knocking his Guarnerius out of his arms.

'Don't make a habit of this, Kate.' He dabbed at a scratch on the back of his hand. 'I don't think my insurance covers it.'

'He's followed us into the gardens,' I hissed. 'What are we going to do?' I peered cautiously between the sword-like leaves of the yucca that I hoped were screening us from Peter's view. I don't think they were fully successful. He looked in our direction and I saw his hand dart to his pocket. He was wearing a linen safari-type jacket and the right-hand pocket seemed weighed down by a sizeable bulge. He was carrying a gun! In those few seconds I knew that my fears had been correct. He was

194

the man Miles was looking for and he was looking for me! He was armed and dangerous and I was alone, apart from Sammy, in the deserted Botanical Gardens, practically a sitting duck.

'If you're really intent on keeping out of his way we'd better leave by the exit over there.' He indicated a side exit which I had not noticed before.

'Oh yes, please, quickly.'

We slipped out through the gap and Sammy consulted his watch and said, 'It's time we were going anyway'.

I had almost forgotten about Sammy's alleged date. I had thought he had chickened out of it or had not really been serious about it in the first place, but apparently I was wrong.

'Where are we going?'

'If you want to avoid everyone, I suggest we go for a walk across the cliffs over the other side of the island. With this wind, most people will be seeking shelter inland or on the lee shore.'

He was right about the wind. As we left the shelter of the trees and buildings and made our way back past the little lagoon and started the climb up the escarpment, it snatched at our hair and clothes and took our breaths away. My scratched arm was bleeding and I wrapped my handkerchief round it and toiled after Sammy. We seemed to have given Peter Brownstone the slip but I still had the uneasy feeling that he had seen us and was secretly dogging our steps. Every bush and stunted tree seemed to hide a menacing figure and I started at every rustle and spent so much time looking over my shoulder that I frequently tripped. Sammy was very patient but he finally called a halt and glared at me.

'Would it be too much to ask why you are behaving like a paranoid? What has Peter Brownstone done to you that you're so scared of coming face to face with him?'

'It's not what he has done, it's what he is likely to do.' Sammy raised his eyebrows in a disbelieving manner and I suddenly wanted to shock him and penetrate that bland, egocentric façade.

'Suppose I told you he has designs on my life?'

And he laughed. A little dry chuckle dredged up from the depths of his chest.

'Oh no, my dear. You really can't expect me to believe that. You've had too much sun.' Then he saw my expression. 'You really mean it, don't you? What have you done to get across him?'

'I have done nothing. Circumstances beyond my control.'

He shook his head, still secretly amused. 'You have nothing to fear from Peter Brownstone. He is one of the most law abiding men I have ever met, terrified of falling foul of bureaucracy.'

'I wish I could believe you. Still, I've nothing to fear with you here to look after me.'

He grunted and looked at his watch and I suddenly remembered his *rendez-vous*.

'Are you really meeting somebody up here?' Sammy smiled enigmatically but didn't reply.

By this time we had reached the top of the climb and were on the rocky headland that divides the lagoon from the sea. The going was rough; large slabs of whitened rock underfoot were interspersed with stunted juniper bushes and straggly scrub. There were no sunbathers or intrepid swimmers on the rocks today and the sea roared and pounded away in solitary splendour. It came to me then that perhaps it hadn't been such a good idea to leave behind the flocks of tourists and strike out on our own. Amongst a gathering of holidaymakers Peter Brownstone wouldn't dare try anything, but if he caught up with us on this deserted headland he could pick us off easily, one after the other, and the roaring of the surf would hide the sounds of the gunshots. I was sure he wouldn't scruple at adding Sammy to his tally of victims and I, by my unthinking actions, had led Sammy into danger. We had got to go back, now, before it was too late.

My decoy duck theory had been madness. I wanted Miles, Pero Njavro and a large crowd of assistants, in that order. Safety in numbers was suddenly a very sensible idea. I now knew who our drugs mastermind was and all I wanted was to leave the action to Miles and the forces of law and order. I turned to explain this to Sammy but he was glaring out to sea and beginning to look worried. I followed his gaze. At first I could see nothing but the heaving waves of foaming spray, then I caught a glimpse of a dark object wallowing in a trough before being obliterated by the next roller. I looked again and this time I could make out the shape of a small vessel, tossing about like a cork as it edged towards the rocky shore where we stood.

'She's coming by boat. How romantic,' I breathed. 'But how rash. She'll never make it. Sammy dear, for Heaven's sake, signal her to go round to the other side of the island. The boat will be smashed on the rocks if she tries to get in any closer.' Get her round to the safety of the harbour, I thought, and let us get there quickly too.

Sammy said nothing but he put down his fiddle and held out his hand to me.

'It's a man not a woman,' I exclaimed as the boat bobbed nearer. 'I beg your pardon, Sammy, but he's being very foolhardy. For God's sake stop him from coming any closer.'

'He'll need help.' Holding hands we scrambled across the rocks and the spray enveloped us like a mist, cutting down our vision. My personal danger was put aside for the moment. There was someone out there in even greater danger and we had got to do something about it.

'We're going to get washed away as well.' I hesitated but Sammy pulled me after him. The figure in the boat was standing up, wrestling with the tiller but his eyes were fixed on us.

I was suddenly reminded of the time when Ivo had dragged me down to the waiting boat at Baošić. Different setting and different people but the sense of *déjà vue* was so strong that I pulled up abruptly, teetering on the edge of a large, uneven rock and nearly throwing Sammy off-balance.

'This is madness. If you're so eager to get with your friend that you'll risk drowning, you can count me out. I'm going back.' I jerked my hand from his hold and started to back away from the sea-washed rocks.

'You're not.' He grabbed my arm and forced me nearer to the water. 'This is where we come to the parting of the ways, but it is I who am going back, my dear, not you.'

For a few seconds I thought I had misheard him. Then I saw his face and the expression in his eyes and I knew.

'It's you!' I gasped, horror enveloping me. 'Oh, no, it's you!'

# Chapter 9

'So you really didn't know?' He dragged me forward inch by inch. 'But you know far too much for my comfort and safety. You'll really have to go. What a pity.'

He sounded almost regretful, and I struggled with him desperately as my mind reeled under the knowledge that I had walked sweetly into his trap.

'Sammy, I don't know anything! You're making a terrible mistake! Let me go!'

But he hung on inexorably, and I was forced nearer and nearer to the edge.

'This bura is – going – to make – things – difficult – for us to – effect – the – exchange.' The words were jerked out of him as he manhandled me forward. 'But – it is – an – excellent – way of – disposing – of you. How – tragic – that – you – should – slip – and – fall – and be – pounded – to – death – on the – rocks.'

I renewed my struggle with the incentive of despair, but although he was not much taller than me he was very strong, his sinewy arms honed to the peak of physical fitness by years of stringent musical practice and discipline.

'I shall miss your cheerful face, Kate.' He accompanied this innocent platitude with a vicious jab between my shoulders that sent me hurtling forward. The sea reached up to envelope me but with a superhuman effort I grabbed a ledge of rock and hung on for dear life. He struck at my spreadeagled hands savagely and I knew I could not resist much longer. The next push would send me over the edge into the boiling maelstrom that was waiting to receive me.

It was the next wave that saved me. It struck with full force completely enveloping us and I felt my fingers loosing their hold and slipping helplessly down the rockface as I choked and spluttered and fought to keep my balance. It flung Sammy sideways and he skidded across the rock, momentarily more concerned with his own safety than delivering the *coup de grâce*. I scrambled back, gained a purchase on the slippery surface and launched myself in the opposite direction. As I broke away from Sammy and got clear of him and the wet rocks I heard a crack and a spurt of dust rose up in front, a little to the left of me. I faltered and there was another crack and splinters of rock showered into the air uncomfortably close. The man in the boat had a gun and he was shooting at me.

I fell behind a juniper bush and risked a look back. He had let go the tiller and was standing braced in the stern with both hands holding the gun, but as the boat was rearing up and down like a see-saw he had no real chance to take aim. It was only a lucky shot that would get me. It nearly did. I gasped as the next shot missed me by inches only and hurriedly tried to get further out of range. I heard a shout and was aware that Sammy was back on his feet and in the chase again and then there was a heavy metallic clonk nearby. I looked over my shoulder as I fled across the ground and my heart sank. The man in the boat had thrown his gun to Sammy and even as I watched Sammy bent down to retrieve it and swung round after me.

200

I hesitated no longer. I must get away. But where to go? I was completely exposed as I pelted across the headland. Sammy couldn't possibly miss me and there was no cover and nowhere to run to. This part of the island was deserted – where *were* all the holidaymakers? 'Please God let someone come,' I prayed as I ran and Sammy took aim. There was a slight incline in front of me and I bolted up this hoping to find cover the other side and expecting at any second to hear and feel the fatal bullet. I burst over the edge and was faced with nothingness. I was on top of the cliff that encircled the lagoon and a sheer drop faced me. Only a tattered pine hanging out over the abyss from a crack in the rockface had stopped me from hurtling into oblivion.

I was trapped. I looked down into the pool far below and vertigo assailed me. I swayed on my ledge of rock, clinging to the sapling with my eyes closed, distantly aware of Sammy scrabbling over the top towards me.

'Kate! Jump!'

The voice from below jerked me back to reality. I looked down once more and groaned with despair. Miles was racing round the strip of beach, closely followed by some uniformed men. He was too late, too far away. By the time he could do anything I would be dead. He waved his arms violently and yelled, 'Jump, Kate! Jump!'

'I can't!' I wailed after another horrified glance at the black water below me.

'For God's sake jump!'

I was slowly becoming dimly aware that I was standing in about the same place as the young diver whom we had watched diving into the lagoon on our first visit. It could be done. There was a sound behind me and I launched myself into space. As I leapt a shot rang out and I plummeted like a stone down into the inky depths.

The water was cold and bottomless and I sunk down and down. They say when a person is drowning his whole life passes before his eyes; all I could think was how strange that I should die here in my favourite spot. My lungs were bursting and there was a fiery band round my chest and then I was spiralling upwards. I broke the surface, gulped down gallons of salty water and sank again. I had been shot. I was mortally wounded and my body would lie for ever at the bottom of Mrtvo More.

Somehow I surfaced again, the light exploding in my eyes, and I was aware of someone reaching out to me and a furious voice in my ear.

'Swim, damn you! Swim!'

'I can't . . . I've been shot!' And I took in another consignment of water and the ripples closed over my head. I was floating away, sinking deeper and deeper into a mindless lethargy but my eyes were open and above me the water glowed golden. The sun reached down through the eddying curves warming and enticing, a tantalising lure. I must get back up there. I struggled feebly and then strong arms grasped me and swept me upwards.

'Kate, for God's sake what is the matter?' Miles's face loomed up above me, his hair plastered over his forehead, a desperate look in his eyes. I choked and retched.

'I've been shot! I'm dead!'

'You haven't – you're not. Sammy has been shot, not you.' At the mention of Sammy, memory flooded back and I gasped and swallowed a lot more water. He spoke slowly as if to a dim-witted infant. 'Pero Njavro shot him before he could take aim at you.'

I couldn't believe that I was whole and not shattered by a bullet. I looked down at my arms and legs writhing whitely beneath the surface. The water was pink-tinged and reddening rapidly.

'I'm bleeding!'

'You can't be.' He stared in disbelief at the pink circle round us. 'Your arm – it's coming from your arm!'

'Oh yes, the yucca.' And then I passed out in his arms. I came to almost immediately and started to thresh about.

'Don't struggle. I've got you.' I opened my eyes and looked straight into Miles's which were only a few inches from mine and black with shock. 'Just relax and I'll tow you back to shore.'

'Sammy?'

'He's dead, you're safe.' I went limp and felt the water surging past my flaccid limbs as, with powerful strokes, Miles propelled me to the beach. Did I imagine that I heard the snarl of a powerful engine coming from the direction of the sea? I tried to ignore the ominous official-sounding voices and activity over the other side of the lagoon. Jammed under Miles's chin, I gave myself up to his rescue efforts and my mind floated as effortlessly as my body, shying away from thoughts of Sammy and the horrible sequences of the past hour.

Miles released his hold on me and I clutched him wildly. 'Steady on, we're there.' He set me on my feet in the shallows and I stumbled and nearly pitched forward so he scooped me up in his arms and staggered out of the water with me clasped to his chest. As I am no lightweight, I thought this was very heroic of him. He spoilt it by tripping over a stone and depositing me abruptly on a slab of rock. We stared at each other for a few seconds and then both of us started to speak at once. Miles waved me on.

'Sammy – it was Sammy all along. I can't believe it! Where . . . ?'

Miles gestured over his shoulder and I followed his finger. Pero Njavro was standing on the beach with another man waiting to receive the dark bundle that was being carried out of the water by two dripping policemen.

'Sammy – Oh God!' And I was violently sick, spewing up some of the gallons of salt water I had swallowed. Some of it inadvertently went down Miles's shirtfront. 'Oh Miles, I'm sorry . . .'

'To hell with my shirt, it's beyond it anyway. You'll feel better once it's all up.' He supported me and I leant over and got rid of a few more gallons, and when I had finished he fumbled in his pocket and then grinned ruefully.

'I've no dry handkerchief to mop you up with today.'

He had plunged to my rescue fully clothed and the water was streaming from his trousers and his thin shirt was moulded to his torso. I was in a similar state, the sodden folds of my skirt clinging damply to my thighs and rivulets of water running from my hair down inside my top.

'Is he really dead?' I looked along the beach to where the body of Sammy lay stretched out surrounded by men.

'Yes, Pero is a crack shot.'

'I really thought he'd got me when I heard that shot. I just went to pieces. I couldn't seem to move after I'd hit the water – I was sort of paralysed . . .'

'Shock.'

'I really think I would have drowned if you hadn't rescued me. I seem to make a habit of ruining your clothes.'

'Remind me to send you my laundry bill.'

'Miles, what about the other man? There's a man out there in a boat who's got the consignment of drugs – Sammy was meeting him.'

'Don't worry. There's a coastguard cutter out there; it

204

will pick him up, has probably done so already.' I started to shiver and he caught me to him. 'It's all over, Kate. There's nothing more for you to worry about. I'll get you back to the mainland and arrange for a doctor to see you.'

'I don't want a doctor, Miles, there's really nothing the matter with me. All I want is a few answers to some questions. Did you get my message? How did you know whereabouts I was on Lokrum? Did you know about Sammy . . . ?'

'Later, Kate. I'll explain all you want to know later, but in answer to your last question, I didn't know for sure about Sammy until a few hours ago. When I think how we were nearly too late . . .' It was his turn to break off and the look on his face was very satisfying to my ego. He brushed a wet lock of hair off his forehead. 'As to how we knew where you were – Peter Brownstone saw you.'

'Peter Brownstone? Hell, do you know, I actually thought he was the villain of the piece? I could swear he had a gun in his pocket.'

'It was probably a guidebook. No, he saw you and directed us over to this side of the island. He indirectly saved your life.'

'And to think I was trying to hide, get away from him, and urging Sammy to flee with me. What will happen? Sammy . . . the orchestra . . . ?'

'Stop fretting, it will all be sorted out.' And he stopped my next question with a salty kiss which rendered me even more *non compos mentis*' When I came up for air he released me and got to his feet.

'Will you be all right for a few minutes? I'll just arrange for someone to take you back to the flat – No damn it all, I'll take you. they'll have to do without me for a while, I've done my bit. Look, just sit here quietly whilst I sort

205

things out; the sun will dry you off.'

'I'm steaming already.' I gave him a watery smile and he walked along the beach to join his colleagues.

I turned away. I didn't want to see again that sodden bundle that was all that remained of Sammy Cohen. It didn't bear thinking about. I looked instead up at the cliff facing me across the lagoon. That was nearly as bad. Had I really jumped from the top? I was suddenly aware that, apart from me and Miles and his colleagues, the beach was deserted. The police or Drugs Squad, or whoever they were, had done a good job in clearing the area. Where had all the holidaymakers gone? I closed my eyes and felt the sun beating down on my lids and drawing the moisture out of my hair so that my curls sprung back like buds unfurling.

'Kate?' Miles's urgent voice in my ear snapped me back to reality and I stared at him anxiously.

'It's all right, there's nothing wrong, but do you know what's happened to Sammy's fiddle?'

'My God, the Guarnerius! He dropped it up on the headland when he tried to pull me towards the sea . . .'

'OK. I'll be with you in a minute.' He shot off again and this time I heard him giving directions before he reappeared at my side a short while later. 'Are you capable of walking back to the quay?'

'If I said no, would you sweep me up in your arms and carry me?'

'Loth as I am to spoil any visions you may have of me as a knight on a white charger, I must seriously admit that I think I am incapable.'

'You might at least have pretended,' I said crossly. 'A woman likes to keep some illusions. I've had enough shattered today.'

'Poor Kate, you've really been in the thick of it.' And he helped me to my feet. I tried to march briskly ahead

206

but my body was not co-operating very well and I was glad of a supporting arm.

There was a shout and Pero Njavro came pounding along the beach towards us. He was carrying Sammy's violin.

'Greetings Gospoda Katerina. Have you recovered?'

'I don't think I shall ever be the same again,' I said feelingly. 'You saved my life. I don't know what to say . . .'

'It was you or him. A pity he had to die so soon. He could have been useful, but I had no choice.'

'I'm not sure how to take that remark. You have the Guarnerius?'

'Shall we share it with her?' enquired Pero of Miles. 'I feel we owe it to her.'

'Much against my professional principles, I agree,' he said.

'What are you two talking about?' I enquired looking from one to the other. 'That violin is hot property. I suppose it will have to be returned to its real owner.'

'Not this one.' Miles undid the case and lifted the violin out. The patina on belly and ribs gleamed tawnily in the sun and I flinched as he inadvertently twanged one of the strings. This was all that was left of Sammy's music-making, the glorious sounds he had coaxed out of this box of wood and gut. Even though he had just tried to kill me, the reality had not yet fully sunk in. I couldn't equate the evil figure of today with Sammy the musician.

'This is where he carried the stuff.' Miles rapped smartly on the tail piece and I looked at him in disbelief.

'In *this* fiddle? But that's impossible. How could he possibly have without damaging it irreparably. What was he supposed to have done – stuffed it down the sound holes?'

He ignored me and ran his fingers up and down the instrument and then Pero produced a pocket knife and handed it to him.

'Miles you can't!' I was aghast, but he smiled enigmatically and continued with his poking and prodding. 'Miles, for God's sake stop!' I appealed to Pero. 'You mustn't damage it – you can't. I don't care how much the drugs are worth, this is priceless, it's irreplaceable!' I think I actually caught hold of his hands but he gently disengaged himself.

'Kate dear, don't get so excited, just take a good look.'

So I looked carefully, and then I understood. The glowing varnish was not the result of centuries of ageing but had been applied recently and bubbles of cheap glue, like beads of resin, clung to the purfling.

'It's not the Guarnerius. But . . . but if this is not the Guarnerius, where is it?'

'Back at the hotel with the other spare instruments.'

'But he always took it everywhere with him, wouldn't let it out of his sight.'

'So he would have had everyone believe, but this was the one he really carried around. Aah . . .' He pressed down on the bridge as he worked his fingers along the ribs and gave a grunt of satisfaction as there was a little click and a section of the waist came away in his hands. He turned the violin round so that Pero and I could see inside the gap. The hollow interior was packed tightly with banknotes.

'Very cunning. This was especially constructed and superficially "distressed" enough to look like the real thing from a distance. He was so insistent on nobody touching or handling it that no one got close enough to discover the deception.'

'But if this was the one he always kept with him, what did he do with the real Guarnerius? I mean, he did have a Guarnerius. He played it – it was genuine.'

'Oh yes. The Guarnerius was his "spare" instrument

208

that travelled with the orchestra.'

'You mean it travelled in the pantechnicon with the other instruments?' I was horrified. 'It was just lying about?'

'You sound more concerned with that aspect of the affair than the fact that he was smuggling drugs on a large scale.'

'But how did he effect the change? With the two instruments I mean. This one could never have been played.'

'Sleight of hand. He was the only one to handle them; everyone knew how obsessed he was with his masterpiece and had no reason to believe things were other than he intended them to appear. He refused to allow the supposed Guarnerius out of his sight so everyone presumed it *was* the Guarnerius and he managed to switch them round when necessary.'

'I can't believe it. You mean he's been carrying that money round all the while on this tour and after he had made the exchange it would have been stuffed with drugs? He would have been sitting on the coach with a fortune in hard drugs sitting on his knee? How did he dare!'

'Our Sammy was a cool customer.' Miles replaced the bogus violin in its case and handed it back to Pero Njavro. 'Come on Kate, I'm getting you home. You look all in. Explanations will come later.'

Although I protested that I was all right Miles insisted on a doctor seeing me when we got back to the mainland. The bura was already lessening and the wind had lost much of its ferocity so the boat trip was not too hazardous. The doctor was young and sympathetic. He had been fed some tale of a boating accident which, on account of the weather, he had no reason to disbelieve;

and after a thorough examination he pronounced me basically fit apart from exhaustion and the after-effects of swallowing too much salt water. He bound up the gash on my arm and for good measure gave me an anti-tetanus jab and assured me with words to the effect that after a good night's sleep I should be fighting fit again. He gave Miles a couple of pills with instructions that he was to make sure that I took them as soon as I got into bed. An order I had no intention of obeying.

Veshna Zuber, who was told the same tale of a boating accident, fussed and fretted round me and promised in sign language that my clothes would be washed and ironed whilst I lay in bed.

'I shall be all right now,' I said to Miles who was hovering in the background, 'Hadn't you better get back to . . . to . . .' I grimaced and he patted my arm gently.

'I'll just see you tucked up safely first.' And he was as good as his word. I was no sooner between the sheets than he appeared on the threshold of my bedroom flourishing the pills and a glass of water.

'Just get these down and they'll help you to sleep.'

'I don't need knock-out pills. Seriously Miles, I've never taken a sleeping pill in my life and I certainly don't need one now. I'm completely exhausted, I shall sleep like the dead.'

'Doctor's orders.' He advanced purposefully on the bed.

'Look, put them there on the bedside table. If I have any trouble getting to sleep I promise I shall take them.' He gave in and left them beside me.

'Are you sure you're going to be all right?'

'Mmm. There's just so many things I want to know.'

'Later. I promise I'll bring you up to date later. Just forget about it all for now.' He bent down and gave me a very nice kiss which I was too tired fully to appreciate, and made for the door. Just as he was about to close it behind him he popped his head back inside the room.

'By the way, what *is* a yucca?'

'It's a plant.'

'Oh.' And this time he really went.

I fell asleep almost immediately but it was a haunted sleep, wracked with horrible nightmares. I was trying desperately to get away from someone or something but my feet were leaden and I felt as if I were rooted to the spot. Just as I despaired of making any progress the ground gave way beneath me and I was falling down, down into a bottomless pit. At this point I woke up, shaking with fright with my heart pounding so loudly in the darkened room that I was sure all the other occupants of the apartment block would hear it. Each time I drifted back to sleep the same dream pounced and held me in its grip. I ran and fell with sickening clarity over and over again. I tried sitting up in bed and fighting off sleep, but I was so physically tired that I could not keep awake and now as I drifted off I dreamed that I was drowning. There were gallons of water pressing down on me and I couldn't breathe. I fought for air and even when I was fully awake again I felt the hot, still air in the room was suffocating me.

Eventually I gave up the struggle and swallowed down the sleeping pills. After a further period of night horrors I finally reached oblivion.

The sound of children playing down below awakened me. I sat up the bed. Light was flooding into the room through the half-open shutters. I had no idea what time it was. I slipped out of bed and padded to the door. The flat seemed deserted and I wandered into the living room. Miles was sitting on the settee scribbling in a notebook. He looked up and a smile flooded his face as he got to his feet.

'Good, you've surfaced. I was just about to wake you.'

'What time is it?'

'Midday.'

'It *can't* be!'

'You've slept the clock round. How do you feel?'

'Rather disorientated. Where is Veshna?'

'Gone to visit one of her daughters. Have you recovered?'

'Let me have a shower and get dressed and then I shall be able to give you a better answer.'

As I stood under the cool jet and washed away the last vestiges of sleep I tried to get myself together. What day was it? When I had worked out that it was Tuesday, shock flooded through me. I – we were supposed to be in Belgrade. With this realisation came another horrible thought: Miles had brought his assignment to a successful conclusion, had "nailed" his man; did this mean his association with the Europa was now over? Would he bother to carry on with his pretence of being business manager? It was surprising how bereft I felt at the thought of this possiblity. What a complete volte-face I had undergone in the last couple of weeks. I hurriedly dressed and plunged back into the living room.

'I should be in Belgrade.'

'Don't worry, we're booked on a JAT flight at 3 o'clock. We should make it. The others left early this morning. I'll get you there in time for the concert.'

'You *are* coming – There *is* going to be a concert?'

'Of course I'm coming. I'm still business manager. And the concert is going ahead but I'm afraid you'll miss the rehearsal that is scheduled for this afternoon.'

'Is there anything to eat?'

'I believe your breakfast egg still has place of honour in the kitchen.'

'Oh no,' I groaned, 'I couldn't face it. In fact, I think I have gone right off my food.'

'That's serious, you must still be under par. Let me try and whet your appetite. Veshna has left a cold colation – is that the phrase?'

'It's the one Jane Austen would have used.'

'There; my classical education coming to the fore.'

'I don't believe you.'

'I'm not just a failed musician and employee of HM the Queen. I've got a degree in classics from Melbourne University.'

'You never cease to amaze me. Just when I think I'm beginning to work out what makes you tick you come out with a remark like that and I realise I have only scratched the surface.'

'Dig away. I am quite amenable to close study.'

I tackled the food with little enthusiasm. 'How can the concert possibly go ahead without Sammy? I'm surprised the entire orchestra is not behind bars.'

'As far as the Yugoslavian authorities are concerned the orchestra is in the clear. And Sven has it written into his contract that he takes over at short notice as leader if the necessity arises.'

'Miles, you can't hush this up can you? I mean Sammy can't just be written off without explanations.'

'No, it will have to come out, but in a strictly edited version. The Yugoslavians are as keen as us to keep publicity to a minimum and protect the working of their drug squad, which means it won't be splashed across the media. What I am hoping to preserve is my own cover.'

'But your part in it must come out surely?'

'No, I think not. The Yugoslavians will deal with this end of the chain. They have made the arrests here and will prosecute and bring the people concerned to trial. What will happen in England is this: the fake Guarnerius containing a consignment of drugs will travel back in the pantechnicon with the other instruments. When it reaches port a zealous customs officer will "happen" to discover it in a routine check and my part in the affair will not be revealed. Other customs officials will then quickly move in and clean up all along the English line. As far as the orchestra is concerned as business manager I would be involved anyway and I hope it will be accepted that I was and am the obvious person to deal with the matter in as much as it affects the orchestra and the tour.'

'Poor Sven. What a responsibility – how is he reacting?'

'He's in a state of shock but I'm sure he'll pull out of it, he's a professional.'

'As you are. Miles, you're not going to clam up on me again are you?'

'I promise you all will be revealed, but not now. We have a plane to catch.'

He helped me pack but in the middle of wedging shoes into my case I sank back on my heels and shook my head.

'It's no good Miles; there's no way I can play in this concert; I just can't. I cannot take my place on stage and perform, not with all those ghosts at my elbow.'

'You can and you will.' He leaned across the bed and grasped my hands. '"Music to soothe the savage breast" and all that, remember? Once you get your fiddle and bow in your hands again you will feel differently.' He gently pulled at each of my fingers in turn. 'You can't waste the talent of these.'

'Miles, I don't think you understand. Sammy *is – was* the Europa orchestra. He was in it from the start, he held the whole thing together. It was as if we were a body;

214

Sammy was the head and the rest of us were various limbs or appendages, unable to operate without him. If you cut off the head, the rest of us are as nothing. The Europa can't function without Sammy!'

'It can and it will, You can't let Sven down. He has agreed to take over and you owe it to him. Is this everything?' He looked round the bedroom and added my violin to the pile of belongings.

'What about the Zubers?'

'I've settled up with them. We really must be going.'

We made Cilipi just in time to check in.

As the JAT DC10 ate up the miles along the air corridor between Dubrovnik and Belgrade, so Miles unravelled the events leading up to my near demise. Even now, with the happenings of yesterday still horribly close and the memory of the subsequent nightmares still haunting me, I could not really take in how close I had been to death; but Miles was only too aware and the concern and horror in his voice was a great boost to my jangled nerves.

'When did you first suspect Sammy was the villain?' I asked, as I unfastened my seatbelt and settled more comfortably.

'Not soon enough, for which I shall never forgive myself. With hindsight, many things pointed to him, but like you, I found it utterly unbelievable. We, Pero and I, went over and over who had the opportunity and, quite frankly, it could have been any of you. There was no one in the entire orchestra who could safely be ruled out. You all move across borders and frontiers with incredible ease and could have a mass of foreign contacts across the world without arousing any suspicion. We decided we must concentrate on the means by which the stuff was shifted; it must be with the instruments, so we took the pantechnicon apart again and found nothing. We even confiscated the brass mutes and the percussion instruments like the maracas and the tubular bells and had them thoroughly investigated but there wasn't a trace, so we had to fall back on personal luggage. Nobody's case had a false bottom or was anything other than what it appeared to be.'

'You *searched* everyone's luggage? Mine?'

'I know exactly what your case contains,' he said with a grin.

'And did you have a search warrant?'

'I'm not a policeman. To continue; having ruled out the pantechnicon and the luggage, we were forced to fall back on the theory that someone was actually carrying large quantities of money or drugs about their person.'

'Do I take it you've been going through everyone's wardrobes searching for secret pockets or body belts?'

'A body belt had occurred to us but it wouldn't be roomy enough to take the amount of currency or drugs we were thinking of. Also, we were now in a hot climate and you were all stripped down to the bare necessities most of the time and you women even seemed to have discarded your handbags. We tried to think of anyone who had a personal belonging he or she clung to for dear life and all we could come up with was Sammy and his Guarnerius. You don't hide drugs in a priceless Guarnerius. You see, even I, an experienced customs officer, was hoodwinked.'

'Don't let it get you down; you got there in the end.'

'Yes, but we were almost too late.'

'How *did* you find out?'

'Yesterday morning we decided to run another check on personal belongings whilst everyone was at breakfast. We were told that Sammy had gone out earlier, complete with violin as usual, so we left his room until last. The first thing we found was the Guarnerius neatly stowed away in his wardrobe. It was definitely the Guarnerius – there was no doubt about it. And then I saw his chart for the Belgrade concert; it was lying there on the bedside table.'

Sammy's charts were a byword in the orchestra. As leader, he bore the chief responsibility for seating arrangements at each concert. According to the shape, size and acoustics of the hall he planned just where he was going to put each deck of instruments. Whereas most leaders would only have an overall plan beforehand and would wait until the rehearsal "in situ" to make final arrangements, Sammy plotted everything out well in advance and drew up complicated charts, positioning everyone on graph paper. Such was his ability, he very rarely had to make any changes once we got on stage. Oh, I knew all about Sammy's charts and I looked enquiringly at Miles.

'The position of principal oboe had been filled in with Marianne Ducros's name and the fourth oboe place was scribbled in with the name of the Yugoslavian oboeist who is standing in at Belgrade; but . . .' He paused, reliving the trauma of the discovery in Sammy's bedroom, '. . . But there were two second violins missing, their names erased: Ivo Tomasic and Kate Bracegirdle.'

I caught my breath. My supposed death had been truly premeditated. It had been no spur of the moment thing, instigated in blind panic. Sammy had planned it all in cold blood and had trailed me round Lokrum for hours until he could carry out his calculated murder at just the right time and make the switch. An icy shudder ran down my shoulder blades and Miles ran his fingers through his hair and continued in a low, tense voice.

'I'll never forgive myself. It had been staring me in the face all the while but it was only then that I realised:

217

Sammy was our man and he had definitely put the finger on you. We rushed downstairs and it was then that the receptionist gave me your message. You can't think how I felt Kate, having just made that horrendous discovery and then learning that you had gone off meekly with him, like a lamb to the slaughter. No one was around, we couldn't find out when you had gone and then Jenny Seaman drifted through the lounge and said if I was looking for you you'd gone off on another date – to Lokrum with Sammy. I asked her if she was sure and she said yes, because you'd turned up earlier that morning expecting to meet Sammy and had been quite put out because he'd left a message saying he'd meet you on the quay at the Old City. She was very intrigued and tried to fasten onto us. Well, we just rocketed out of the hotel leaving her standing there. Actually, I think I may have knocked her aside in my hurry.'

'Did you really?' I asked in delight.

'Pero had his car outside but he stopped first to make a phone call summoning help and then he drove us down to Pilé. If,' said Miles, fingering his hair again, 'you discover my locks are prematurely white and not sunbleached, some of it can be put down to that ride. We did it in *five* minutes. You may look disbelieving but I can assure you that we did it in five minutes. We just left the car by the Pilé Gate and rushed through into the Old City and tried to run down the Placa. Have you any idea what it was like, trying to *hurry* through a seething mass of people that was content to idle and saunter to its heart's content, enjoying the sunshine and the sights? It was a nightmare; and the heat! We eventually reached the Old Harbour and then we had to wait for a ferry. The rough weather conditions were slowing everything down and the ferries were taking twice the normal time to make the crossing.

218

'That immediately threw up another worry; had Sammy taken advantage of the freak conditions and pushed you overboard on the way over? Pero insisted that if this had happened it couldn't be kept secret and as there was no fuss about a young woman having been lost overboard from one of the ferries we tried to shut our minds to this possibility. We reached the jetty at Lokrum, and then where do we start looking? It is a big island.'

'Yes, the northern part, where all the holidaymakers congregate, is only the tip of the iceberg.'

'If he had taken you off into the interior we could search unsuccessfully for hours. We couldn't understand how he had managed to lure you away in his company after all my warnings.'

'I thought I was safe with him, that his presence would protect me from my unknown enemy. How stupid can you get?'

'He fooled us all with that image he had built up. It was probably why he managed to get away with it for so long. Anyway, we decided to split up and do a quick recce round the tourist area and meet at the restaurant. Our main hope was to meet up with someone from the orchestra who might have seen you both.'

'The only person we saw was Peter Brownstone and I thought it was *he* who was after me.'

'Thank God you did. He told us he had seen you and Sammy behaving in a most suspicious manner in the Botanical Gardens. He said you appeared to be hiding from someone or something and he seemed to think you were leading Sammy astray. He also insisted that he was sure he had seen you both a little later heading up beyond the lagoon.'

'And to think I thought he was the villain of the piece and was trying to persuade Sammy to keep out of *his* way!'

219

'It was very lucky he saw you, and being Peter Brownstone was glad to have a moan to a willing ear about your behaviour. Anyway, you know what happened after that. Reinforcements had arrived by this time and we raced across to the lagoon. I saw you appear over the top of the cliff facing us and for one horrible moment I thought you were going to fall. Then I saw Sammy with the gun and I wished you had. I nearly died when I saw him take aim but Pero got in first. Thank God he had a gun.'

'The Yugoslavians obviously don't have the same scruples as us about arming their men.'

'You've seen the Milicija. Anyway, you both dropped like stones and neither of you came up. When I got to you and forced you above the surface you were babbling something about being shot and there was blood in the water and for a few minutes I thought Pero had been too late.'

'What happened afterwards?'

'There was a coastguard cutter patrolling offshore and it picked up the man in the dinghy and arrested the ship he had come from which was lying at anchor further off. This had come from Libya, which was the starting point in the chain. We, and I'm talking now about a combined operation involving several nations, moved in and picked up all those along the line who hadn't already been apprehended.'

'A real clean-up?'

'You could put it like that. The ring is completely smashed. Sammy was the missing link and once we had him there was no reason to delay the clearing-up process.'

I digested this in silence and turned my attention to the window. We had been flying over mountainous regions and far below us the river Drima had coiled in and out of rocky plateaux. Now we had left the mountains behind and were flying towards the Danube Basin over the Morava Valley. We would soon be touching down at Belgrade Airport. I sneaked a glance at Miles sitting beside me. He looked relaxed and complacent.

'I suppose Sammy's death fits in nicely with your tidying-up operation?'

'It certainly makes things easier in a way. At least he won't be brought to trial and you won't have to stand as witness.'

I hadn't thought of that.

'How did he get caught up with it in the first place?'

'Greed. That is always the motivation.'

'But he had a fulfilling, worthwhile career and earned good money. What made him put it all in jeopardy to join a filthy racket like that? Perhaps he got a kick out of it.'

'He probably did, but I'm sure greed was at the basis of it; greed and insecurity due to his traumatic childhood. It doesn't excuse him but it provides a reason. His early years haunted him. He felt hard done by and reckoned the world owed him a living. He was determined his later years were going to make up for his beginnings. I'm sure we will discover that he has a numbered Swiss bank account and several desirable properties tucked away in various parts of the Continent. Don't waste your sympathy over him.'

'I'm not. You still haven't told me where Ivo and Adrian fitted into the scheme.'

'Now that is the most extraordinary part of the whole thing, they didn't. Unlikely though it seems, the little racket they were involved in had nothing to do with Sammy and the hard drugs. As smokers they got caught up in the pot scene and were recruited as couriers. Sammy must have been horrified when he found out.

There he was with his nice little network running beautifully and two bungling amateurs come on the scene
threatening everything he had worked for and set-up
over the years. He knew it was only a question of time
before they brought the authorities down on them and
exposed the orchestra to investigations and enquiries –
the last thing he wanted; so they had to be eliminated.'

'Just like that.'

'He didn't do his own dirty work though, apart from
the attempt on you.'

'Thinking about it, what makes it so ghastly is the way
he behaved so normally all the while I was with him on
Lokrum. He even bought me a slap-up meal and
watched me eat it – like a condemned man's last meal, it
seems now,' I gave a shudder. 'And all the while he was
planning the exact moment to do away with me. He must
have hated me, apart from the threat he thought I posed
him. Why?'

'You did get across him.'

'All good, clean, innocent fun. Or at least it was on my
part. I thought we had a beautiful relationship. God!
How mistaken can you be – he must really have got it in
for me. In his twisted way he was really enjoying the
situation, savouring the moment when realisation hit
me. I shall never trust anyone again.'

'You trust me, don't you?'

'I'm not really sure whether I do, or should.'

'That is a stab in the back after all we've been through.
Try and look on the bright side of things; a very nasty
drug ring has been smashed.'

'And your part in it has been brought to a very satisfactory conclusion.'

'But the fight goes on. This one has been scrubbed out
but another one will pop up tomorrow and another one
and another one. It's a filthy trade and is reaching epi-

demic proportions worldwide.'

'And the lone ranger, alias Miles Bretherton, lives on to fight another day.'

He grinned but made no reply and I wondered if and where I came into his scheme of things.

# Chapter 10

Belgrade is an arboreal city. A city of parks, wide tree-lined roads and green avenues, although at this time of the year it is humid and dusty even in the leafy shade. As we left the plane I felt as if I were being immersed in warm soup. The heat was a palpable thing, suffocating and viscous and very different from the dry, clear heat of the Dalmation coast. On the drive from the airport to the city we traversed very flat terrain with field upon field given over to the cultivation of sweet corn, grown strictly as animal feed here, and sunflower. The sunflowers were in full bloom and the sight of thousands of golden, dark-centred discs raised to the sun was a glory to be seen and savoured. In the city itself, the ubiquitous oleander had given way to hibiscus, but the masses of bushes flaunted the same pinks, whites and reds as their southern cousins.

To me Belgrade is a charming city; an impression first formed on my fleeting visit of several years ago and now confirmed. In the course of its history it has been frequently burned, sacked and rebuilt. The guide books may deplore the rash of high-rise buildings, a legacy from the fifties, and decry the lack of planning continuity, but to me it all hangs together and gives the impression of a dignified, spacious town with cultural overtones. The Europa had been booked in at the Slavija Hotel which is a modern skyscraper building in the southern section of the city, not far from the Belgrade motorway.

Miles had wheeled and dealed and managed to secure me a single room, for which I was very thankful. I was not yet ready to face the comments and sympathy of my friends, especially Sarah. I must say he had pulled out all the stops to ease me back into the orchestra with as little angst and embarrassment as possible. He had insisted that I was still in shock, which was probably correct, and I was not to be questioned or harassed in any way. I had a brief meeting with Sarah in the foyer. She hugged me wordlessly then said warily, 'I've had my orders, but are you all right?'

'Yes, I'm OK. How did the rehearsal go?'

She pounced thankfully on my lead. 'My dear, it was a complete fiasco! Two hours of unmitigated horror! A full complement of first and second violins, part from you, playing their hearts out and no two of us bowing together.'

'Sarah, that's impossible.'

'You should have heard us! And I won't touch on what woodwind, brass and percussion got up to.'

'Poor Sven – how is he?'

'Walking around like a zombie. If he's got any sense he'll get himself blind drunk – it's the only way he'll get through this evening. As for Willie, I don't have to tell you how he is reacting.'

I could imagine it. I felt sorry for Sven. Willie was probably one of his biggest problems.

'It must be hell for Sven. I mean, he's really laying his career on the line.'

'And the Europa's too. I declare we'll be booed out of

the city tonight and we'll never get another engagement.'

I hoped Sarah was exaggerating. The thought of Sven taking his place as leader instead of Sammy, sent a *frisson* of anguish through me and I wondered how I would react that evening. If all the other members of the orchestra felt the same way, no wonder Sven was on the verge of falling to pieces. But I should have known better; Sven was made of sterner stuff.

He is a large, untidy Dane. Shaggy, I suppose, would be the adjective to describe him. He has a shock of ruffled hair, light eyes and a crumpled face and although he sports no beard or drooping moustaches, it is easy to imagine him in the horned helmet and gartered leggings of his Viking ancestors. He looks as awkward and out of place in his evening clothes as I do. He called us to attention as we waited to go on stage, fixed us with his glittering eyes, like the Ancient Mariner, and said tersely:

'You will play. You will play correctly and beautifully and you will ravish our audience.'

And we did.

The Zuzoric Art Pavilion was packed. People had flocked from the city centre to the Kalemegdan Park to attend our concert. Many concerts are given out of doors in the summer months under the shadow of the mighty Kalemegdan Fortress with its military museum, but we were lucky to be housed in the Pavilion that evening. The concert in the square at Dubrovnik had shown how difficult an outside venue can prove to be and here there was an added distraction: a panoramic view of the convergence of the Sava and Danube rivers, just beyond the boundaries of the Park.

The first half of our programme was devoted to Beethoven and as the sonorous notes of the Leonora No.

3 Overture rang out I settled down and relaxed. Beethoven, so lavish and majestic and predictable, has a very calming effect on overwrought nerves and I immersed myself in the music and let it take over. I don't know whether it was desperation, the sheer will-power of Sven and Willie Bode or the authority of the music, but we gave our all that evening and by the time our soloist, a young Hungarian pianist, was into the first movement of the 4th Concerto, a neurotic, tense orchestra had pulled itself together and was playing superbly.

During the interval I wandered outside to escape the heat of the hall, gratefully clutching my iced drink. The floodlights painted the grass and foliage in lurid shades of green and drained the buildings of colour. It was very still but there was a background hum from the bustling, evening city. I turned back and was suddenly aware of Miles standing in a doorway watching me. I had not seen him since he had whisked me into the Slavija that afternoon. In his evening clothes he looked remote and splendid but there was a watchfulness about him, something almost forbidding, and when he raised a hand to acknowledge me he did not smile. Tomorrow the orchestra would be back in England and Miles would skilfully ease himself from his temporary position of business manager and hand back the reins to Richard Godbold. Was he also planning to ease his way out of my life? I had fallen for him, but although he appeared to reciprocate this feeling he had not commited himself in any way. He had kissed me, seemed concerned about me, and surely I hadn't imagined his horror at the drama on Lokrum? But he would probably have felt equally upset and responsible if it had been any other female member of the Europa.

I had probably read far more into his friendship than I should have done and he was now trying to think up ways

227

of extricating himself from the situation with as little embarrassment as possible. This was a sobering thought, a horrible thought, and I determined then and there not to wear my heart on my sleeve any more. Thank goodness this was the last concert of the tour; in the short time left I would avoid Miles as much as possible. It shouldn't be difficult as he was sure to be very busy in more ways than one. But I felt despondent as I took my place back in the hall and as the lilting, pastoral melody of Mahler's 1st soared around me I felt as if I were being mocked by the cuckoo motive ringing from the oboe.

At the end of the concert I cased my violin and made an undignified rush for the exit and the coach. Miles grabbed my arm and swung me round as I was mounting the steps.

'Where do you think you're going? Anyone would think you were running away.'

'I am.' I even struggled with him, so full of good intentions was I and so weak from his touch.

'What about the reception?'

Of course, there *would* be a reception, the full works. 'I'm tired. I don't feel equal to it.'

'Neither do I, which is why I'm kidnapping you.'

'What for? Surely I don't still have to keep in purdah?'

'This is purely for my own pleasure.'

'But shouldn't you stay around? I mean, this is your big moment.'

'I probably should, but I'm not going to. I have better things to do.'

'Where are you taking me?'

'Skadarlija – do you know it?'

'Never heard of it. Where or what is it?'

'Wait and see. Do you feel capable of walking a short way or shall I get a taxi?'

228

'I shall be glad of an opportunity of stretching my legs.'

'Good, let's get going.' He slung my violin inside the coach and re-possessed my hand. I went with him willingly, all scruples laid aside, reassured by the delightful smile he beamed in my direction.

A short way was a gross understatement. We seemed to walk for miles, traversing streets and avenues still pulsating with heat. Tramcars clanked past us and roadmen hosed down the dusty pavements. We walked across squares, past statuary and along streets teeming with people, then we turned down a road away from the main thoroughfare and I heard music. I looked enquiringly at Miles and he smiled and led me round another corner. We were in a sloping, cobbled street. Old-fashioned, wrought-iron street lamps lit the curves and complementary lanterns hung from the walls. The street was lined with restaurants, each one marked with a terraced area that sported tables and chairs amidst pots of oleanders and citrus trees. I read the names as we sauntered past; Tri grozda, Three Bunches of Grapes; Tri Sesira, Three Hats; Zlatni Bokal, The Golden Pitcher. The scent of food and wine was quite overwhelming and from each establishment came the sound of music; music from another era.

'Skadarlija,' announced Miles, 'the old Bohemian quarter of the city. This is where all the artists and musicians used to congregate.'

'And do they still?'

'Well, *we're* here. This place looks as good as any. I take it you would prefer to eat outside?'

'Oh yes, I want to soak up the atmosphere; it's positively oozing with it. What a fantastic place.'

We were shown to a table lit romantically with red candles beneath a tracery of leaves. Pools of light in the shadows indicated fellow diners at other tables and I heard snatches of many languages circulating through the langorous night air.

'I hope you've recovered your appetite?'

'I'm ravenous.'

'So am I.' We picked our way through the enormous menu card which was set out in English, French and German as well as Serbian, and not completely succeeding in any tongue, and chose a veal dish as our main course. Miles ordered a carafe of red wine and when it had been poured he lifted his glass and said:

'*Ziveli*!'

'*Ziveli*!' I solemnly replied and remembered there was something I wanted to ask him.

'Miles, how come you can speak a half-decent Serbo-Croatian?'

'I've got an ear for languages and I went on a crash course.'

'Which didn't include the Cyrillic alphabet?'

'They overlooked that. How is your veal?'

'Delicious.'

From across the street came a burst of merriment and the clink of bottles and glasses as waiters scurried amongst a jovial party.

'They are celebrating,' I said, trying to keep the envy out of my voice.

'So are we.'

I didn't ask what, presumably it was the smashing of the drug ring, but applied myself to the veal. To follow, we had palačinke, which is the national dish of pancakes, stuffed with walnuts and syrup. We drank a lot of wine and I gave myself over to the pleasures of the moment. I was here with Miles, being romantically wined and dined and I was determined to make the most of it. Tomorrow was another day.

There was a dream-like atmosphere about the place. I

felt as if I had been transported back into another era. Where the light from the street lamps spilled onto the cobbles I expected to see women in long dresses and men in frock-coats toting easels and canvasses. Surely, if he had forsaken his precious Montmartre, Toulouse Lautrec would have felt at home here. There was a definite air of *fin de siècle* about the setting; the tall, mysterious buildings from whose ground floors burst lights and music; the wrought-iron furniture beneath canopies of leaves; the laughter and patter of contented boulevardiers. I drank in the scene as I sipped my wine and then I looked across at Miles. He was watching me with an intense look on his face and I felt a little twist of anguish curl through me. This is where you get the brush-off, I thought. At any moment now he's going to start mouthing platitudes and putting you down and you will then smile brightly and thank him for the meal and for his recent protection and trot back to the Europa as if you had no cares in the world, but with a big, gaping hole inside you.

Would I have the guts to carry it off? I felt glued to my seat and suddenly very sick. I put down my wine glass abruptly, splashing crimson drops across the white tablecloth.

'What is the matter? Are you all right?'

'Nothing, just a goose walking over my grave.' I forced an artifical smile to my lips.

'Kate, have all these recent happenings spoilt Yugoslavia – Dubrovnik – for you? I know you had a special feeling for the place.'

'I suppose I shall never think of it in the same way again; but no, I think it still exerts the same pull. It's just that everything came to such an abrupt stop – a lot of loose ends, and I never re-visited half the places I intended to or did half the things I had planned.'

231

'Then how do you feel about going back to Dubrovnik for our honeymoon?'

A dark, furry moth blundered within our orbit and started to gyrate wildly round the candle flame. I spun round with it, dizzy with the shock of what I thought I had heard.

'*What* did you say?'

'I said, how would you like to honeymoon in Dubrovnik?'

I drew my gaze away from the moth and tried to focus on the face across the table. His silver-blue eyes were dark with intensity although his face was dead-pan.

'Miles, are you *proposing* to me?'

'Well yes, I suppose I am. I mean, you *are* going to marry me, aren't you?'

A burst of joy shot through me and I gripped the edge of the table. 'I don't think I could bear not to.'

'Oh Kate!' And then somehow I was in his arms, getting all mixed up with the table and the abandoned crockery. There was candle-light and lantern-light and surely moonlight, flickering round us and illuminating his dear face and the kisses we were exchanging. And music too. Wild, romantic gypsy music swooping around us, tugging at the heart strings and seducing with its unrestrained beat. I surfaced slowly and a trio of faces swam into view; dark, villainous faces framed by black locks, split by delighted grins beneath bristling moustaches. The faces belonged to gypsies. They hovered over us, playing their fiddles wildly and wearing the most exotic costumes ever seen outside Ruritania all flowing sashes, embroidered waistcoats, tasselled caps and twinkling boots.

'Miles, you *fixed* it!'

'I didn't, I swear I didn't – this is just part of Skadarlija.'

232

The music rose to a lilting climax and the serenade finished with a flourish of bows. The three musicians bowed deeply from the waist, bade us '*Laku Noć*' which means good night, and moved off. There was more to come. An elderly woman clad entirely in black, complete with shawl swathed tightly round her head, appeared at our table carrying a large, flat-bottomed basket full of crimson roses. They were the hot-house variety; tight velvet buds on long stems. Miles gave her some coins, selected one and handed it to me. I touched it with my lips and drank in the heady fragrance.

'Is this romantic enough for you?'

'It's like a fairy-tale. What girl could resist being wooed like this? Have you been here before?'

'No, but its reputation has gone on before. Do you want some more wine? Champagne?'

'I'm high already. I daren't answer for my actions if you ply me further. Are you sure you really want to marry me?'

'Quite sure. I don't go around shedding proposals to just anyone you know.'

'Not the other twenty-seven female members of the Europa?'

'I don't know what I've done to earn this reputation. It's most unfair. Are you going to turn into a nagging wife?'

'Probably; and are you going to be a faithful husband?'

'Yes Kate, I promise you.' He was suddenly deadly serious and gripped my hands tightly. 'I don't know if I am being fair asking you to share your life with me. My work presents difficulties; I am frequently away and I don't work office hours.'

'My music means a lot to me.'

'I know, and I'm not asking you to give it up. There

233

will have to be a lot of give and take on both sides. Are you sure?'

'Miles, are you having second thoughts? Trying to wriggle out of it already?'

'Will this prove my good intentions?'

It certainly did. He stopped my mouth with kisses and it was some time before I got back the power of speech.

'What about your daughter? How will she feel about it?'

'She'll be delighted. She'll have two mothers as well as two fathers. I'm sure you will get on well together and she'll want to cultivate you if only because she is an ardent stamp collector and will hope to add to her collection through you.'

'Miles, how am I going to explain you away to all my orchestral friends?'

'But they know me already.'

'Yes, as a temporary business manager. If they discover after our wedding that I'm really married to a customs officer your little charade is really going to be made public.'

'I'm sure we'll be able to think up some simple explanation in due course. We'll cross that hurdle when we come to it. Are you sure you really do want to visit Dubrovnik again?'

'Yes, the place exerts a fascination over me and there is a lot of unfinished business. I never said goodbye to the Zubers or to Pero Njavro.'

'Pero Njavro exerts far too much fascination over you, if you ask me. What's he got that I haven't?'

'Broad breast, full eye, small head and nostril wide,

High crest, short ears, straight legs and passing strong.'

'Surely that refers to a horse? I'm not a jealous man but it's a bit much to find my wife-to-be entertaining lecherous thoughts about another man before she's even married me.'

'Not lecherous thoughts. It means I have a discerning eye, and having looked the market over, I've chosen the best.'

'Well, I can't resist that one. We'll go back to Dubrovnik after we're married and visit the Zubers and Pero Njavro *and* his wife and four kids and go swimming on Lokrum.'

'Lokrum! Oh God! Lokrum will haunt me for the rest of my life.'

'Then we must lay the ghost. I'm not sharing my wife with a dashing Serb or a villainous phantom.'

'I shall never be able to forget Sammy.'

'Neither shall I, but I promise you the horror will fade and the nightmares cease.'

'How did you know I had nightmares?'

'Because I have too a discerning eye. Now let's talk of something far more pleasant; you for example.'

'I'm all for that.'

'Have I told you that your eyes are like Delft saucers? And that you have a most irresistible dimple in your chin when you smile? I could go on for ever about your attractions and my feelings for you but you won't want to hear all that corny patter.'

'Do go on,' I breathed.

And he did.

If you have enjoyed this book and would like to receive
details of other Piatkus publications please write to

Judy Piatkus (Publishers) Limited
5 Windmill Street
London W1P 1HS